Praise for
SAINT MAZIE

"Full of love and drink and dirty sex and nobility...Attenberg takes Mitchell's witty, colorful piece and spins it into something equally lively and new." —*New York Times Book Review*

"Tender-hearted and loose-living, Mazie is the unlikely guardian angel of New York City's Depression-Era down-and-outs. You'll love this smart, touching novel that brings her world to life." —*People*

"This novel is as boisterous and compassionate as the woman it canonizes." —*O Magazine*

"Attenberg is a nimble and inventive storyteller with a particular knack for getting at the heart of outsized characters...[she] proves her chops as a historical novelist by perfectly capturing Mazie's jazz-age voice, which ranges from clipped and vulgar to melancholy and lyrical. Attenberg also sidesteps many of the pitfalls of the form: no day-by-day plodding through the decades, no unedited research notes masquerading as dialogue. She resists any plot twist or final revelation to provide a tidy psychological explanation for Mazie Phillips-Gordon sainthood." —*Washington Post*

"Attenberg captures Mazie's voice so vividly you can close the book and still hear her talking. She is a tremendous achievement...[A] bold, magnificent book about family, altruism, women, and freedom, as well as a love letter to New York and a timely social manifesto for the 21st century." —*Guardian*

"Attenberg's style, at turns lyrical and blunt, is a strong match for Mazie...This voice—pleasantly tinged with jazz age argot, refreshingly modern in its honesty, and always intimate—is Attenberg's great achievement in SAINT MAZIE...[A] boisterous, deep, provocative book." —*Boston Globe*

"A winning novel and a lovely tribute to a New Yorker whose only claim to fame is her outsized kindness. Her Mazie is richly imagined and three-dimensional, and in these pages she lives forever." —*Los Angeles Times*

"Fresh and witty...SAINT MAZIE looks deep into the spirit of generosity. Jami Attenberg's Mazie lives a very big life in a very small space, turning her darkest experiences into something inspiring." —*Wall Street Journal*

"A raw, boisterous, generous novel with a heroine to match and New York in its soul, SAINT MAZIE offers proof again that Jami Attenberg is a brilliant, lion-hearted storyteller."
—Maggie Shipstead, author of *Astonish Me* and *Seating Arrangements*

"With SAINT MAZIE, Jami Attenberg has crafted a tale that is somehow both a love song and a gut punch at once, and will leave you all the better for having read it. When I finished reading, I wanted to start all over again."
—Therese Anne Fowler, author of *Z: A Novel of Zelda Fitzgerald*

"A funny, touching novel." —*Vanity Fair*

"An exuberant portrait of an unforgettable woman and the city she loves." —BBC.com

"Delightful...[an] often ebullient tale about the simple pleasures of a working life...Thanks to the wonderful Jami Attenberg (with an assist from the legendary Joseph Mitchell) Mazie does live on, an actual 20th century New York City saint." —NPR

"SAINT MAZIE is a novel with as much style and moxie as its titular character. I missed Mazie Gordon-Phillips and her family when I was finished reading, but I missed New York, too. By telling this one woman's story, Jami Attenberg has managed to write an ode to New Yorkers of every generation. She is a true poet of the city."
—Gabrielle Zevin, author of *The Storied Life of A.J. Fikry*

"Attenberg has an impressive ability to capture unique voices and make these characters authentic and distinctive...The voices in SAINT MAZIE ring out and linger, bringing to life this specific place and time in New York—and American—history." —*Dallas Morning News*

"Ingeniously constructed...An attentive character study that also happens to be rich in city lore and period detail, SAINT MAZIE is an edifying, companionable, and moving novel."
—*Kansas City Star*

"*The Middlesteins* author Jami Attenberg has traded writing about the Midwest for Jazz Age New York—and, oh, what a glorious swap it is. If you love historical stories with bold language that vividly paint a picture of another era, you'll be so happy to spend your summer days alongside Mazie Phillips, the real-life proprietress of a downtown NYC movie theater called The Venice. Take a peek inside Mazie's diary, and get swept away."   —*Bustle*, "The 17 Best Books of Summer"

"[Attenberg] nails Mazie's irresistible combination of sweet and seedy, tough and tender."   —*Miami Herald*

"Impressive...Attenberg excels at developing Mazie's voice as she grows from an impetuous, witty girl, into a shrewd-yet-selfless character. But the book is largely about the silent tragedies of womanhood, and the different forms love and loneliness can take...What SAINT MAZIE is most concerned with: how to be a human being."   —*Bust Magazine*

"Mazie continues to grab the lapels and hearts of readers—and we are all the more glad for the shake-up she gives us...Mazie fittingly achieves immortality in the minds and hearts of readers."   —*Milwaukee Journal Sentinel*

"Unflinching examinations of some of people's more unflattering qualities, compassion for the same, and a clear love and respect for the journeys we all must go on...[Attenberg's] work has the same sense of bonhomie and joy as did the original 'Saint' Mazie."
    —*The L Magazine*, #1 on the "50 Books You'll Want to
Read This Spring and Summer" list

"I loved it to pieces...Through an incredible cast of voices, Attenberg gives us the story of Mazie Phillips, the bawdy, brassy broad who runs a New York theater from the Jazz Age through Prohibition and into the Great Depression...The frame and structure Attenberg gives her story are as interesting as the story itself, and the whole experience is a delight. Highly recommended!"   —*Book Riot*

"SAINT MAZIE is a love letter to a New York City that doesn't exist anymore—the gritty, working-class Lower East Side and Coney Island that your grandparents might remember...genuine and relatable."   —*Condé Nast Traveler*

"I'd love to be Jami Attenberg for a day to see what she sees. The next best thing is to read the touching, funny, and wise SAINT MAZIE, which is as difficult to categorize as the hard-living, heart-breaking, soul-saving ticket taker it is about."
                                —Charlotte Rogan, author of *The Lifeboat*

"A terrific novel—touching, funny, big-hearted, just like Mazie herself. It's written with great verve and brio, and I loved the way we circle around and then dig deeper into Mazie's life through the multiple voices and sources. It's Mazie herself, though, who shines the brightest, and who lingers on in the mind and heart, a real diamond in the rough."   —Monica Ali, author of *Brick Lane* and *Untold Story*

"SAINT MAZIE moves with joy and wonder through the past. This book has such brio, warmth, intelligence, and personality it seems a wonder it is made of mere words."
                        —Rebecca Lee, author of *Bobcat & Other Stories*

Also by Jami Attenberg

The Middlesteins
The Melting Season
The Kept Man
Instant Love

SAINT MAZIE

A Novel

JAMI ATTENBERG

GRAND CENTRAL
PUBLISHING
New York Boston

Copyright © 2015 by Jami Attenberg
Reading group guide copyright © 2015 by Jami Attenberg and Hachette Book Group, Inc.

Cover design by Brian Lemus
Cover copyright © 2016 by Hachette Book Group, Inc.

Grand Central Publishing
Hachette Book Group
1290 Avenue of the Americas
New York, NY 10104
grandcentralpublishing.com
twitter.com/grandcentralpub

Originally published in hardcover and ebook by Grand Central Publishing in June 2015.
First Trade Paperback Edition: June 2016

Grand Central Publishing is a division of Hachette Book Group, Inc.
The Grand Central Publishing name and logo is a trademark of Hachette Book Group, Inc.

The publisher is not responsible for websites (or their content) that are not owned by the publisher.

The Hachette Speakers Bureau provides a wide range of authors for speaking events. To find out more, go to www.hachettespeakersbureau.com or call (866) 376-6591.

Book interior design by Marie Mundaca

Library of Congress Cataloging-in-Publication Data
Attenberg, Jami.
  Saint Mazie : a novel / Jami Attenberg. — First edition.
    pages ; cm
    ISBN 978-1-4555-9989-9 (hardcover) — ISBN 978-1-4789-0381-9 (audio book) — ISBN 978-1-4789-0382-6 (audio download) — ISBN 978-1-4555-9988-2 (ebook) 1. Women—New York (State)—New York—Fiction. 2. Nineteen twenties—Fiction. 3. New York (N.Y.)—Social life and custom—20th century—Fiction. I. Title.
PS3601.T784S25 2015
813'.6—dc23
                                        2014041173

ISBNs: 978-1-4555-9990-5 (trade paperback), 978-1-4555-9988-2 (ebook)

Printed in the United States of America

RRD-C

10 9 8 7 6 5 4 3 2 1

Book designed by Marie Mundaca

Mazie's Diary, March 9, 1939

Fannie brought one of her fancy friends down to the theater last night. First she handed me a beer then she had me shake his hand. Bribery. He gave me a cigarette, the first one I've had in weeks. It tasted as good as I remembered. All of these things I'm not supposed to be having and there I was, having them. Rosie would kill me. We smoked for a minute, shooting the breeze. Then the fella told me he was there on a mission and he wouldn't take no for an answer. He wanted me to write a book about my life.

I said: Who cares about my life? I just sit in this ticket booth all day.

And he said: Plenty of people care, you run these streets.

Fannie stood back, quiet, unlike usual. She was watching the both of us, or maybe it was only him. She likes these young boys around, and I guess I can't blame her. I'll hand this one a few points for his looks. He was real slick, tan, a Mediterranean fella in a bespoke suit. He's twenty-five if a day, but it didn't matter, he carried himself like he'd known everything about life since birth. It must be so easy to have all the answers already. It must be so easy to think you know the truth.

I said: I'm not so interesting. It's the bums that have the real story.

And he said: No, the bums are interesting because of you.

If he can't see why they're worth talking about, then what kind of story would he want me to tell? Ten years of my life I've been helping those bums, I couldn't ignore them. And this guy, with his suit and his hair and his eyes, he wants me to forget their names.

I started closing up shop. Counting the change I'd already counted, just so he'd get the hint.

Fannie said: I'm sorry I brought him here.

I said: Everyone's welcome at the Venice Theater, even the snobs.

He said: You have a story to tell. I'm never wrong about these things. You're the queen, so tell the story of your kingdom.

That cigarette was perched on his lips like it was part of his flesh. I wanted a hundred more of them but the doc says no. He slid his hand through the slot of the cage before he left. We shook, but then we still kept holding hands, and it made me feel young again under my skin, like I was a piece of ice melting in the sun. Just a pool of me left behind. We stood there like that. He held my hand, I held his.

I'm a sucker. An old lady. A fool.

He said: Think about it.

Then this morning I dug you out of the closet and dusted you off. So all right, I'm thinking about it.

PART ONE
Grand Street

1

EXCERPT FROM THE UNPUBLISHED AUTOBIOGRAPHY OF
MAZIE PHILLIPS-GORDON

People ask me why I spend so much time on the streets. I tell them it's where I grew up. These streets are dirty, but they're home, and they're beautiful to me. The bums know about the beauty of it. The bums love it like it's their own skin. The ruddy dust from the streets, the mud in the parks where they sleep, sunk deep in the lines in their foreheads, jammed up under their fingernails. The sun and the dirt mixed up with their sweat and the booze. All the dirt. It's the earth. If you can't see the beauty in the dirt then I feel sorry for you. And if you can't see why these streets are special, then just go home already.

Before she was the Queen of the Bowery, walking around in those brilliantly colored dresses, with her floppy felt hat and dangling bracelets and walking stick, helping all those homeless men for years and years, and before people started writing about her in magazines and newspapers, calling her an important New Yorker, a hero is what they said, before all that, she was just Mazie Phillips, the girl who lived upstairs from me who maybe I had a little crush on but wouldn't give me the time of day.

Mazie's Diary, November 1, 1907

Today is my birthday. I am ten. You are my present.

I am the daughter of Ada and Horvath Phillips. But they live in Boston, far away. I never see them anymore. So are they still my parents? I don't care. My father is a rat and my mother is a simp.

I live in New York now. Rosie says I am a New Yorker. You are my New York diary.

George Flicker

First it was just Louis Gordon in the one big apartment on the third floor, alone for a long time, I remember. He was a giant man, filled with red meat. You could smell it in the hallway. Him cooking it, I mean. And he was a sweaty man, too. Dead of winter, he'd be sweat-stained before noon. He always wore this brown fedora with a blue feather in it—that was the flashiest thing about him, that feather. He was not a man who liked to draw attention to himself, but that feather let you know there was a little something going on there. So there was Louis, the big man, all alone, right above us.

Now there were five of us in our family, my mother, my father, my aunt, my uncle, all crammed into one small room. Plus another uncle, Al, my mother's brother, he lived under the staircase and he was always up in our apartment, taking up more of what little space we had. I see your face, but those days we really packed them in there. And actually Mazie was of great service to my uncle Al later on, so he's important to this story. He's not just my crazy uncle Al who lived under the stairs.

Okay, so sometimes there were six of us in this one room, but Louis, he had two rooms to himself. It's oppressive, living in a small space like that. On the one hand, we were used to it. I never knew anything else but that room; I had been born into it. And we had our small joys. We all had food. No one got sick, no one died. All around us tenements were soiled and reeking. But we got lucky with this one building. Even if we were crammed together we were still safe and clean. The family remained intact. But we envied those with more room.

So there was a little jealousy, but still, he was our neighbor.

Be nice to your neighbors was what we were taught. My mother used to call him "The Quiet Giant" on account of him being so tall but never making a noise. You never heard the floor creak once, and this is one creaky building we're talking about. Every ache and pain you could hear. Sometimes she'd go upstairs and knock on his door just to make sure he was still alive. She was worried about him being single; she worried about that all the time.

Then he marries Rosie. The story goes he met her at the track, out of town, in Boston. Oh, let me think...the track was called Readville, which was a big deal at the time, but it hasn't been around for many years. It's not much of a story is it? [Laughs.] So he marries her and brings her to New York. And Rosie's a real knockout when she shows up, this fine, dark hair wrapped around her head, her eyes are lined with kohl, her lips are dark red. She looks exotic, like a gypsy, but she's a Jew, of course. And she smiles at everyone, because everyone's smiling at her. She's just a good-looking girl.

And now there's two people in two rooms, and now the floor is creaking. Every night! Now he's not so quiet, and my mother never knocks on his door. This goes on for, I don't know, a year? But then the creaking, we start to not hear it so often anymore, and Rosie, who had been so happy, now we see her around the neighborhood, and she's never smiling. She's shopping, and she's sad. She's taking a stroll with Louis, and she's sad. You say hi to her in the hallway, and she is joyless in her greeting. I remember my mother saying, "The Quiet Giant and The Royal Sourpuss."

Once I was in their apartment. Only once though. I was running down the stairs in our apartment building and I tripped and fell, skinned my knee right open. Kids do this kind of stuff all the time. Well Rosie was walking up the stairs with groceries and saw me fall. So she hauled me into her apartment to tend to me. The thing I really remember was this giant wooden table with all these chairs around it, this beautiful shiny wood. When Rosie was in the bathroom finding a bandage for my knee, I walked around the table, counting the steps, sliding my hand against it. What did they need that big of a table for?

Anyway, Rosie took good care of me. She cooed over me, took me into her arms, pressed me against her chest. She held me so tight, and then she very suddenly let me go, sent me downstairs to my mother. I remember it very distinctly. She said, "You belong with your mother."

After that, I don't know, a month or two maybe, Louis and Rosie leave town for a week. They ask my mother to keep an eye on the place. They say they're going on the honeymoon they never had. My mother thought he had money buried in the floorboards. "Ill-gotten gains." She joked about pulling up the floors while he was gone, but she wasn't kidding. She thought he was pretending to be something he wasn't so that no one would suspect him. She never thought they were ill-gotten before Rosie got there. Look, I liked Louis. He had legitimate business too. He owned the movie theater, he owned the candy shop. He invested in the community. And he was always giving everyone a nickel. Ill-gotten, who is anyone to talk?

Then when Louis and Rosie come back to town, they have two girls with them, Rosie's little sisters. This is when I meet Mazie and Jeanie, the Phillips girls. About six months after the girls arrived, the whole family, Louis and Rosie and Mazie and Jeanie, moved across the street to a bigger apartment, a whole floor, five rooms I heard, but never saw. And *then* you should have heard my mother.

Mazie's Diary, December 3, 1907

I lost you! And now I found you. But I don't have anything to say.

Mazie's Diary, March 13, 1908

I'm no good at this. Remembering to write in you.

Mazie's Diary, June 3, 1908

I ain't no liar, I don't care what anyone says.

George Flicker

When they first got to town, Mazie was probably ten years old, Jeanie's four or five years old. I must have been nearly seven by then. The two girls were always very nice to look at, although they weren't necessarily prettier than anyone else. They looked not so different than the rest of the curly-haired, dark-eyed Jewesses on the Lower East Side.

But Rosie bought them beautiful dresses, and bows for their hair, and they were well fed. So they were not sick or sallow like those who could not get enough to eat, which was more than a few people on the streets those days. And Jeanie took ballet classes when she was very young, which seemed crazy to my whole family when there were no extras for the Flickers, and Uncle Al was sleeping under the staircase. But there she was walking around dressed up like a tiny ballerina, which we could all admit was at least nice for us to see, a little girl looking pretty.

Mazie had no use for me. I bored her. She always was looking for excitement, looking ten feet behind you like there was something better out there. And she seemed so much older than me. I guess there's a big difference between seven and ten, but now I think it was just that she had been through more than the rest of us. Mazie was very smart. It wasn't like she was book smart, none of us were. And she was street smart, but all of us were that, being city kids. It just seemed like she knew more about the world, and always did. She ran with the older kids on the rooftops of the tenements. They were a tough gang. Of course, my mother wouldn't let me anywhere near them.

So no, I didn't play with the Phillips girls. I just admired them from afar. Or from across the street, anyway.

Mazie's Diary, July 8, 1909

I can run faster than any of those boys from the block. I told them I would prove it and I did. I raced them all tonight on the roof and won. I beat Abe and Gussy and Jacob and Hyman and not a one of them were even close. They were all spitting in my dust. Even in my dress I can beat those boys. Gussy said I cheated but how could I cheat? He's a cheater for even saying that. He's a crummy lying jerk. After, Rosie yelled at me for getting dirty but I told her I didn't care. It was only a dress.

Louis told her to leave me alone, it's what kids do, they get dirty. Rosie told him not to say another word about children, not one more word. That clammed him up. Then she started crying. Jeanie was hugging her, begging her not to cry. I started yelling that it was just a stinking dress. I ran outside, they couldn't catch me. I ran a block, I ran another. I ran as fast as I could. It was just a dress. Why did she have to cry?

Mazie's Diary, August 8, 1909

Gussy got a piece of my fist tonight. Call me a cheater one more time, I told him. Just one more time. Well he did and now he's sorry.

George Flicker

She drew blood more than once. This scared us, and it impressed us. She was beyond being a boy or a girl.

Mazie's Diary, January 4, 1911

You're where the secrets go. I mean to write in you all this time. I mean to tell you everything. I mean to tell someone everything about my life but I forgot until now. I got all these secrets inside me. Only I just forget to let them out.

Mazie's Diary, February 3, 1913

I wouldn't let Rosie throw you away. She's got nothing better to do than go through my personal private things all day. But you're mine.

Mazie's Diary, November 1, 1913

I turned sixteen today, and I've already fought with Rosie twice. I can't listen to her another minute. She's always yelling and screaming when I come home late. Treating me like I'm a brat. I'm not a brat! She's an old cow. And I've been good for weeks. I've been doing everything she's asked for days and days and weeks and weeks and years and years. One night I go out, and it's my birthday. One night I come home late. One night!

George Flicker

Of course then she grew those bosoms of hers and everything changed.

Mazie's Diary, May 12, 1916

I dug you out of my closet so I could scream at the top of my lungs without anyone hearing.

Rosie doesn't understand what it's like to love the streets. She doesn't see the shimmering cobblestones in the moonlight, she just wonders why the city won't put in another street lamp already. She doesn't see floozies trying to sweettalk their customers, earning every nickel they get, working as hard as the rest of us. She just sees crime. She doesn't see the nuns and the Chinamen and the sailors and barkeeps—the whole world full of such different people. It's just crowds to her, blocking her way. She sees a taxi whisking by and she thinks, what's the hurry? And I think, where's the party?

This is what I want to tell her! There's a party.

Mazie's Diary, June 1, 1916

All the girls I know have a fella except for me. But why would I want just one person loving me when I can have three?

George Flicker

Was she any wilder than the rest of us? She was wilder than me, I can tell you that much. But that wasn't hard. I was a good boy, and she was a good-time girl. You see the difference. She was very...touchy-feely. What does that mean? You seem like a smart person. You know what it means.

She was still a brunette then, and she wore her hair in waves. Sometimes she pinned it up, but most of the time it was loose, though still tidy. Her eyebrows were plucked thin, and she powdered her cheeks white. She wore bright pink and red dresses, the brighter the better—she'd have liked to burn your eyes when you looked at her, I think. New dresses all the time. She was always swirling them around, flirting with her body. Day or night you couldn't miss her. She wouldn't let you.

She did a little of this, a little of that. Once in a while she worked in this candy shop Louis owned during the day, but not anything you could count on if you were trying to find her.

But mostly you'd see her on the streets, looking for fun. She went to all the bars on the Bowery, even the bars where the girls weren't allowed. My mother used to say she had no sense of propriety, but I've always thought propriety's for people who need rules. And Mazie had been making her own rules for too long.

Lots of times she'd come home right when my father was leaving for work in the morning. I should explain that my other uncle, my uncle Barney, had a terrible back and he'd get laid up from time to time, so eventually my father had to take on a second job, this one at a pickle factory. I didn't get to see him that much after that, so I'd started watching him leave from the window. I wanted to see him every last possible second. Isn't that crazy? All of us were packed together in that apartment, one bed next to another, no privacy, no quiet. Half the time you'd wake up in the morning under someone else's covers. And still the minute he left I was missing him. But he was a good man, of course I missed him. He liked his pipes, he had a nice set, and I would watch him pack the tobacco in there. He'd let me pack it too, and then my fingers would smell like tobacco. I loved that smell. I smoked a pipe well into my eighties. I thought about him every time I smoked. He was a workingman—life was work to him—but he had his small joys.

Anyway, he'd be walking down the steps when Mazie'd be walking up hers. She'd wave, he'd nod. Now she was an adult, so all the grown men were scared of her too. No men in the neighborhood would be caught dead talking to her while she roamed the streets like she did. The mothers didn't like her, the fathers didn't want to talk to her. But once upon a time she used to be a little girl they all loved. It was not hypocrisy, but it felt something like it.

Mazie's Diary, June 14, 1916

I sat on the front stairs before I went home. I knew what was coming. Oh boy did I know. I could be standing across the

East River and know when that woman opens her mouth. So I waited for a minute. I wanted to see the daylight hit the stairs. I like watching it spread across the street and then the sidewalk. I smoked. I closed my eyes. I let the sun hit me. The sun's some kind of gift. Another day we're all alive. I wish she could understand. I'm just happy to be alive.

She was asleep on the couch when I came in, tucked into a quilt. When she's quiet, she looks like a girl again, with that pudge around her chin. Louis was in the kitchen like always. He had a plate of hot eggs and leftover steak in front of him. He was peppering the steak. He just gave me a nod. He wants nothing to do with the arguing. Poor Louis. He'd give us every cent he has just to keep the peace.

I stumbled into my room. I knocked into a wall. All right I was drunk I guess. So it was my fault I woke her up. My fault, my fault. Everything's my fault. A minute passed, then there's Rosie in my room. Didn't even knock! Just walked right in. Started talking about the neighbors knowing too much, worrying about them being in Louis's business. Nobody wants anybody's nose in anything. I couldn't argue so I didn't. I just shushed her for Jeanie's sake.

But then Jeanie was up. She had slept in one of her ballerina outfits again. No one could sleep then so it was into the kitchen with all of us. Rosie got back on the couch, stuffed in her quilt. I braided Jeanie's hair while Louis made us eggs. Jeanie told us jokes and made us laugh. Louis went to work and I did the dishes while Rosie stared at me from the couch. She looked mean.

Rosie said: One day that door won't be open.

I told her I'd crawl through the window. I told her she'd never ever get rid of me.

Jeanie danced in circles around the room. Fast, spinning. Jeanie's braids came out. Rosie was wishing ill on me. I wasn't going to change a thing.

Rosie said: Enough, Jeanie.

But you can't stop that girl from dancing.

Lydia Wallach, great-granddaughter of Rudy Wallach, manager of the Venice Theater (1916–1938)

First of all, obviously this is all secondhand information. I'm certainly fine with speaking on the record, but most of this was told to me by my mother and by my grandmother, and a lot of this information came, I believe, from my great-grandmother, whom in fact I never met, or if I did I don't recall it. There's a chance she held me when I was just a baby. I vaguely recall having heard that she did once from my mother.

But anyway, essentially, this is all rumor and gossip, family lore, I suppose you could call it, although I don't know how interesting any of it is. I guess we take what we can get for family lore. And Mazie was the closest thing to a celebrity any of them knew. She was a celebrity because she was written about, and was sort of known about town as this downtown fixture, but beyond that she was a celebrity in my family because she was charismatic and generous, and led a very big life for someone who barely left a twenty-block radius.

One little thing I can tell you for a fact is that Louis Gordon bought the Venice Theater in 1915, and my great-grandfather became the manager of it the following year. For the first few years Louis's wife, Rosie, worked the ticket booth. There were some other employees here and there, but Rosie was the one who ran the show.

George Flicker

After Louis bought the movie theater, the girls really started running around on the streets. Rosie was too busy working the ticket booth to keep an eye on them. Always Jeanie had been a good girl. But then she became a handful too, in her own way. Sometimes you'd see her dancing on the streets, hustling for change. Bella Barker sang, Jeanie danced. We all clapped and threw a penny or two at them.

And what a pair they were. Jeanie had a smile as long as Broadway. And Bella, even when she was a little girl, had these dark, heavy, sexy eyes that made her look older than she was, and of course that wise woman's voice. She was born ready for something big. Her voice made everyone stop and listen to her.

Of course Bella was always more of a solo act. She left the neighborhood for a while when she was a teenager. She was off to Pennsylvania for a year or two, working the vaudeville circuit out there. When she came back she was married to a man named Lew, her manager, who seemed like an old man next to her. And she has a new name, a grown-up name. So she's Belle Baker now, and that's when she started to get famous. But Jeanie was still just playing at dancing. Nobody believed for a second she had the same hunger in her as Belle did.

Mazie's Diary, September 12, 1916

On the way home from work who did I see but our little Jeanie twirling around on a street corner. I stood off to the side and watched her for a while in her candy-colored tutu. Our little sweetheart. Her cheeks were flushed pink from the sun. Our father loved to dance, is what I was thinking. You can't dance on the street forever, is also what I was thinking. But I want her to anyway.

Mazie's Diary, September 23, 1916

Tonight I met two sailors from California. San Francisco seems so far away, how can it even be real? One was tall and one was short and that's all I can remember. Names, I don't know. I got so many names in my head all the time.

They said New York reminded them of home, it being so close to the water. But in San Francisco the mist and the fog come off the ocean so thick you can't see one foot in front of you, that's what they told me.

I said they were lying, and they laughed.

I said: What's so funny?

But then they never answered.

I danced with the tall one while the short one watched us, smiling hard. He looked like he was burning up. When the tall one dipped me, the tie from his uniform tickled my face. I love a man in uniform. Any kind. I think they walk taller when they got something formal to wear. When they got a place to go. The tall one asked me how old I was.

I said: Old enough.

He said: Old enough for what?

Then they both laughed at me some more. But I'm old enough for anything. They don't know but I know.

The tall one tasted salty when I kissed him but later I saw him holding hands with the short one. They were so slim and pretty in their uniforms. Sometimes I just want a uniform of my own.

George Flicker

She was unapologetic about who she was and haughty to those who questioned her, even if they didn't say anything out loud. Like my mother for example. The two of them did not like each other at all. People sometimes think "chutzpah" is a compliment but not the way my mother said it. Sometimes she would cross to the other side of the street when she saw Mazie coming, and she did not do it quietly. She coughed and she stomped. My mother was a tremendous noisemaker. If Mazie cared she didn't show it. Once I heard her shout, "More room for me," after my mother had sashayed her way across the street.

Mazie's Diary, November 1, 1916

Jeanie bought me a birthday present, a pretty dark purple bow, nearly the color of the night sky. I asked her where she got the money, and she told me she saved every penny from dancing next to Bella.

She said: She lets me keep a penny for every ten we make.

I said: That doesn't seem fair.

She said: It was her idea to have the show in the first place. Bella says people with the brains make the money.

I said: You got brains.

She said: I just love to dance.

I asked her how much change she had and she told me it was a lot. I told her I'd show her where I hid you if she'd show me where she hid her change.

I said: We could trade secrets.

Jeanie showed me all the change she had, a few bills at least. Hidden in her suitcase in the closet, the same suitcase we used when we came to town from Boston. I asked her if she was saving for anything. She didn't say anything. I told her she could tell me anything, that she was my sweetheart, my little girl. Finally she got very close to my ear.

She said: I wouldn't want to go forever, but I'd like to join the circus.

I told her I'd come with. I'd ride on top of a horse with a crown on my head and she'd be an acrobat and fly high up above me. The Phillips Sisters, the stars of the show. All the men would swoon at our feet. That part I liked the best but I didn't tell her that.

Jeanie said: But what would Rosie say?

I said: She wouldn't say anything. She'd just be in the audience clapping like everyone else.

Jeanie said: Do you think that's true? Wouldn't she miss us?

I said: We're just daydreaming here, Jeanie. Don't ruin it.

Jeanie said: All right. I guess she'd be in the front row then.

I said: She'd be our biggest fan.

Mazie's Diary, November 7, 1916

I have to work in the candy shop again today. Boring. Only little kids coming in there all day long, dirty change, sticky paws. The bell rings on the front door and I look up and it's the same thing over and over. I feel like a dog when that bell rings. Waiting for someone to feed me with something interesting to look at.

I'd rather be running errands for Louis at the track. I like the track. There's grass and trees, blue sky cracking above us, but then everyone's smoking cigars, too. I like the way it smells clean and dirty at the same time. Plus everyone's having a nip of something. The flasks those men have, jewels crusted in them. Whatever it takes to hide the money. But they're generous though with sharing what they got. Makes it so I don't even mind the horseshit.

But Louis doesn't like it when I come. The track's no place for a woman, that's what Louis says. Of course he says that. He doesn't like the way the men there look at me. I thought he wanted me to get married, but Louis doesn't trust any of those men, at least not with me. But he's one of those men. I like to kid him.

I said: Rosie found you at the track. How'd she find you?

I poke him with my finger.

I said: Is it cause you're so tall, Louis?

He doesn't answer me.

I said: Cause you stick out like a giraffe?

Nothing. Louis keeps his cards so close it's like there's no deck at all.

I think I'll eat all the chocolates in the shop today. All the chocolate kisses, all the chocolate bars. I'm going to tear off their wrapper with my teeth. And I'll eat all the Squirrel Nut Zippers and Tootsie Rolls. Chew till my jaw hurts. And all the caramel creams and butterscotch twists and peanut butter nuggets and those sweetie almond treats. I'll suck on all the hard candies, cherry, strawberry, grape, orange mint. Lick all the lollies till they're gone.

I'll eat and I'll eat and I'll eat just so I never have to look at any of those stinking candies ever again.

Mazie's Diary, January 3, 1917

Last night Rosie and I split a bottle of whiskey. This was after I came home, on time for once. I came in to say good night and the bottle was next to her in bed. I couldn't tell how long she'd been drinking. All I knew was she was already knee-deep in it. She was mourning something, I didn't know what. Louis was nowhere. Jeanie was sleeping. I got under the covers with Rosie, and she handed me the bottle.

I said: What are you thinking about?

She said: Our parents.

I said: Well that'll do it.

She said: Do you remember what happened in Topsfield?

That story again. She and I had talked about it before, when Jeanie wasn't around. Topsfield, that was right before she left us behind.

We were all out together, a real, happy family for the day. Papa holding me with one hand, Jeanie in his other arm, Rosie wedged between him and Mama. Papa was not handsome. His eyes drooped, and his skin was the color of cold, watery soup. And those lines around his mouth and eyes made him always look furious, which he was. Lines don't lie. But he was tall and young and had so much hair, and I remember him as strong. That day, out in the world, he was our father.

We walked together like that. A ruddy-cheeked barker

called us close and bragged about the world's skinniest man and his wife, the world's fattest woman. There was the dark-skinned rubber man, skinny as stretched taffy. His face was so calm, like turning himself inside and out was nothing to him. He was born to bend. I remember the sun was bright, and it was nearly fall, but it was still warm. I was squinting, seeing the world between tiny slits in my eyes. Men with low-slung hats waved hello to Papa. Everyone knew Horvath Phillips, for better or for worse.

But to Rosie I said: I remember that he left us that day.

Because I knew that she wanted that to be my only memory.

He told us to stay put, said he'd be back, sliding that flask from his pocket as he walked away. There were men in white face paint pretending to tug on an imaginary rope. The sun began to set. Jeanie was tired and we found a bench and Mama took her in her lap. My skin stung from the sun, my stomach was sick from sweets.

Mama said: Should we try to find him? I don't know.

She was talking to Rosie, who was the only one of us old enough to understand that the question was not a simple one. But I can't remember her saying anything. She was just simmering.

Mama said: Yes, we'll wait.

Then it was dark and the mimes were gone, most of the families too. Just young people floating around, also some lonely-looking men. Mama still kept turning her head around, thinking he'd come back.

Rosie said: If you don't go find him, I will.

They argued about Rosie wandering around at night by herself. Rosie started fighting for us to just go home already. Mama didn't want to walk the roads by herself. She was still scared of this country, had been since the day she got here. Found the most terrifying man in town to marry, that couldn't have helped much either.

Mama finally gave in to Rosie, and agreed we should try to find him. I remember this sigh of her shoulder, and then Jeanie nearly rolled off her lap.

She wasn't pretty anymore then, Mama. Her hair was thin. She pulled clumps of it out, and so did he, when he was mad. She still had the knockout hips though. I walked behind her as we went to find him and I remember those hips, because I have those hips too. A little girl with her arms around her mama, her face sunk in her hips.

Rosie had known where he was all night. Mama did, too. Those two had just been playing a game with each other for hours. Because back behind the big top was an open field lit up with lanterns and white candles, and filled with people dancing in a frenzy. There was a small stage in the middle of it, packed with men playing all kinds of instruments, accordians, fiddles, guitars, a washboard and spoons. A man sang in a deep growl, French, now I know, but I didn't then. There was a sign at the front of the stage, the Cajun Dancers is what they were called.

The audience was so caught up in the moment, moving faster and faster, laughing and grinning, they were almost hysterical. I could feel the heat coming off their bodies, and then I was nearly hysterical too. The lust of those people is a lust that I hold in my heart. They were gorgeous and free.

Mama put Jeanie down next to me, and we held hands, and then we looked at each other. While Rosie and Mama scanned the crowd, we began to dance our own dance. We were never going to sit still, Jeanie and me. Not like good girls did. I twirled her around until she fell, dizzy, and then I fell, too. The grass tickled the backs of my legs.

I looked up and there was Rosie, pulling away from Mama, and working her way through the crowd. She had found Papa. He looked happy, is what I remember thinking. His eyes were closed, bliss, and his face was relaxed, the lines erased for the moment. He embraced a young, plump, black-haired woman in a long green gown. The dress rose and crashed while they danced. I don't know if he knew the woman or not, if she was the reason why he was so content, or if it was just the dancing. Maybe he just loved the freedom. More than once I have wondered if it would have been easier to forgive him for all that he did if he had just up and left our home, rather than stayed put and laid his cruelty upon us.

I said: I remember you grabbing his arm, and I remember you pointing to us. You shamed him. You were so bold.

Papa bowed to the woman he had been dancing with, and then walked with Rosie back through the crowd, which somehow managed to keep moving and part for them at the same time. Or at least that's how I remember it: Everything faded into the background except for Rosie and Papa.

I said: It was a long ride home.

Rosie said: I felt like I aged ten years in that time.

I said: She tucked us in so quietly that night. She kissed every part of our face.

Rosie said: I didn't get to go to sleep. He took me out back.

I said: I know.

Rosie said: Until I passed out from the pain.

I said: Oh, Rosie.

Rosie said: Was I wrong that day? Did I deserve it?

She was too drunk. She sounded confused.

I said: You were right, and he was wrong.

Rosie said: I'm sorry I left you there.

I said: We didn't blame you for leaving us. I didn't, anyway. Jeanie didn't even know what was happening.

Rosie said: And I came back for you didn't I?

I said: You did.

Rosie said: I was always trying to do the right thing by us even if she wouldn't.

I said: You did.

She said: I take care of you, right?

I said: Rosie, we love you. You know we love you.

Rosie said: I'm not bad, am I?

I said: You're not. You're a good girl.

We drank until we slept. Rosie more than me. When I woke, there was Jeanie, sleeping between us. I don't know if she heard us. I wouldn't want her to hear it. I wouldn't want her to remember any of it.

Mazie's Diary, March 1, 1917

The sun was rising when I took off my shoes this morning. Rosie stood at the door and stared me down. I turned my back on her and wrapped the covers around me, put my head on the pillow, and prayed for peace. God heard me.

I don't know much about praying. It feels like you could be trading on one thing for another, and maybe the thing you're trading isn't really yours in the first place.

Rosie just crawled into bed with me. No yelling. We started whispering to each other.

We curled our hands together. They were cold like always. I remember when Jeanie and I were little we used to crawl into bed with her and Louis and rub her blue-tinted fingers and toes, breathing on them with our hot breath. All I wanted was to be warm and close like that forever.

She said: What if you get a baby in there?

She rubbed my stomach. When she touched it I felt ill. The last thing I wanted was a baby to lug around all day. And I'd never fit into my pretty dresses again.

She said: Then no respectable man will ever want to marry you.

I didn't want nothing to do with marriage with a respectable man or any other kind of man. Not once in my life did I ever dream of my wedding day, no white dresses, no goddamn diamond rings. I only ever dreamed of freedom. The love I have is with the streets of this city.

Mazie's Diary, March 20, 1917

Oh, Rosie. My poor, dear Rosie.

This morning she took us girls to a dusty little gypsy parlor on Essex, empty except for a few plants and a folding table and chairs and a vase with a peacock feather in it. I didn't want to be there, and neither did Jeanie. Golly, Jeanie's so pretty now, skinny and pretty, with her pale skin and puffy lips and moony eyes. I swear she floats when she walks. Still she had a sour face, just like I did. After being sweet for so long, turns out she's a Phillips girl, after all.

The gypsy pushed aside some curtains and came in from the back room. She was wearing a chain of thick gold coins around her neck, and the coins clinked together as she moved.

Dark hair, dark skin, her skirts flowing around her. Some people find that glamorous. To me it's just another gypsy, but Rosie has always had a thing for them.

At first she acted like we weren't there. We could have been ghosts. She lit some incense on the table in front of us, watered some plants in the front window. Then I noticed the plants were dead, gray leaves, stems tipped over. I felt like I was nowhere all of a sudden.

The gypsy sat down at the table with us, told us her name was Gabriela. She smiled at Rosie, and Rosie smiled at her. There was a love there. She looked into my eyes and held them there. The long stare. Searching for something, but I didn't give her a damn thing. Then she looked at Jeanie's eyes, and then back into Rosie's eyes. We were just sitting there waiting, all of us. All right already, is what I was thinking. We get it. You know how to hold a room.

She told us we were there for our sister, like I needed to be reminded Rosie existed. How can I forget?

She didn't have an accent, like other Roma I'd met. She had thick eyebrows, and they made her look serious. She could have been old, she could have been young, I couldn't tell.

She said: I needed to meet you in order to help your sister. You are all in the same home. You are living one life together. You are family. You are sisters. You are connected in this life, and the last one, and the next one, too.

A scam if I ever saw one, I thought. I couldn't wait to tell Louis when I got home. I looked at Jeanie, thinking she'd be on my side. But she was drooling over everything the gypsy said. What a sucker.

Then she held out both of her hands toward me. I sighed and I groused, but finally I put my hand in hers. With her index finger, she traced a few lines on my hand.

She said: Life, money, good.

She was nodding her head.

She said: Well, money will come and go. Mostly come though.

Her hands were cool and soft. Her nails were clean. I admire a well-kept hand. She rubbed a thumb along a line across the top of my hand, and then a line beneath that.

She said: But this is no good.

She squeezed my hand tightly and released it.

She said: No love for you. You will spend your life alone.

I pulled my hands back.

I said: I got company whenever I like.

Rosie shushed me. I don't care, I don't need anyone telling me about my life.

Jeanie said: Now me.

She shoved her hands in the gypsy's. Gabriela smiled at Jeanie like she loved her. The warm glow of a con artist. She told her she had a strong love line, and she pointed to something on her head. She told her she will marry well. A rich man. She asked if she liked rich men. As if she wouldn't want a rich man! I watched Jeanie's face. She was considering it, though she didn't answer. But she smiled. Maybe she smiled like it was funny. I would have said, Who cares? But nobody was asking me. Nobody was telling me I was going to marry someone special.

Gabriela turned to Rosie, and Rosie slid her hand in hers so easily it was like they were husband and wife.

Rosie said: You already know what it says.

Gabriela said she did. Rosie asked her to look again. I didn't know why it was so serious.

Rosie said: Now that you've met them, look again.

Gabriela said: They are strong these two, as you said, but who they are will not change what will happen to you. They love you. I don't need to look at their palms to see that. They're going to be who they're going to be.

Then she brought Rosie's hand to her lips and kissed it. It was a sweet vision.

She said: I still think it can happen, Rosie.

Rosie started crying and then Gabriela swept herself up into the back room, and came back with a handful of bottles. She smacked each bottle down in front of Rosie.

She said: I've asked everyone I know, and they've asked everyone they know too. I went uptown, I went downtown, I went across the river, and I gathered these for you.

She handed Rosie a piece of paper.

She said: I wrote down instructions. How much, how often. And there's an address on there, a Chinaman. He sticks needles in you and they say it lights a fire within your womb.

She held Rosie's hand again.

She said: I lit candles for you, my friend.

Now Rosie was sobbing, and then we held her. So our poor Rosie can't have babies. I never knew, but how could I? We were her babies all along, I thought we were enough for her. I didn't know she wanted anyone but us. She watched over us better than our own mother ever did. She's our sister and our mother. Oh, all this time her heart was breaking and we didn't even know.

George Flicker

Oh you want to know about the gypsies? What do you think you know about the gypsies? That they're a bunch of criminals, probably. That's what people always thought about them. My mother swore they spoke the truth. My friends from Little Italy, they wouldn't go anywhere near them. They're superstitious, and they were afraid of the curses. I have only ever been afraid of what I could see right in front of my face. Because I have seen enough. I don't need to imagine anything worse.

But the gypsies were just the same as you and me. They lived here just like everyone else. They walked the same streets. It's true that some of them were criminals. But you can't judge a whole people by the actions of just a few. But that's what we do here in this country. We do it in this world. I've lived such a long life. I thought things would be better by now. Every day I still watch the news. I listen to people talk. Things are not as bad as they once were, but not as good as I had hoped they would be someday. It's the year 2000 already, and there's still all kinds of messes in this country. I had higher hopes for this world. Eh, but what are you going to do about it anyway?

Mazie's Diary, June 16, 1917

Rosie's sick on the couch again. Hands on her belly. She swings from happy to sad in a heartbeat. We wrapped her up in blankets. I told her to stop taking whatever the gypsy gave her. Rosie, please stop, I was begging her.

She told me I was a fool and didn't know what I was talking about, that things take time, life takes time. But it doesn't seem right, this much pain.

What would anyone do to hold on to a dream for a little longer? Gypsy con or not, it doesn't change Rosie's dream.

I can't blame her for having one, though. I would never blame anyone for wishing for something more from this life.

George Flicker

Then I was old enough to go to war, or at least I told them I was. I was a few months shy of legal but they didn't check too hard. I would have said anything though to get out of that cramped apartment! The taller I got, the smaller it seemed. And I wanted to see the world. That I would be fighting in a war didn't scare me for some reason. Maybe I wasn't so brave, maybe I was just stupid instead. I won't talk about what happened though, what I saw there. You know, we're not like your generation where we need to talk about every little thing. Sometimes a bad thing happens and then you're done with it.

But anyway I didn't see Mazie again for five years, so I can't help you out during that particular time period. Because I went to France and then I stayed there when the war was over and lived there and worked there and had a life there. I lived with a French girl for a year even. And she was really something, I'll tell you. Ooh-la-la, I know. [Laughs.] I've had my fun, I've had my fun. Eventually I had to come back though. My mother got sick, and of course, there was all that trouble with Uncle Al.

Mazie's Diary, November 1, 1917

Twenty years old. I'm sure I should be having more fun.

What is this pull in me that makes me want trouble? Months I've been quiet and good, even though the heat on the streets was making me feel sexy, wanting to dance and drink. To kiss someone. Passing by alleys at night and seeing girls and boys playing. Fingers on lips, fingers on tits, I miss it. It's been so long since I've lain down with someone. Most nights are with Rosie now. I lost this summer to her belly.

Mazie's Diary, December 13, 1917

Rosie lost another baby. This time it felt like she was pregnant for only a minute.

Now she's flat on her back again in the living room. Weeks and weeks of it, and there's a dent in the couch now, I can see the mattress sagging beneath her. I swear the springs will sink straight through the floor.

She grabs my hand but squeezes too hard and it hurts but I try not to make a noise. She asks me to stroke her head but shifts her head, squirms beneath my fingers. Rub my feet, she tells me.

But then she says: No, you're doing it wrong. No, don't touch me.

Watches me with her eagle eye, thinking I'll leave her.

Louis sits in the kitchen, head down, in the food. He closed the theater for a few days this week. Jeanie's nowhere I can see, smart girl.

I take nips in the bedroom. I can't go to the whiskey, but the whiskey can come to me.

Mazie's Diary, December 16, 1917

Something's going to break soon. I got no control over myself and I like it.

Mazie's Diary, January 4, 1918

I wasn't ready to go home yet but there was nobody left in the bar worth talking to. Talked to a bum on the street instead, an old fella. We split whatever was in his bottle and I gave him a smoke. I was feeling tough. I asked him how long he'd been on the streets.

He said: Longer than you've been alive, girlie. You gotta be tough to last that long.

He beat his chest.

I said: I could survive out here.

He said: You don't want to try.

I said: I could do it. You wanna see me?

He said: You got a home, you're lucky.

I said: Why don't I feel that way?

Then he got gentle with me.

He said: If someone loves you, go home to them.

A bad wind blew in and I grew suddenly, terribly cold. I couldn't bear the night for another minute. I handed him the rest of my smokes and wandered home.

Mazie's Diary, January 5, 1918

Rosie was trying to sweet-talk me early this morning. A nice change from yelling I guess.

She said: Don't you want a sweetheart?

I said: The whole world's my sweetheart.

Mazie's Diary, January 18, 1918

Now she's sharp and angry. She told Jeanie the dancing was done. No more classes, she said. And she told me I'd be on the streets if I came home late one more time. A month ago she didn't want to lose me, now she'll throw me on the streets?

I said: I know the streets. I've been there before.

She said: You can't take those dresses of yours on the street.

I said: I don't need none of it.

She said: You'd be nowhere without me.

Jeanie and I looked at Louis but there was nothing, no help. His heart is broken too, I think. His giant heart, exploded.

Mazie's Diary, January 21, 1918

Took a few turns at the snuffbox of some rich man slumming downtown tonight. I can't say I didn't like it. Slapped his hand away from my tit though—he didn't earn nothing just by sharing. He's no hero like the sailors. Just a spoiled rich prick.

Everything started tumbling around me. I left when the fistfights started. I couldn't help but laugh even as I lifted my skirts over the drunks bloody on the floor. That was not the right bar for a girl like me, though I couldn't say it was the wrong one either.

But then I was walking down the streets and the moon was judging me, it was staring at me and judging me, I swear it was. I stood on the corner, and I let it judge me. I'll judge you back, too, moon. What do you know? Stupid moon. Horrible moon.

I came home and got down on my hands and my knees in front of Rosie, still on the couch. She put her hands in my hair.

She said: Why can't I have a baby?

I said: I don't know.

She said: Why won't you be a good girl?

I said: I don't know.

We stayed like that until I came in here to write this down. She clawed at my neck when I walked away.

It's her pain, not mine.

Mazie's Diary, January 22, 1918

I was gone all day and all night. No candy shop, no track. Just the streets and the bars and the men and the women and the whiskey and the beer and the smokes and the snuff. Nothing but these things, and then more of these things, and then bed.

Mazie's Diary, January 24, 1918

When I woke up this afternoon I went into the kitchen and Rosie was sitting at the table with Louis. Maybe the fever broke, I was thinking. I looked in her eyes and they seemed clear. But my eyes were hazy, so what did I know? I couldn't trust what I saw for nothing.

She sounded clear though.

She said: I've tried everything with you. Louis, you know I'm right.

He didn't want no part of it, I thought, but he nodded. He was pressing his fork against his eggs.

She said: Something's gotta change. You know I'm right too, Mazie.

I felt bad about interrupting his eggs. Louis loves his eggs.

He said: Here's the thing.

At last! The big man speaks.

He said: It's a favor more than anything else.

Favor's a word I can't refuse when it comes to Louis, and he knows it. He's taken care of us forever and he didn't have to. He waited to say that word. He waited till he couldn't wait anymore. Kept the favor in his pocket. Bet he's got more than a few in there.

He said: Rosie's been sick and I've been needing help down at the theater.

He put down his fork and then he took Rosie's hand. Or did she take his? I couldn't tell. They were propping each other up now. That's what it meant. That's how that works when you're together with someone. I get it, even if I don't have it.

He told me he wanted me to work the ticket booth, that it was true that the hours were long but it was important work to him. He had put a lot of money into the theater.

He said: You're good with numbers. There's money coming in and out all day. And I need someone I can trust there. There's sticky fingers all over this city, you know that.

He told me it would just be for a little while and when I asked how long he told me he didn't know, and I don't think he was lying, it wasn't exactly a lie.

I said: It's a cage and you know it. You're putting me in prison.

He said: Tell me what I ever ask you for.

Rosie said: He gives you everything!

I could not argue with either of them about anything. I know they were right. They had me cornered. Finally, Rosie had me.

I said: Death is upon me.

They laughed at me like chickens.

Rosie said: It's good that you're funny. It's good that you find things so funny. You'll be needing that sense of humor.

But I wasn't kidding around. That ticket booth! All day, hours and hours, the whole world going on around me. I'm going to miss everything. The world will pass me by. I will grow old and then die in that cage.

2

I chose only to help the men, not the children. Men, I can help. I can give them some change, a place to sleep. I can call an ambulance. Their needs are simpler. And if they still fail, there's no one they can blame but themselves. But the kids I steer clear of. There's people better at it than me, who have the time to give. I've got a jar full of lollies for them, and that'll do. I got nothing to say to them. Every kid on the Bowery knows they can come to me and I'll give them a treat, and that's all. Give them a treat and then shoo them away.

Lydia Wallach

So she and my great-grandfather Rudy Wallach worked together for two decades at the Venice Theater. I have seen pictures of the theater, both the interior and the exterior, but none of these pictures are in particularly good condition. I know that the theater was beneath the tracks of the Second Avenue elevated train line, which I imagine made it quite noisy. I can also tell you the theater was in the style of the era, which is to say it was a classical-style movie palace, with European design influences. There were velvet seats—I presume they were red, though it was obviously impossible to tell from the photos I saw—and high ceilings with some ornate decor. The theater seated approximately six hundred people, and there was a ground floor as well as a balcony level. In its initial conception, it was, for lack of a better description, a very classy joint.

Mazie's Diary, February 1, 1918

Today was my first day at the ticket booth in the theater. Glass cage is more like it. Prisoners would complain if it were their cell, that's how small it is. A chicken would squawk if it were his coop.

I said: A dead man would complain if he knew this was his coffin.

Rosie was moving things around lightning quick, a lockbox, a roll of tickets, a tin can full of sharpened pencils. She slapped a notebook on the counter.

She said: Then I guess you'd better rest in peace.

She stepped outside of it and ushered me inside. I bruised my hip on the countertop squeezing in there. That countertop had already marked me for life.

I flopped down on the swivel chair and spun myself slowly around. There was just enough room for that. There was a heater in one corner, already blowing like it had been waiting for me all along. A clock ticking off the minutes before nine in the morning. A calendar on the wall. One month gone, February lay blank. Life was going to happen all around me. The truth of the moment struck me. I started to tear up like a stupid baby girl.

Rosie said: Oh, you poor thing, putting in a hard day's work

I said: It ain't that. I'm not afraid of work.

She knew I was telling the truth. I'd always done what Louis had asked me to do.

I said: It's just that I'll be all alone in here, and everyone else will be out there.

I suppose I was being a little dramatic and I flung my arms out. Of course they bumped right up against the window, only proving my point further.

Rosie started laughing at me, and it just sounded so good, to hear her laughing. I almost didn't care what she was going to say. Even if she was teasing me, I was happy to hear her laugh.

She said: Mazie, there's one thing you'll never feel in this job, and that's alone.

She squeezed in next to me, and showed me my tasks. How I'd keep track of how many tickets I started with in the morning, and how many I ended with in the evening. She taught me the combination to the lock. She slid open a small drawer underneath the countertop. Inside was a flask. She looked at me and shrugged.

She said: It does help move the day along.

I said: Well, well.

Then it was ten all of a sudden and there was a line of people building up in front of the theater.

She said: Don't let anyone give you any trouble.

She left me with a small paper sack, lunch for the day. I settled myself. My hips and chest and belly all shifted into some kind of position and I tried to sit up straight but I knew I'd be slouching by the end of the day. The train rumbled on by over my head again, a thundercloud rolling through. I couldn't even hear myself think but what was there to think about anyway? It was just me and the line. Rosie was still standing there, off to the side, watching everything. She was smiling so hard I thought her face would split in two, straight down the middle, two cheeks floating off in the sky. She had rearranged me. I was a movable part to her. And now I was in this cage.

I slid aside the front guard to the cage and slotted it into place. The whole of the line took a step forward all at once, like they were taking one big breath together. I looked at them all. Women holding hands with their little ones, a few sailors and soldiers, more than a few men in suits looking like they might be trying to sleep off their night out on the Bowery.

Then I got a little dizzy for a second. It's just a job, is what I was thinking.

Finally, Rosie spoke.

She said: This is Mazie, and she's in charge now.

And damn if they didn't all wave at me and say hello.

Lydia Wallach

My great-grandfather was responsible for the movie selection, staff management, concessions, and the care of the theater itself. Basically anything that was contained within the doors of the theater, he managed. And Mazie sold the tickets and handled the money, and if anyone got out of line, she also ran security. Rudy was a tiny, gentle man. I have seen pictures of him and he looks much shorter than everyone else around him. He had immaculate skin and hands, as did my mother, and I do, too. Look at my hands. Look at how tiny they are. [Holds up hands.] Those are the Wallach hands. So Rudy wasn't in any place to be roughing up any of the bums. Also he was the child of intellectuals. That's right, I always forget that part. My great-great-grandparents were Russian intellectuals escaping some sort of persecution I never quite understood, and they moved to New York when he was just a baby. He was just this fine, sensitive man, fair to everyone, and he wasn't interested in any of that rough-and-tumble business. So I guess it happened quite naturally that it fell to Mazie.

Mazie's Diary, February 5, 1918

The movies make me sick in my gut.

I knew this before and then I forgot but now I remember, oh buddy do I remember.

I shut down the cage last night early. All day long I'm sitting there, wondering what's going on inside. So I wandered through the theater. The high ceilings made the place feel like a castle out of a storybook, somewhere far away. Europe is what I was thinking, although what do I know of Europe?

I wanted to watch the last show of *Tarzan*. I slipped into the theater, onto those bruised red velour seat cushions, soft under my fingertips. There was a romance to it, I could see it. All those rows of big, beautiful, round bulbs that lined the walls. Rosie shows up once a week and tells the ushers to dust the lights. Sweep and dust, dust and sweep, she repeats it. She should ask that gypsy of hers if she were a general in a past life.

The movie was just starting, and everyone hushed up. At first I liked seeing all the animals, the giraffes and the lions and the snakes and the alligators. They looked like trouble. It was dreamy, watching something wild and alive and different than my own life, up high, so much bigger than anything I know.

But it only took a minute till I started to feel wobbly. The animals on the screen swelled up, then they floated and waved around in front of my eyes. Something gooey started to boil in my stomach. I turned my head away from the screen but it was too late. I was retching in the aisle like a bum on the corner after the bars closed for the night. Someone shushed me, but then there was someone else by my side, a small hand holding my hair. Some lady, I figured. When I stopped retching I looked up and there was Rudy.

I said: I don't know what's wrong with me.

He said: Let's get you outside, Miss Mazie. Get some air in you.

I put my arm around his neck and we stumbled together through the lobby and out the front door, and then he leaned me up against the cage.

He asked me if I was sick and I said no. He asked me if anyone in my house was sick and I said no.

He said: Sometimes one of the boys gets sick, and then we all do. Just out of nowhere.

I said: It's not that, I'm fit as a fiddle. It's looking up at the movies. I don't know what to tell you. All that jumping around.

He said: No more movies for you.

I said: Who needs to go to the movies anyway? Real life's more interesting. Flesh and blood.

I was getting my spunk back in the cold air. I was feeling a little humiliated too. Bending over that like that, him seeing me weak, I didn't like any of it.

I said: It's just a movie, who cares.

He said: So you stick to tickets and I'll stick to the movies. Front of the house, back of the house, that kind of thing.

I said: It seems fair.

We shook on it and it was like his hand nearly disappeared in mine. He's a strange little doll of a man, that Rudy.

Mazie's Diary, February 8, 1918

It's one thing to walk the streets, and it's another thing to watch them. I used to be just one of the crowd, stretching my legs, mixing with the rest of those lugs. But now I'm sitting still while the world moves on around me, and I'm seeing things a little differently through the bars of this cage. Hustlers and cons I knew here and there but not so much. Now I watch them every day and I'm learning. They don't care where they land as long as they get what they're looking for. Maybe they never hit me up before because I was always on the run on the streets, but now I'm a sitting duck and they won't leave me alone. I must have a bright red target on my forehead that says Easy Mark. But that sign would be wrong. I'll teach them soon enough not to mess with me.

Mazie's Diary, February 10, 1918

A charmed life's what I've had up till now I see.

Thirteen-hour days, and all I can do is drink myself to sleep lately. Rosie says it gets easier. Rosie's got it easy herself right now. Jeanie's been going to the track instead of Rosie. I can't say I'm not jealous. How long could it go on though, me sitting here? It's been two weeks. I'm sure they won't want me to stay here forever. Whatever lesson they want me to learn I'll swear I learned it.

Jeanie doesn't even like the track that much. She says there's a man there who's sweet on her though, always tipping his hat at her, running after her, opening doors she didn't even know needed opening.

She said: It's like he made these doors up out of thin air.

She told me he was a horse doctor from Long Island. His name's Ethan Fallow.

I said: What kind of name is that?

She said: I don't know, but he's taller than me, so I don't care.

Mazie's Diary, February 12, 1918

That train, that goddamned noisy train. I have to yell all day long to be heard over it. People lean in with their hands on their ears to hear what I have to say. At least I'm making them pay attention to me.

Mazie's Diary, February 22, 1918

I don't know what to make of that fella Rudy. He's nice and respectful, so I can't say as I mind him. But he's always creeping around late. I can't wait to leave when it's closing time, and he's still there after dark. He's free to do what he likes. He's not ripping anyone off I don't think. Only what about his family? All those little boys running around afoot. He and that wife of his are baby machines. You'd think he'd want to go home to them. Or maybe not.

Lydia Wallach

As I said, he was dead long before I was born. I'm sorry I don't have a "he bounced me on his knee in the theater" story or anything like that. But yes, he was a legendary cinephile at that time, as legendary as one can be for that sort of thing. I know what you're thinking. Oh he *really* liked movies, good for him. But he was part of a network of movie theater managers who had late-night screenings of art films imported—or sometimes smuggled, depending on the state of war—from Europe. Of course it's not really a big deal to anyone. He's not in any history books, or anything like that. It was just this sort of very cool thing that he did—cool if you find people being obsessive about things cool, that is. Which I do, a bit.

But I don't know terribly much beyond that. I do know that it was something that drove my great-grandmother crazy, because she had wanted him home more with his sons. It became something that my grandfather and his three brothers treasured because eventually they were permitted to attend these late-night screenings. It was influential on them to a certain extent. One of my great-uncles did move to Hollywood for a short period of time, I think just a few years, and he was an extra in movies though he never got a speaking part. And then there was another brother who eventually ended up in the Midwest, in Madison, where he helped to start a film archive, and he stayed there until he died, which was not that long ago actually. I did not go to the funeral, because I had a lot of funerals last year, and one more seemed unnecessary.

And, of course, I work as a lawyer for a cable company, the name of which I don't feel comfortable stating in this interview, on rights and issues for their original programming. I minored in film at NYU—we were in a class together there, right? I thought you looked familiar. And I always thought I would do entertainment law, the whole time I was in law school. There was really no question I would do otherwise. My family has always relaxed by watching movies. When I think of my childhood, I think of my hand in a bucket of popcorn. It's quite visceral, this memory. Whenever I smell butter I feel small and comforted and safe. Just talking about it now makes me want to lick my fingers.

Mazie's Diary, March 1, 1918

I met a nun today. Holy moly, my first nun.

It's not like I've never seen a nun before. They're all over the place, those Catholics, trying to save everyone's soul on the Bowery, all the people having too much fun for their own good. But they've always left me alone before. I don't know why. Maybe my dresses are too fine for them to bother with me. But I'm sitting in that booth all day, a working stiff, doing what I do. So now they're after me I guess.

All right, I was taking a nip from the flask, it's true. A nip and a cigarette, no one can blame me. I'd read all my *True Romances*, and there wasn't another show for twenty minutes. Jeanie had already stopped by to drop off my lunch, she was off to the track. People were hustling by on the sidewalk, but no one stopped to say hello. Cars choking on the street, cursed train rumbling above. Nothing left to do but drink.

So I lift the flask to my mouth, and then out of nowhere, there she is, her face pressed up against the glass of my cage, her hands to the bars. I screamed.

She said: Before you drink, think.

I caught my breath, but then I was seeing red.

I said: I'm thinking just fine.

I tipped the end of the flask into my mouth. She shook her head, judging me on behalf of Jesus. She had honey-blond hair, a little wisp of it sneaking out from her habit. Her eyes were like blue glass, they had a shimmer to them. No makeup, just her face. She wasn't much older than me, and she was short like me, but I didn't know if she had the same curves under that habit. There we were, two girls on Park Row. Only one of us was showing a lot more skin.

I said: I ain't hurting anyone.

She said: Except yourself.

I said: Oh brother.

I started blowing smoke in her direction and she took a step back.

I said: What's your name, sister?

She said: Sister Tee.

I said: What's the Tee for?

She said: It's T-e-e not T. Tee's for Theresa but there's ten Theresas in the church so we all have different nicknames and I'm just Tee, because I'm wee.

This made me like her. She's just a kid, I thought. I'm one too, I guess.

She said: We're not talking about me though. We're talking about you. And your soul.

I said: I'm Jewish so you can stop worrying about my soul.

She said: Everyone can be saved.

I said: Sister Tee, you wouldn't even know where to begin with me.

It made her laugh a little bit. She was sweet. I'd have liked to see her out of that habit, all dolled up, in a club on Second Avenue, dancing up a storm with the sailors. Slap some rouge on those baby cheeks of hers and she'd grow up real fast. But it was not to be, me and Sister Tee.

A line started to build for the next show.

I said: All right, go find another drunk to help. I got work to do.

She said: Remember to think about what I said.

I said: Scram.

I waved her off with my hand.

She swished off in her skirts, and I was missing her already.

I said: But come back sometime. Come back and say hi.

She was bold, and I liked it. For a nun, she had flair. And I liked how she seemed both old and young. I thought maybe

she would be my first friend on Park Row. Even if she thinks
I'm no good, I bet she'd still be my friend.

The war's coming to an end, everyone's saying it, on the radio, in the papers. I'll believe it when I see it. But it's putting
everyone in a good mood. There's a parade every other day. I
think folks think we throw enough parades we can make anything happen. There's been soldiers coming home, for weeks
and weeks now. Hurrahs floating in the air. I can sometimes
hear them. It's all off in the distance, though. It's out there
and I'm in here.

In here I deal with the bums and the stragglers and the
cons. The men in suits sleeping off the night before. Why
they don't just go home I'll never know. I have to say
they're all starting to make me laugh. Except the ones with
the children. The mothers with the kids for the funnies,
that's fine, that don't get to me. I'll give them a lolly, sure.
I've got a jarful just sitting there. They pay full price and
move along. But the cons with the kids, saying they're begging on their behalf, using them. I can't tell what's true or
not.

This woman Nance has been coming around more lately,
I've seen her for a few weeks. I'd heard of her before, back
when I used to have a lot more free time on my hands and
I knew all the gossip from the bars. She says she has children
but I've never seen them. I shoo her away from my line.

Off with you, I tell her. Stay away from my paying customers. We're running a business here.

She scatters from the theater. Park Avenue, across the street to the King Kong Bar, a pause at the window, around the corner and she's gone. Just a skirt in the distance. Too old to be a street urchin, too pretty to be a common whore. Only thing left's a con.

Mazie's Diary, May 10, 1918

Where's our Jeanie, we've all been wondering lately. In the arms of Ethan Fallow, I suppose. He came by Grand Street last night. He brought her a bouquet of tea roses, and she held them in her lap for an hour, and then they went for a walk and I didn't see her again before bed. There's a first, me beating Jeanie to bed.

It seems like it takes a lot of time, courting. You sit and wait for them to call you. Then you sit and wait for them to come to your home. Then you sit and wait for them to tell you how beautiful you are. Then you sit and wait for them to fall in love. I've no patience for any of it. I want instant love.

Jeanie's been spending a lot of time at the track, too. Making up errands she needs to run. And she's been hanging out with Bella Barker now that she's back in town again. Only now her name's Belle Baker, like that makes any difference. She's still got the same voice, the same eyes, those pits of sadness. Barker or Baker, you are who you are.

Jeanie does whatever she wants now. She works Rosie and Louis like a con. She took all my tricks and made them perfect. I'm not jealous of most of it. I wouldn't want to hold Ethan Fallow's hand for hours on end. I wouldn't want to nod my head at everything Belle says.

Only the freedom I envy.

Jeanie gets to do whatever she wants, I told Rosie last night.

Rosie said: Jeanie I don't worry about.

Mazie's Diary, May 15, 1918

That little Nance came back again today. She stood in front of me after the line for the last show had died out. A dried-up girl, younger than me. The bottom of her dress was in tatters. Her hair was long and unbrushed. Her tan overcoat was stained with something purple. Still, I wasn't buying what she was selling. She was no beggar. There was lipstick on those lips.

She said: Please, ma'am, please. I'm broke and hungry and I've got two little ones at home and we haven't had food in a week and can you please please please help us. A penny, a nickel, something, anything.

Her voice was too singsongy for me to trust her. She'd made that speech too many times before.

I said: Scram, little miss. I know what you'll do with any scratch I give you.

She said: I swear on my life it's for my kids.

She reached down the front of her dress and pulled out a rusted locket on a chain. She struggled to open it, and it was then that I could see her hands were shaking. But when she finally released it, she pressed it up against my glass cage. There were photographs on both sides, a boy and a girl. Two faded babies.

Looking at the pictures, I got a choke in my throat. I might have lost all the air in my body if I didn't go to these children straightaway and help them. I couldn't help but think about Rosie. All the sadness. Her on the couch all those months.

I had a bag of chocolates sitting in the cage and I slid them to her. She grabbed it and stuck her filthy fingers in it. Keep it, is what I was thinking.

I said: Where's their father?

She said: Their father went to war and never came back.

I said: My condolences.

She said: No condolences. He's in France, the bastard. He met some girl there, surprise of the century.

I felt sorry for her. It's easier to let things go when there's no reminder of someone. But she had two babies in a locket.

She said: He couldn't wait to get away. He got me hooked, and then he joined up to get away from it and from me and he left me behind with those two babies. Isn't that funny? Easier for him to go fight the Germans than spend another minute with me.

She started licking her fingers.

She said: Sweet Jesus, it's good.

I watched her eat. She put one chocolate after another in her mouth. She was a greedy child, is all. A hungry brat.

She asked me for money but I said no.

She said: They're real, I swear on my life.

I said: Then let me see them. I'll lock up right now and go there. Last show's nearly over.

She had eaten all the chocolate. She could have run. But she didn't.

So I gathered together all the food I had in my cage, another bag of candy, half a sandwich. Then I followed her home through the pitch-black streets. We didn't talk about her problems, we talked about the city instead. How different it was now that there were cars everywhere you looked. Can you believe the noise? Can you believe the dirt? We talked about how we both loved the rain because it washed the streets clean. Even for a few hours New York City would sparkle again.

She said: What I wouldn't give for the rain to clean me up.

We picked up our skirts over some garbage in a back alley off Mulberry Street, and she led me to a metal door, brass buttons around the edges, the center painted red. There was a thick, rusty keyhole. Nance pulled a key from the front of her dress. I guess she kept everything down the front of her dress.

She said: It's Mama.

She stood there for a moment, as if she were afraid to enter. Which made me afraid to enter, too.

It was quiet, and it was quiet, and it was quiet, and then suddenly there was squawling and screeching, and I covered my ears.

Nance said: Oh come on now.

There was one candle lit and she walked toward it. There was the smell of piss and I breathed through my mouth. My eyes adjusted and I could see where the howls were coming from. There was a boy with white-blond hair, a thin sliver of flesh in the dark.

He said: You've been gone all day.

She said: I was getting you food, wasn't I?

She gathered the boy and a little girl to her.

She said: This nice lady brought you some candy.

I opened my purse and handed them the chocolates. My eyes grew used to the dark, and I could see the girl was frail and curly-haired, a sprout of a thing. She stopped wailing when she took the candy. Even by candlelight I could see they ate just as their mother did, with greedy desperation, salivating like animals.

All I wanted to do was steal them and give them to Rosie. She would have loved them. She would have fed them.

Later Nance and I shared a cigarette outside in the alley.

I said: They can't live on candy forever.

She wasn't paying attention to me, though. She had her eyes on my cigarette. She wanted her own.

I told her I'd bring her food tomorrow, and I asked her what she'd do after that. I gave her a cigarette and she didn't say thank you. I told her I couldn't help her forever.

She said: Are you sure you can't? Come on, Miss Mazie.

She stroked my arm for a second. She had this sleepy smile. The lipstick held steady.

She said: I can tell you're a girl who likes to have a good time. Everyone knows Mazie Phillips likes to have a good time.

I swatted her hand away. Then I shoved her up against the wall. I could have punched her. The only reason I didn't was because of those babies.

I said: You better be thinking of your children now. Else you'll end up like the garbage in this alley. All of you.

She started to cry.

She said: I'm sorry, it's the only way I know how to be. I ain't bad, I swear it.

I felt bad for shoving her. She wasn't much different than me, just like Sister Tee wasn't different either. Just a turn here, a twist there. No one to love you.

I said: That's how I feel too. I ain't a bad girl.

She said: I'm just hooked. It makes you desperate.

I said: Stop thinking about you. Think about them.

I promised to bring them food tomorrow morning. I left the stinking alley behind. It was past midnight when I got home and Rosie wasn't happy about it. She had her arms crossed, and a cup of tea in front of her at the kitchen table. She was squinting at me. She didn't look pretty. Louis was slouched back in his seat, his hands behind his head, just waiting for it.

But I had a good reason! I was sad and full of life at the same time, thinking I could help this family. For once they couldn't be mad at me for coming home late.

So I told them the story, about Nance and these children, locked in this dark basement all day long with nothing but a candle to light their way. I asked them if there was something we could do to help. Louis, with all his connections, had to know someone. I was looking back and forth between the two of them. I was waiting for them to tell me I did something right for once.

Then Rosie stood up from the table.

She said: I don't want to have nothing to do with it.

She was calm and icy. She picked up her cup of tea and left the room.

Louis sat there for a minute, just shaking his head at me.

He said: Why are you telling this story in this house? I don't understand you.

He wasn't talking much louder than a whisper.

He said: After everything we've been through. After everything she's been through. You're just throwing it in her face.

Then he got up and left me there. It stung me all over. I'm crying now while I'm writing this. Sitting in the candlelight, while in the other room the two of them are thinking I'm some cruel, vile girl. When all I want to do is help.

I won't mind them, though. I won't. I will help those children.

Lydia Wallach

Part of Mazie's legend within my family can be attributed to her charitable contributions, not within the community where she lived, although my understanding was that she was ultimately exceptionally charitable, but more specifically, she was giving to my great-grandmother, and to my uncles after Rudy passed away. "Legendary" [puts her fingers in air quotes] doesn't cover it actually. There were pictures of her on the wall, framed photos of her and my great-grandfather. My mother said there was a shrine in the living room. Sadly, none of them exist anymore, or if they do, I don't know where they are. There have been too many apartment moves along generations. Things get thrown away. I know you've been trying to find a picture of her. I wish I could help you. I'm sorry, that's all I can say.

I think it meant a great deal to my mother to hear all these stories about Mazie and Rudy. She loved her uncles very much and they didn't have any other family around—they were the only relatives that made it over. My great-grandparents were trying to create their own universe by the force of procreation. But none of my great-uncles had children except for my grandfather, and then it was just my mother, and then she only ended up having me. So their grand experiment to populate the world with Wallachs failed and ends with me as I have no intention of having any children because number one, there are too many people on this planet already, and number two, who has time for it? You have to really want it, and I do not.

It broke my mother's heart when I told her that I was uninterested in childbearing, but, to be fair to me, she had a heart that was easily broken. But that was because she had a beautiful soul. A gorgeous, gorgeous soul. I think this was because she grew up with all that attention from her uncles. There is something about being beloved by men from a very young age, being made to feel special, that makes a girl blossom in a particular kind of way. I did not have that same kind of attention. I had just my father, and he loved my mother most until he did not love her at all.

You know I think I was always fond of hearing these stories about Mazie in part because she went down an unconventional path. Marriage and children, they just weren't important to her. It's important to be exposed to alternate lifestyle possibilities, even if you don't embrace them for yourself. It's just good to know the possibility exists.

Mazie's Diary, May 16, 1918

Jeanie worked my morning shift for me today.

I said: You don't need to mention it to Rosie.

She said: Oh I wouldn't dare.

Her tone was sweet but I'll likely have to repay the favor someday. A sister knows the difference between a gift and a favor.

Then I went shopping on Hester Street for the babies and Nance. I bought a loaf of bread, a jar of strawberry jam, a bushel of crisp, rosy apples, and a fistful of dirt-lined carrots still on their stems. I wanted to give them the earth. More chocolates, butter, milk. I tried to buy food that would keep. Food they wouldn't have to cook. Food they could just shove in their hungry little mouths. I was delivering to them a wish with this food. A hope for good health.

The door was open an inch when I got there. I pulled it

wide open and let the sunlight stream in. There was no stove in the room, no fireplace, no icebox, no sink, nowhere to wash. It was nothing more than a box, and inside it this small, sad family.

The children ran toward me saying my name over and over again. Nance told them to give me a hug. She was jammed up in a corner, her knees pressed against her, a cigarette in her fingers. She was blocking the light from her eyes with the other hand. The little girl reached up toward my waist and rested her head along my backside. She felt like a feather. The boy grabbed the food from my hands. He tried to rip the loaf of bread in half but his hands were too small, and he was weak. I took it from him and broke a hunk off and handed it to him, and another to her. The whole world disappeared for the children while they ate. In the sunlight I could see that both of their eyes were runny and pink, with crusts around the edges. Oh I'm crying now writing this, just as I was then.

I realized I didn't even know their names, and I asked Nance. Rufus and Marie, she told me.

I handed them the jug of milk from my purse, and I told them to drink it. The boy let the girl go first. She drank until she spit some milk down the front of her dress, and then she started retching, and everything she ate started coming up. Nance stayed in the corner. I burned. I pulled a handkerchief from my purse, and I tried to clean her up as best I could. She was crying. I told her it was going to be all right, and so did her brother. I told her to eat slowly, and she did.

I have no plans beyond but to keep feeding them. Before I left I handed them a fistful of lollies, a box of crayons, and some paper. I told Nance I'd be back tomorrow.

She said: What about me?

I said: What about you?

She said: Don't I get any lollies? Don't I get anything?

She sounded no older than her children.

I threw one at her.

Mazie's Diary, May 17, 1918

They were spread out all over the floor coloring when I got there. Marie had drawn a circle with swirling rays surrounding it. I asked her what it was.

She said: It's the sun. It's the outside.

I asked Rufus what he was drawing and he told me it was a forest of lollies.

I'd steal them if I could. I would.

Mazie's Diary, May 18, 1918

I only had a few moments before work today. I was thinking I'd show up and everything would be better, that some magic would have healed Nance. But I was a fool of course. A sick person doesn't get better overnight.

The door was locked when I got there and I had to bang on it for a while. Finally Nance pushed it open. The room smelled of retch. She crawled on her knees back to the corner where she had made a nest of blankets. Her children were curled up with her.

I asked her how I could help. I said I'd call a doctor.

She said: There's no doctor's going to help me. I'm just going to feel this way for a while until I don't anymore.

I said: Maybe I should take them home with me. Just so they'll be safe.

She said: You'd love that, wouldn't you? Taking my babies away from me.

I said: I only meant to make it easier. I'm here every day trying to help you, missy. You don't want my help, fine. But you should be looking after those children of yours. They didn't do a thing wrong. They don't deserve this.

Christ, maybe I was yelling too loud, I don't know.

I said: You asked me for help, remember?

She said: Well now we don't want it.

She struggled her way to standing. Her legs were quivering but still she stood.

She said: You don't come in here and tell me how to live my life. You don't tell me how to love my children.

I said: Nance, I didn't say you didn't love them.

I was trying to be softer with her. I didn't want her to throw me out.

She said: You think I don't know what you think of me? I know the truth.

Marie started crying, and then Rufus did too.

I said: You're just sick right now. You're not thinking straight. I'm here to help.

Nance pulled those babies tight. It was the strongest I'd seen her.

She said: Say good-bye to Miss Mazie. Saint Mazie's more like it. Thinks she's better than all of us.

I said: I'll be back tomorrow. I'll bring you more milk.

She said: We don't want it.

I said: I'm coming anyway.

She said: See what I care. I don't have to open the door for nobody.

I'll throttle her with my own two hands if she hurts those babies.

Mazie's Diary, May 19, 1918

I went early this morning to Nance's. The alley outside their front door was quiet except for the strays, the rats, and the cats, scuttling, tussling. The door was shut tight. I pressed my face up against it. It was early and quiet. I was sure I could hear Marie crying inside. I had milk with me, and lollies, too.

I started pounding on the door.

I said: I'll leave the milk outside. You don't have to speak to me, only please take the milk.

I hid around the corner to see if Nance would open the door. Finally two enormous stray cats, spotted gray and filthy, knocked over the jug and took to lapping it. Then cat after cat came out of every corner of the alley, and the milk was gone. Nance had never opened the door.

I took it upon myself to do a little nosing around today—as best I could from that cage. I talked to a beat cop, Officer Walters. He's stopped by a few times to share a nip from the flask, and to flirt. He's an old dog. His hair's turning gray and he's got a big belly. I'd worry he'd crush me if I let him hold me. But he's good for a laugh and he's got a nice set of thick lips on him, so all right, he can have a nip. He tells me to call him Mack but I never do.

I asked him if he knew about Nance. He knew Nance, oh yes he did.

He said: Sorry to tell you this, Mazie, but if she wants to keep her door locked she's entitled to it.

I said: But those children are living in darkness all day I'm telling you. And she's not feeding them right. Can't you just go knock on her door?

It occurred to me that his breath was thicker with liquor than mine.

He said: I think we know how to handle this. It's our jobs to know.

I said: Well then I know how to handle you.

I snatched the flask from his hand.

I said: Go on, get out of here. I'll find someone else to help me. What are we paying our taxes for?

I yelled and yelled, but there was not a hint of guilt in his step. Just another man in a uniform, just another man with a swagger.

All day I asked those who came to my cage their opinions on the matter. Everyone said the same thing: It's her door. I reminded them about the children but it didn't matter. All you can do is knock, they told me.

A rule-breaker on my side is what I need.

Mazie's Diary, May 20, 1918

Sister Tee! Sister Tee.

Mazie's Diary, May 21, 1918

I tracked Tee down last night. I saw one of the other Theresas on the street. Sister Terry, this one was called. She was older, with a thin gray mustache. I suppose they don't give a care what they look like when they're married to Jesus. I called her over and told her I'd give her free tickets for a week if she'd go find me Sister Tee. She said I didn't need to bribe her, and that salvation was right around the corner and it was always free, no matter what. She rushed off, her habit in ripples. Ten minutes later, there was my Sister Tee, loose strands of golden hair coming out of her wimple. I didn't even know I had missed her until I saw her again, and I think she felt the same. She smiled like she knew me well. Maybe she already does.

I said: I know I'm technically a sinner and all. But I could use a little help.

She said: God has love for everyone.

I told Sister Tee everything, ending with the part about the big red door being locked. I told her Nance no longer trusted me, that she'd never open the door for me again. The whole time her eyes were set tight, her face too. I told her I couldn't stop wondering what was happening in there. Locked behind the door. At last, Sister Tee cried out in some kind of pain. I put my hand on hers, I asked her if she was all right.

She said: I've been grinding my teeth lately. I used to do it at night, and now I've started doing it during the day. When things are bad. When I hear a sad story. A story of ungodliness.

I said: A story of unfairness.

She said: A story of injustice.

I said: A story of inhumanity.

Her eyes were wet with inspiration. The air between us churned into something new.

She said: We must save those children.

Tomorrow, she promised, she would return with news.

Mazie's Diary, May 22, 1918

Not a peep.

I might die from the waiting. Stuck in a cage, waiting.

After dinner Rosie was teasing Jeanie about Ethan, and Jeanie didn't even blush.

I wonder if he'll propose someday. An engagement. Rosie would be beside herself. Then it'd be just me left for her to worry about.

Mazie's Diary, May 23, 1918

It was hot today, too hot, spring's gone already, and I never even had a chance to love it. I sent one of the ushers to get me a beer from across the street, and then another after that, and then another before closing, and I let Officer Walters buy me one to take home with me, which I'm drinking right now by the open window. There's a big pack of pigeons cooing on the roof across the street. The moon is nearly full. I'll drink until I know I'm done. What else am I supposed to do with myself? No Sister Tee. The waiting is killing me.

Mazie's Diary, May 24, 1918

Louis won big at the track and bought us all new purses. Mine's pink and has a jeweled clasp and it's very pretty and I don't care because I haven't heard anything.

Mazie's Diary, May 25, 1918

Sister Tee brought me no good news today. I can't stop crying to save my life.

She and some of the other Theresas were switching off shifts, all day and all night. Some sisters from an uptown church relieved them twice. The first two days the red door didn't open. They knocked and they waited. There they all were, huddled amongst the rats in the alley, waiting for this hophead to open the door. I can't believe I asked them to do this. I was feeling shame all over me. I apologized and Sister Tee told me not to worry. The weather was so pleasant they didn't mind at all. And then finally, the third day, the door opened.

Sister Tee said: It creaked and moaned like a waking demon.

There was Nance, blinking in the sunlight. She was staggering. Her head hung down, and her arms drooped, and she was swaying. Sister Tee imitated her. Like a dead woman risen, is what Tee told me. The nuns rushed from their corner nest and pushed past her into the spoiled room.

Sister Tee said: The stench.

I asked if the children were dead.

Sister Tee said: Not dead, but not much alive either. The littlest one is too small for her age, and it might be too late, is what the doctors are saying.

She started talking about malnutrition and bruises and bad blood. I couldn't pay attention to the details through the sting of my fury. I know what it means now to see red. I could feel the hellish flames within me. It was blinding me. I punched my fists against the counter and I couldn't even feel a thing. Sister Tee took a step back. I had scared her, and I was sorry for it. I tried to calm down but couldn't.

Sister Tee said: I'm sorry I didn't come sooner to see you, Mazie. We had some praying to do.

I said: Where's Nance? I'll kill her.

Sister Tee said: Mazie, you need to be more forgiving. She's an ill woman.

She told me Nance was in the hospital drug sick, her two children on a different floor. The little girl's dying, the little boy's fighting.

I started to cry. The faded babies, fading.

I said: What can I do?

She said: Same as us, just pray.

I didn't tell her I wasn't one for prayer but I'd give it a shot. I'm saying it now, this counts as my prayer. Please let them get well.

Mazie's Diary, May 29, 1918

The youngest one died. Little Marie. Sister Tee says Nance will go to jail as soon as she's able. She says the nurses won't even look at her. They'd sooner throw her on the street. I'd do the same if I could.

Red-eyed in the cage all day long.

Lydia Wallach

Everything's packed away in the guest room and I can't bring myself to dig through the boxes. I'd have to unpack them all. I just can't leave them half packed, or half unpacked, as it were. Once I start I'd have to finish the whole project. So it would be a whole thing I would have to do. And I don't really have the time for it now. Or I guess the space, the mental space. It was enough to come downtown to meet with you. I'm happy to do it, don't get me wrong. I'm not trying to make you feel bad. It's just an exertion. Like there's taking the train to work, and then there's work, and then there's taking the train home again, and that's all I've got in me. When I think of all those boxes it seems insurmountable. It could take days. And I'd have to find a place for everything. How will I know exactly where things will go? I'm just not prepared to make that kind of decision. This is why I can't help you. It's the boxes' fault.

I know you wanted a different answer than that. I don't think there's much in there. I'm certain I've only ever seen one picture of her, and I have the faintest memory of it in my mind. But it's been decades since I've seen it.

I'm sorry. I wish I could do this for you, but . . . right now I can't. I've just moved into this new house in Westchester. I'm divorced. The marriage was brief, shockingly so. His mother died last year, and mine did as well, and a friend of ours who was very sick, suddenly, pancreatic cancer, and was given three months to live, and then was gone. And we just looked at each other at the end, and we should have been holding each other through all of it and instead we were separate, we were in opposite corners of the room, and we simply couldn't find our way back to each other. It felt physical. There were all these ghosts between us. Everyone always thinks of ghosts as being invisible or like air but they take up so much space in a room, you've no idea.

I know you didn't ask about this, I'm just offering this as an explanation. So there's all these boxes from my mother in the guest room, and my husband would have been the one to unpack them. I'm organized, of course, but I can't face my mother's things right now. Another thing to face. All I have done is face things for months and months. So there they sit, in this room, I guess it's a guest room. Maybe it will be a study. Honestly, I have so many rooms. This house is much bigger than I needed. It feels a little preposterous and self-indulgent. But there's this deck out back, and I sit there in the mornings with coffee, and the birds are chirping in the trees, and there's a little stream past the trees, etcetera, and it feels like a thing that I wanted, I'm sure I wanted it, and now I have it, but I do not think I wanted it all alone.

Mazie's Diary, June 15, 1918

Sister Tee can't find Rufus. She thought he was at an orphanage uptown, and she went up there looking for him, but he'd never made it there. She's going to check three more orphanages tomorrow. She says there's no point in calling. She says you've got to go there and see for yourself. I offered to go with her, but she says she can get more done looking the way she does.

At least he's been released from the hospital. At least he's well enough. But where has he gone to?

Lydia Wallach

I was a child when I saw the picture. I can imagine how frustrating it is for you to not be able to secure any photographic evidence of her. Truly. My entire job is to deal with evidence and facts. But my memory won't help you much, because I only saw the picture for a moment. Okay. Let me think. The one thing I can recall is this—and I'm not sure it will be much help to you at all—I had heard many times that she was a bottle blonde. Brassy, sassy blonde. That was supposed to be her schtick. But in my memory, in the photo I saw, she was a brunette. She was young, and a brunette. She was standing in front of a ticket booth, her ticket booth, I am assuming, and my great-grandfather is standing next to her. They're both saluting, as if they were soldiers. Oh, and there was a cross around her neck. That's in my memory, but I don't know how it could be true. Because she was Jewish.

Mazie's Diary, July 3, 1918

I thought if I waited to write until I had good news it would make the good news happen. But there's nothing good to report. I've been drinking cold beer all day long for weeks, waiting for Sister Tee to come back into my life. But she had disappeared until today.

She said: We've lost him.

I gasped.

She said: No, no, no! Not passed away, lost. But lost in the system. He could be anywhere.

She told me she would keep trying to find him. I thought, well, I won't hold my breath.

I was sweating. I wasn't even going to cry. I had promised myself I wouldn't cry. I've been holding it all in. I didn't cry. I feel like I'll never cry again.

She put her tiny hand into the ticket booth.

She said: I brought you something.

I put my hand out and she opened hers and dropped a chain of light blue beads into it. I saw the cross immediately. It was a rosary.

I said: I told you this soul's not yours for the saving.

She said: I'm not worried about your soul. I'm worried that

you're sad. You could just think of this as a pretty thing you could hold on to sometimes that will make you feel better. Sometimes that's all it is to me. But please, Mazie, don't tell anyone I said that.

I promised I wouldn't. My promise is gold. I said she was my friend now, and she agreed I was hers, too.

And it is a pretty thing to hold on to, it's true. I left it behind in the cage though. It's becoming a home of a kind to me. I didn't mean to get comfortable there. I didn't mean to be there so long. But there I am. Here I am.

3

EXCERPT FROM THE UNPUBLISHED AUTOBIOGRAPHY OF
MAZIE PHILLIPS-GORDON

Heartbreak's one thing that leads these bums to the streets. But by the time they get there, the bums don't care about loving nothing but their booze. Coupling up is good for a night or two. It'll keep you warm, if warming up is what you're looking for. But when you're a drunk you never want to share that bottle for too long with anyone. Love requires you to share. To these bums, love looks prettier from afar. They believe they're better off in their sad lives with just the memory of love—and they're probably right.

Mazie's Diary, July 12, 1918

Rosie got word from Boston. Our mother's sick. I haven't seen her since I was a little one, Jeanie either. She never came to see us, though I'm sure he wouldn't let her. We weren't angry when we left, just scared.

So Rosie's off to Boston for a few days to check on her. Nobody knows how bad it is, or what's wrong. It could be anything. Just a telegram from him saying she wasn't well.

This morning she and Louis were back and forth on whether she'd be traveling alone.

He said: May I remind you about the last time we saw him?

She said: May I remind you you've got businesses that need your attention?

He said: I could send a guy with you.

She said: What guy?

That was what I was wondering, too. Since when does Louis have guys he can send out of town?

I said: I could go with her.

But no one even listened to me—when do they ever? So I just smoked another cigarette and watched the two of them hash it out.

It's been ten years! More maybe. How old are they? I wonder if they'd look the same. I wonder if she was even quieter now, if that was even possible. I wonder if he got meaner.

Benjamin Hazzard, Jr., son of Captain Benjamin Hazzard

So what Johanna told you is true. I did meet Mazie Phillips once. I had this wild hair for a moment after my father died, and I thought I should meet this woman I had heard about. I felt very much that I'd been living my life to impress, or sometimes *not* impress him. Because he was the kind of man you wanted to impress, either way, good or bad. And I think in my sadness I started to resent that desire. Oh I don't know...it's probably even more complicated than that but I can't even remember my exact feelings about that time in my life, and frankly I'm not even sure if it matters anymore. I only know that I hopped in my car after my father's funeral—leaving my mother behind, mind you, still wiping her eyes at the loss of my father—and drove to New York to meet this woman my father never stopped talking about, even in front of my mother. He was so brazen, so insensitive. Who talks about another woman in front of his wife and kid? What kind of man is that?

Mazie's Diary, July 14, 1918

Cat's away, and this mouse is putting on her dancing shoes. I'm going out on the town after work. Forgetting everything I've seen these past few months for just one night. Louis can't do nothing about it, and he knows it. Rosie knows it, Jeanie, too.

Mazie's Diary, July 15, 1918

My eyes are green. I've been told they sparkle in the sunshine and glitter in the moonlight. Also they look like jewels, emeralds, and tiger's eyes, too. Captivating, mesmerizing, hypnotic. Every fella's got a little something they like to say. But they're just plain green. And the truth is, in the dark you can't tell anything at all. That's what I always want to say to these men with all their fancy ways of talking about a very simple thing. You know you won't care when the lights are out. They're just green, you fools.

So last night this man starts asking me about my eyes, and I could not give two good goddamns. He sat down next to me, taps two fingers on the bar, like he was announcing his arrival. I was drinking gin, which was making me feel pretty and mean. I should know better, but some nights nothing but gin will do. I pulled out a cigarette and tried to light it myself, but he was quick on the draw. I nodded a thank-you. I wasn't giving him anything more than that, but I did give him the smallest of glances. He was in uniform. Me and the men in uniform.

He said: Now are those eyes green or blue?

I said: The color of money.

He said: The color of luck.

I said: I wouldn't hold your breath.

Then he sucked in his breath. His chest was broad and mighty. His uniform fit him snug, fit him bold. There was not a speck of dust on it. He was a handsome, big man. His hair was wavy and slick at the same time. He had worry lines on his forehead and between his eyes. What did he have to worry about? Oh, and his eyes were green, too.

I said: The color of trouble.

He waved his hands at himself, then made like he was praying with them. Begging for permission to exhale.

I said: All right. Breathe.

He was docked at Chelsea Piers, and had wandered through the city looking for a good time, which is not what he said, but what I believed to be true anyway. I asked him if he was a hero. He said everyone serving overseas was a hero. I touched his arm for a second. Oh lordy, it was a nice arm. I went from mean to smitten fast.

He said: I'm a sailor. I sail ships. Big ones.

I said: I run the Venice Theater. I sell tickets, I count the change, I keep the books. When there's trouble, I kick out the riffraff. I'm the first thing you see when you come to the theater, and the last thing when you walk out the door. You can't miss me. I'm always there.

I hate that I wanted him to see me in my cage, but it's the only thing I can call my own, even if it's really Louis's place. I know they're there to see the movies, but lately I've been pretending the crowds have been lining up to see me.

He said: You're a businesswoman then.

I said: That's right I am.

He said: You run the show.

I said: Yes.

He said: I run the ship.

I said: Yes.

He said: Both of us are used to being in charge. How will we ever get along?

I said: I don't know. I never give an inch.

He said: Not even one?

So we set to drinking, and we did an excellent job of it for many hours. We were real professionals. Then the barkeep kicked us out for our own good and we decided to walk across the Brooklyn Bridge because he'd never done it before. I gave him the business about it, teasing him for missing out on something special.

He said: I guess I've just been waiting for a pretty girl to take me.

It didn't even matter what he'd said or if I'd heard those lines a hundred times before. He was twice my size and he was handsome and he was a hero and I wanted to throw my arms around him and feel him against me. The pop of those brass buttons against my chest.

We reached the middle of the bridge and leaned against the railing. We were all alone. The smell of the river stung my nose. The Captain put his arm around me and pointed out the stars, and even though I already knew them all I pretended that I didn't, which I only hate myself for a little. I thought he needed to teach me something so that whatever would happen next would happen next. I kept calling him Captain. Captain Captain Captain. I couldn't stop myself for nothing.

He said: Call me Benjamin. We're getting to know each other here. No need to be so formal.

I said: Captain, don't ruin the best thing you got going for you.

It was nearly a full moon. That moon was watching me and I didn't even care. Watch me, just watch, I was thinking.

He talked and talked. Now I knew he was part Mick, part Italian, and part parts unknown. Now I knew his mother had passed last year, and his father was heartbroken, and he was too. Now I knew he had gone to the Naval Academy, and that someday he hoped to teach there.

He said: I'll slow down in ten years. Maybe five. But right now I've got the lust for adventure.

Now I knew all the countries he'd been to, and all the oceans he'd sailed. Now I knew how many men were on his ship, and that they were good men, except for the few who were only just fine.

He said: Not every man's meant to be a hero. Doing the right thing's different than being noble. But at least I can count on them to be right.

Now I knew he had been engaged once, but it was over. She had started working for the first time in her life while he was away at war, and he said it had changed her.

He said: She forgot about me.

I said: How could she? I would never.

He took a step back on the bridge and turned me to face him. Those meaty hands warm on my shoulders. I blushed and looked down at the ground.

He said: Aw shucks, Mazie. Come on and look at me. Now you're shy? You've been bold all night. You get me all the way out here on the middle of this bridge and now you can't look at me?

I looked at him. Trouble meets trouble.

He moved his hands up to the sides of my face and he pulled me toward him and kissed me. I kissed him back. We pecked at each other for a minute, figuring each other out. Finally he kissed my upper lip, and then my lower lip. I opened them a little bit. Then he forced them open entirely. He put his tongue where he liked. I could not argue. I did not even try. Then he moved his hands slowly from my face down my neck and to the top of my dress. There was a gentle swell of cleavage there and he put his finger in the space between my breasts. He stroked up and down. He looked around and then bent his head down and started kissing the tops of them. Then he licked them, dipped his tongue between them. I put my hand on the back of his head. I did not want him to ever stop.

He said: Oh, Mazie, these are beautiful. You're beautiful. All of this. Beautiful.

There was his hand ruffling up my dress, and my hand on the waistband of his uniform. I've lain down with men before. Not many, not as many as Rosie thinks. Not many at all, really. But the point is I've lain. In a bed. Now I was pressed up against the bridge. He lifted me up easily and I wrapped my legs around him. I felt common and special at the same time. We were both laughing because it felt so good. He kept pushing and pushing into me. I was delirious. But I told him to stop. I had the good sense. I told him I didn't want a baby in me.

He said: I can't. Don't make me.

I said: I won't. But be careful.

He told me he'd be careful. We kissed. It was a deep, long kiss, and then we were laughing again. He pulled away from me, and pushed even harder, very quickly, and then he wasn't looking at me at all. He was looking over my shoulder, maybe at the river, maybe at his ship, maybe at the moon, maybe at nothing at all. Then he closed his eyes, groaned, and pulled out of me lightning quick. Then there was a mess on my legs. He said he was sorry and I told him not to be sorry. Then he dropped down on his knees and buried himself beneath my dress and licked me. He didn't miss a spot. It felt brutal. Eventually I made a noise and out there, in the middle of the river, in the middle of the night, I thought it almost sounded like a cry for help.

He's gone now, back to his ship. Louis wasn't at the kitchen table when I got home, Jeanie wasn't in bed either. Looks like I'm not the only mouse in town.

Benjamin Hazzard, Jr.

He was a particularly likable man, my father. He was a war hero, of course, and Americans love their heroes, and I think he felt that love in our community. He was *received* in a certain way, shall we say. But also he was warm and charming, not your typical stiff military type. Of course he cheated on my mother for years. Not just with Mazie, but with women in many different cities, as well as in our own town. Over the years he did little to hide his infidelities, and he gave me terrible advice about how to treat women, which haunted me for much of my life. He had a sense of entitlement to women. He just sort of took as he pleased. It was really remarkable and nearly admirable if it weren't so goddamn despicable.

I've been married twice before Johanna. Three wives! Johanna's had me in counseling for years though. She seems to feel this will keep me on track. I'm seventy-four years old, and I've insisted to her that I've had all the kinds of feelings I'm ever going to have. But still I go because she has asked, and I would prefer not to die alone.

I thought I had lived long enough that I had earned the right to some peace and quiet, but it turns out I have not; not yet, anyway. I also thought I was too old to change, but again, I am wrong, as my wife frequently informs me. I promised myself I'd live longer than my father, and I have; much, much longer, though that wasn't hard, because he died when he was sixty. We think of that as young to die now, though people did die younger then.

Would I prefer not to be in therapy? No. Would I rather just live the rest of my life happily in retirement, reading the works of the presidential scholars, sailing on the weekends, gazing at my bride, those plummy lips, that petite derriere, and telling her how lovely she is and how lucky I am to have her? *Instead* of discussing my feelings? Absolutely. I would like to eat steak every night for dinner, and that is not to be either. Another doctor entirely. [Laughs.] All these doctors, destroying my dreams.

Mazie's Diary, July 16, 1918

Delirious and decadent all day. Seemed like everyone in line had a gag or a funny word for me. All I wanted to do was think about the Captain, and the two of us on the bridge. I could dream about it for days and never get bored. Today was the first time in weeks I hadn't started the morning by crying and thinking of that little girl.

Mazie's Diary, July 17, 1918

Tee came by the cage, told me a sob story about a war widow she found sleeping in front of her settlement house, three babies wrapped up in her arms.

I said: I ain't getting involved ever again. No way. I learned my lesson.

But I handed her everything in my purse. Tee's the con and I'm her sucker.

Mazie's Diary, July 18, 1918

Rosie's not returned home yet. She sent a telegram to Louis but he wouldn't tell us what it said. Only that Rosie was fine. If we were waiting for a tragedy, he had nothing to report.

I was still feeling sort of dreamy so I stuck around late. No point in going home to an empty house, and I've cooled on saloons for the moment. Nothing can match my night with the Captain, why bother looking?

I saw the late-night lineup of Rudy's people in front of the theater. I guess they're the other theater managers in town. They were still tidy in their uniforms. Not my kind of uniform exactly, but at least they wore them with pride. They were sharing cigarettes, sipping from flasks, talking in low voices. I finished counting up the money for the night. I teased them.

I said: We're closed for the night, gentlemen. There ain't no more shows till morning.

One man said: Aw, you know us, Miss Mazie. We're waiting on Rudy.

I said: Don't you boys have anything better to do than stare up at a big screen all night? You spend all day in front of it. Go chase some girls!

They all laughed at me. They don't care nothing for girls. They just like to watch movies. They're hypnotized by them.

Rudy came and let them in and they all shuffled off. Silent and mysterious creatures of the night. That part I understand. I locked up my cage and wandered through the lobby. What could be so good, I was thinking.

I stuck my head in the theater. I tried not to look up for too long. But I'd never seen anything like it before. The movie was in color! Of course it wasn't much of a movie. There weren't any actors in it. It was just a bunch of circles and waves moving across the screen. But it was definitely in color. I know color when I see it.

Two seconds later, I was hunched over, retching up my guts all over again. Rudy came over to help me, walked me out front when I could make it.

He said: You trying to make yourself sick?

I said: Being nosy always gets the best of me. But Rudy, that was color up there.

He said: Someday there's going to be color all the time. People talking too.

I said: Then you boys will never go home.

He said: Speaking of nosy, I forgot something.

He pulled a letter out of his pocket.

He said: Who's this captain friend of yours?

I grabbed it from him. Postmarked the day after he met me. It was addressed to Miss Mazie Phillips, The Beautiful Proprietress of the Venice Theater. No return address.

There wasn't much to it. Just that I was special and lovely, and that he would think of me whenever he saw a bridge, and that in his line of work, he saw a lot of bridges.

I hurried home after that. The house was empty. I read the letter again and again and then I got under the covers and put my hands between my legs and thought about bridges.

Benjamin Hazzard, Jr.

I understand from an intellectual perspective why he had such fond memories of her. They met at a moment in time where everything was perfect. He looked at her and told her she was gorgeous and then sailed off on his boat. They were both allowed to be perfect for each other forever.

Mazie's Diary, August 2, 1918

Rosie's home now, came back late last night, angry and weary from her travels. Jeanie and I wrapped ourselves up under a quilt on the couch. Then Rosie said our mother's brain was slowly bleeding. We found each other's hand under the quilt.

She said: I barely recognized her. Her face doesn't look the same anymore. It's all mashed up.

Rosie was holding on to the arms of the chair. Claws into fabric. She was tough and grim, and she was breaking my heart with her pain.

I said: Do you think he did it to her?

Rosie said: Of course he did! Of course he did. He said she fell, the liar. Fell a hundred times, more like it. She'll die for sure and then he'll be a murderer too. And he'll never be held responsible for his actions.

Jeanie said: I don't even remember her. I wish I could remember her.

I was thinking about when Rosie came to get us, when she brought us to New York. I could see it, still, even though it had been at night, and late. Jeanie had been a toddler, what did she know? But I could close my eyes and see it. The house had dirty floors...or made of dirt, maybe. We'd lived somewhere nicer once, closer to the city. He drank us into the country, that's what Rosie said once. Maybe the floors were made of dirt after all.

There was Rosie picking me up whole from my bed, blanket and all. She shushed me, took me through the kitchen, and it was light and I opened my eyes. I saw Louis and my father standing there. Louis was counting out cash. The trees in front of the house bent with the wind, and there was a rushing noise in the leaves. Then we were all in the car, and then we were driving. All night we drove. I wasn't scared, because I was with Rosie.

My mother was nowhere in all of this. I don't think she said good-bye. I can't remember it if she did. I can't remember what she looked like either. Except maybe like the rest of us girls. A hazy, dark-haired lady. I can see her eating quietly by herself in the kitchen. A dark head hunched over a bowl. I don't remember her smiling. A mother is supposed to smile at her babies.

We don't even have any pictures of her here. Rosie walked out with us, and that was it. She didn't want nothing from them but us girls.

I said: I wonder what would have happened if we had stayed.

Rosie said: I would never have let that happen.

Jeanie said: How did you know when it was time to leave? When you left the first time?

Rosie didn't want to answer any more questions. She just sent us off to bed. Told us she'd be tightening the screws again now that she was back.

Mazie's Diary, August 15, 1918

Nothing but drinking and working for days and days. Not a letter for the Proprietress, not a one. The drinking's making me sick I think. I'm waking up queasy. But I can't seem to stand a second of my lonesome life without it.

Mazie's Diary, August 18, 1918

Last night Jeanie and Rosie got into it. Oh boy did they ever.
I can't say I enjoyed the yelling but at least it wasn't me caus-
ing a fuss for a change.

Jeanie wants to work for Belle Baker. She doesn't like traveling to the track, it's too long a journey, she's bored on the
train, bored when she gets there. Belle's got a new show on
the Bowery. She's a headliner now. She's the queen of the
Thalia Theater. She needs a lady-in-waiting, says Jeanie.

Rosie said: You've got a job.

Jeanie said: A job you picked for me, not a job I picked for
myself. Why do you get to pick everything all the time?

Rosie said: Maybe because I know what's best.

Jeanie said: Please let me do this one thing. Please, Rosie.
I'm always on time, I'm always where I say I'll be. I'm always
pretty, I'm always sweet, I don't drink, I don't stay out all
night, I'm a good girl. Please, Rosie.

She got down on her hands and knees on the kitchen floor.
I saw it with my own eyes. She put her hands in Rosie's lap.
She was begging her.

I said: Go on, let her have some fun.

Jeanie started to wail. This is the end of your childhood,
I was thinking. You are using it up right now. Rosie reached
out to her, put her hands on her head. Promised she would
talk to Louis.

I know I'll be jealous of Jeanie, doing what she likes. But at
least she knows what she wants. I can't begrudge a soul their
desires.

Mazie's Diary, September 1, 1918

I was a little queasy this morning. I'm a sturdy wench, strong as an ox. I keep hoping the whiskey will kill whatever germ is inside me.

Mazie's Diary, September 15, 1918

Rudy told me this morning about this influenza, it's been spreading across the country and it's hit New York. He's got his entire family wearing surgical masks, and he handed one to me too. He told me there were too many strangers in our midst, and I was handling all their money, breathing all their air. I told him I'd look a fool if I wore it. In my mind I was thinking that maybe I already did have it. But I couldn't bring myself to say it out loud.

Mazie's Diary, October 4, 1918

There's new rules now for theaters, courtesy of our public health department. They're closing us down during the day and staggering our openings at nights. Rumor is they'll start shutting us down if we're not up to snuff. More and more people on the streets in surgeons' masks.

I retched again a few times. They're quarantining people all over the place. I might offer myself up for it. I don't want to, but I'll do it.

Mazie's Diary, October 8, 1918

Rudy came to the cage this morning, just to tip his hat to me. We were making our pleasantries and then the sickness in my stomach started up again and I retched in front of him. Just once, it was violent and it was over. I had time enough to make it out of my cage.

I said: It comes and goes. Just for a few weeks now.

He said: Is it in the mornings?

I didn't say anything and then he didn't say anything. I watched him control his mouth until he couldn't anymore.

He said: I got four kids at home. Four times I've seen my wife have morning sickness. I don't want to make any assumptions or assertions of course.

I said: Of course you don't.

He said: I'm just telling you. Sometimes when women get sick in the morning it means something.

I didn't say a goddamn thing after that. He told me he'd send someone to clean up my mess. I just wanted him to leave and then he finally did.

Mazie's Diary, October 11, 1918

More rules for the theaters. We're to leave our doors open during the day, and the building must be well ventilated and clean. We have to instruct all our patrons not to cough, sneeze, or smoke. Good luck with all of that.

Rudy saw me retching again. Told me if I had the influenza I'd be dead by now.

He said: All I'm saying is, maybe it's something else.

I said: Shut up, Rudy.

Lydia Wallach

The other reason why my family was so enamored with Mazie was her scandalous existence. This was a group of people in love with the drama of the cinematic experience. They loved a good show. And, from what I heard, Mazie put on a really good show for a while there.

Mazie's Diary, October 12, 1918

It ain't the flu. Well at least I ain't dying. At least there's that.

Mazie's Diary, October 15, 1918

There are two kinds of doctors for babies. I asked around. I got names of both kinds. I could walk out my front door and walk five blocks one way or ten blocks another. One way I got a baby for life, the other way I got nothing in my belly but room for the next drink.

Mazie's Diary, October 16, 1918

I'm a fiend for cigarettes right now. I can't take a lick of booze so the cigarettes are the only thing keeping me calm. Rosie doesn't like the cigarettes in the house.

She said: You're a chimney these days! Your teeth'll turn yellow before their time. You'll be a young woman with an old woman's smile. Think about that before you light another one.

I try to steer clear of her when I can. I don't want her to know. I don't want to hear it from her. I can't bear to hear it from her.

Mazie's Diary, October 18, 1918

Goddamn that captain. Goddamn him to hell for showing up and screwing me and leaving. His postcards don't mean a thing to me.

Mazie's Diary, October 21, 1918

She knows. They all do.

I came home tonight, hoping to hide. There's a chill out there now, a fall chill, but still I was drenched through and through. I'm a mess lately, nothing to be done about it. But they were all sitting around the living room, Louis and Rosie and Ethan and Jeanie, playing cards. Louis was showing them some sleight-of-hand tricks. A bottle of something or other was open. The two happy couples coupling. I had someone once too, I wanted to say. But I didn't even know if that was true. It was only for a night. Rosie called to me, told me to come sit with them.

I said: I'm tired.

Rosie said: Come on now, we're having a good time.

Jeanie said: We never see you anymore.

I sat down next to Ethan on the couch. He and Jeanie were holding hands, and she had her head on his shoulder. Aren't they sweet, I was thinking, but I was being sour in my mind. Ethan grinned at me. He has so many teeth in that mouth of his, and he's so eager with his smiles. He's like a giant child. Sometimes friendly is too friendly if you ask me.

Then I smelled him. I wasn't trying to, but the scent came right off him. Earth from a stable. I don't mind that smell usually, but tonight it seemed like death, like a dead body was sitting right next to me on my own couch. I started to gag. Somehow I kept it down. But when I looked up, everyone was looking at me.

Rosie said: Are you sick?

I said: I'm not sick.

Rosie looked me up and down. Oh that woman is so sharp! Why does she have to be so sharp?

She said: You look fat.

I said: No, you're fat.

She said: Even if I am fat, I am the exact same fat as always. You, however, are not the same as always, Miss Mazie.

I said: Why don't you mind your own weight and leave mine out of it?

She said: I've heard you retching too, not just now. You think I don't hear what's going on in my own home?

Ethan pulled back and stared at me, and Jeanie too. Louis was just shuffling and cutting the cards, not looking at a thing. I was not holding up my end of the argument.

Rosie said: I never knew anyone who liked her pretty dresses as much as you, Mazie. What happens when you can't fit in them anymore?

I said: I suppose I'll be buying some new dresses then.

Rosie said: Why are you getting fat, Mazie?

And then we came to the end, I thought.

Louis said: Ethan, did I ever tell you about the time I met Rosie?

Ethan said: Not as far as I can recall, Louis.

Louis said: It was a beautiful day at the track.

Rosie said: We're talking about Mazie here.

Louis ignored her. He was having his say.

He said: It was a beautiful day at the track. Rosie was

seventeen years old, and she had her hair up in braids around her head and a dress that fit just so.

Louis outlined the shape of Rosie's body with his hands.

He said: I could not have ignored her if I tried. Girls didn't wear makeup then like they do now, but she had her face on. You were like a young tigress is what you were, Rosie Phillips.

He said this in such a passionate way it was like his desire for her became physically present in the room. Maybe it was my heat and maybe it was my hormones but I swore I saw little heart-shaped arrows darting from his eyes in her direction. Oh lord, he's a sweaty, bald, fat man, but I would have melted for him too. All anyone ever wants is to be desired, but especially girls like us, the ones with the meanest father in the world.

He said: You were a beer wench. I was there on business.

Rosie said: I was the boss of all the other beer wenches.

He said: You were the boss of me is what you were. A bossy bitch. And I loved you from the start.

Rosie said: You did. You chased me the whole season.

He said: I did, and I caught you. And do you remember what I told you when I finally caught you? When you finally agreed to be my bride? I said that your family was my family, and your joys were my joys, and your problems were my problems. And that I would take care of you.

Rosie said: I remember that.

Louis said: And you liked that about me.

Rosie said: I loved that about you.

Louis said: Everybody hear that?

We all said we heard it.

Louis said: So, Mazie, you sick?

I said: No, I'm not sick. I'm pregnant.

Louis said: Mazel tov. A new member of the family. What a blessing. Now let's let her get to bed. She's tired.

It's not as simple as that, though. And we all know it. I hear Rosie in the other room right now talking about how I don't want a baby, how I've never wanted a baby, how there's no mother in me. And why her and not me. And why is life this way and not the other.

And she's right.

Louis says: Sometimes blessings are indiscriminate.

I whisper: Good night.

Mazie's Diary, October 22, 1918

Rosie brought me lunch today at the cage, between the first and second shows. It was a bowl of beef stew. She walked it all the way from our home. Brought me a spoon and a napkin and everything. That spoon was shined up nice. And she nearly tucked that napkin right into my blouse till I slapped her hand away.

I said: What do you want?

She said: We need to talk about it.

I said: Can't you see I'm working here?

She said: I know you don't want it.

She doesn't know anything. I don't want it, it's true. But sometimes I think about the Captain and then I do. I never wanted anything to love before. It's all mashed up in my head. All I'm doing is crying when no one's looking.

She said: But I do want it. I want this baby. Have this baby for me, Mazie. For me and Louis. Give us the baby. We can all live together and be one family.

How desperate was my Rosie? I was thinking about that time she took us to the gypsy, all those months she spent on the couch all clutched up in pain. Today she looked just as desperate, but now there was an extra layer of fire. She was nearly murderous.

I said: You can have it.

She was looking at me so steadily I thought she might break in two, two Rosies collapsing before me on Park Row.

She said: Are you sure?

I said that I was. She finally gasped. And then I did, too. I guess I've been holding it in for months and months, what was happening, what I've been thinking. What was I going to do, I didn't know that whole time. But now I know. One kind of choice over another, it didn't matter. But at least with this one I please someone else.

Mazie's Diary, October 28, 1918

Rosie says I can wear an overcoat to work every day and no one on the streets will be able to see my tummy. Rosie says I'll be behind a counter in the cage all day and no one will ever know and that won't ruin my reputation and someday a nice man will still want to marry me. Rosie says I've got to go straight to work and home again and get plenty of rest and she'll bring me meals every day to make sure I'm well fed. Rosie says that I've got to cut down on the drinking and the smoking so this baby will be born healthy and strong. Rosie says Rosie says Rosie says.

George Flicker

I remember my mother telling me, "She thinks we didn't know? We knew."

Mazie's Diary, October 31, 1918

Now there's a lot of talk in this house. New kinds of talk. There's no room for a baby in this apartment, Rosie keeps saying. We got more room than anyone on this block, says Louis. Rosie wants a house somewhere far away in the country, but Louis says it's impossible with all his business dealings. What about Coney Island, that's the newest talk this morning. What about living near the ocean? Jeanie says she'd die if she lived far away from the city. Rosie tells her if she gets married she can live anywhere she likes. We sit around the kitchen table and plot. I light a cigarette, and Rosie pulls it from my fingers. This is what we are doing now, every day. Talking.

Mazie's Diary, November 1, 1918

Twenty-one years old today. Old enough to do anything I like.

Mazie's Diary, November 3, 1918

I know that I'm supposed to feel something alive inside of me but it feels only like a weight I have to carry with me wherever I go.

Mazie's Diary, November 5, 1918

Rosie puts her cold hands on my warm belly at night. She says I warm her up. She says it's like I'm her furnace. She stares at my belly. She wonders what it looks like on the other side. She holds her hands there until I tell her to stop.

Mazie's Diary, November 7, 1918

They announced the end of the war today and the whole city cheered at once. I've never seen anything like it. I probably won't again in my lifetime. The end of the war! We shut down the Venice. No one was bothering with the pictures today. I roamed the streets with Jeanie and Ethan. One parade bled into another. People kissing and hugging on the corners. Bottles of booze in the air. Children with lollies in one hand and balloons in the other. I couldn't stop laughing for nothing, none of us could. It was one kind of relief at last. Do you see this, I whispered to myself, but I knew I was talking to my belly.

By the time we made it home though, the radio was saying it was a fake armistice. We had a party for nothing.

Mazie's Diary, November 11, 1918

Today the war was really over. The papers said so. No more war. I can't believe the whole city celebrated again, but they did. Any excuse. We laughed all day, but then tonight we cried. Too exhausted to be anything but grateful.

I never believed these words could come out of my mouth, but I'm ready for the party to be over.

Benjamin Hazzard, Jr.

I suppose I had this idea that I might try to seduce her, or toy with her. In my devastation from his death she seemed to be at fault for something. I was nineteen years old—that's a good age to blame the wrong people for your problems.

I wanted to see her face. That I know. I had seen some of

the others. A few women from the club, these boozy, bored wives, and there had also been this young widow down the block who was constantly breaking things in her house that only my father could fix, of course. And I am nearly certain he slept with my seventh-grade math teacher, although I'll never be able to confirm it.

But she seemed mythic to me. The woman from New York. The famous Mazie Phillips. She'd been in the papers. He'd met all manner of politicians and war heroes, and he was an important part of the Republican Party in Connecticut. But Mazie was a real celebrity to him, and she had known him in his prime, during that war, the one he had actually fought in as opposed to watching Stateside. Everything after that war bored him, I suspect. Or maybe he really loved her. He could have loved her. I'll never know that either.

I'll tell you, I plumb my feelings regularly, but I can't seem to define this moment precisely, though I can see it in my mind, everything about it. I had a bottle of whiskey at my side in the car, and the more I drank the less upset I became. My sadness began to solidify into an angry darkness. I arrived at the theater at midday. There she was in her ticket booth. I stood in line and waited my turn. She waited for me to say something and I had prepared nothing. The whole car ride there I'd just been having a conversation with my father in my head instead.

Then she said, "Step aside if you're not buying a ticket, kid." I *was* a kid then. I was nineteen years old. I said, "Are you Mazie Phillips?" She said, "Yeah, who's asking?" I said, "I'm the son of Benjamin Hazzard." She didn't say anything, but she lit a cigarette. And then all I could do is blurt out that my father was dead. And then I remember this vision so specifically I can squint my eyes right now and see it: This quiver started in her hand, the one that was holding the cigarette, and the cigarette began to shake, and then this quiver sort of rolled through her body if that makes sense, all the way up to her face, and then she began to cry.

Mazie's Diary, December 1, 1918

The baby died. Rosie keeps throwing her arms around me like that will change what happened. Like her arms can bring it back.

She says I should say something, anything. I don't want to talk about it ever. No one can make me.

Mazie's Diary, December 11, 1918

They took the mattress away while I was at the Venice. I slept on the couch the last ten days, and Jeanie slept next to Rosie. No one wanted to be in the same room as it.

Mazie's Diary, December 13, 1918

I came home from work tonight and Louis was sitting quietly at the kitchen table with a glass of something strong in front of him. He looked like he'd been waiting for me to show up all night. Rosie was stretched out on the couch. She had a small pillow over her eyes. Louis told me to come join him. His voice was crumbling. I sat next to him and put my hand on his arm. I said his name.

He said: I am devastated for you and for this family.

I said: I'm going to be fine.

He said: They made us memorize poems in school. They just sit there in my head waiting for me, waiting for me to need them. My favorite was always Wordsworth. Do you like Wordsworth?

I said: I've never read him.

He said: You should read him. He was smart. I'll buy you a book of his.

I told him I would like that.

He said: I can't stop thinking of this one line of his from a poem called "Intimations of Immortality." Our birth is but a sleep and a forgetting. And I believe that baby slept right through it, and doesn't remember a thing now. I've got to be right. Don't you think I'm right, Mazie?

He was crying then. These big gusts of tears from this big man. He was nearly choking on it. His whole body shaking. Rosie rose, I did too. We threw our arms around him. Our dear Louis.

I don't know if we will ever be happy again. It doesn't feel that way. I can't imagine what that looks like anymore. Happy.

But I think we will feel better than this someday. We have to feel better than this someday.

Benjamin Hazzard, Jr.

What did I do? I went home. When she began to cry I realized instantly that I had made a terrible mistake, and that I was not where I was supposed to be. Of course I should have been with my mother all along. So I went home.

Mazie's Diary, January 1, 1919

I dyed my hair blond. New year. I will leave the past behind. Jeanie didn't recognize me when I walked in the door.

I said: Good.

Benjamin Hazzard, Jr.

She ended up being sort of tough-looking in the end, which surprised me a little bit. Certainly you could tell she had once been enormously sexy. I was admittedly a randy nineteen-year-old when I met her, but I can assure you she filled out that cage nicely. And having any attraction to her when she was my mother's age makes me feel a level of discomfort I refuse to parse.

I will say this: Most of the other women in my father's life were a bit better maintained. I haven't used this word in a long time, but she was a real broad. I imagine she had bleached her hair for many years, and it was wiry, and the ends were split. All of the smile lines around her mouth were pronounced, and there was this pinkish color to her skin. She was somewhere between rosy and boozy. We all fall apart no matter what, obviously, but some of what we consume leaves a more vivid trail behind than others.

Mazie's Diary, January 16, 1919

They passed Prohibition today. Just what all those soldiers fresh home from the war need—sobriety! Sister Tee came by the cage, pretending like she just happened to be in the neighborhood, but I knew she wanted to brag about it a bit.

I said: You got anything to do with this Prohibition business?

She said: Just said a prayer or two.

I said: Great, now I'll know who to blame when I'm thirsty.

It won't make a lick of difference though. People will find booze if they want it bad enough. This is New York City. We like our drink here. I know I'm not planning on giving it up.

Mazie's Diary, March 16, 1919

We're moving to Coney Island soon. Rosie told us tonight. Louis has business there now. Just like that, he has business. They're looking for a house near the ocean.

Rosie said: And I think it'll bring us all closer together. There's too much city out there, getting in the way of this family.

Jeanie said: I feel plenty close to you right here.

Rosie said: I can't keep track of you girls anymore.

Jeanie said: But I'm happy here.

I couldn't bring myself to argue either way. I haven't slept through a night since I lost the baby. Maybe this home was ruined for Rosie as much as it was for me.

Rosie said: You can work for Louis out there, it'll be fun.

Jeanie said: Doing what?

Rosie said: He bought some bumper cars at Luna Park.

Jeanie lurched a little bit, like she was going to be sick.

Rosie said: You don't like it, you got ways out.

She was talking about Ethan. We've all been waiting for him to propose.

Jeanie tried one last time.

She said: Didn't you raise me to be something more than the girl who runs the bumper cars?

Rosie said: I raised you to be a part of this family. Don't be putting on any airs with me. You came from the same house I did. You're not too good for anything.

Jeanie said nothing after that. I thought she'd put up a fight, being far away from her beloved theater. But she just kept calm. Quiet face, quiet hands, still and calm. Give in like the rest of us, was what I was thinking. It won't hurt but for a minute.

Mazie's Diary, May 1, 1919

The Captain is here.

I looked up this morning in the cage, and he was smiling at me, and then he laughed. Was there a joke that was funny because I hadn't heard it.

He said: Happy May Day.

There he was, as if nine months hadn't passed at all, and it was perfectly normal for him to be waiting in line to buy a ticket for the matinee. I had thought of him so often it was like he had become some kind of dream.

He said: Did you get the postcards I sent?

I wished I didn't have them hanging up behind me in the cage.

I said: I might have seen a postcard or two. Bragging about your travels while I'm just sitting here in this cage.

He said: I just wanted you to know I was thinking about you the whole time.

First time I met him, I knew he was full of lines. Second time I met him, it still didn't matter. They all just sounded so good coming out of his mouth.

My hands were in fists and I didn't even notice it until he

slid his hand through the cage and on top of them. His voice got real soft.

He said: I don't write just everyone.

I looked up at him and I kept my mouth tight but then I batted my eyelashes at him anyway. I couldn't help it. He stirred something in my loins, or at least close to that area.

He said: Come on, how could I forget a girl like you? The most famous girl downtown. I bet people come from all over just to see that pretty face of yours.

I said: Well I do get a line.

I couldn't let him touch me for a second longer. I pulled my hand away and lit a cigarette, and then held my other hand to my wrist to keep it from shaking. I was feeling so much and I couldn't tell if it was hate or love or both.

He said: I'd stand in line to take you out to dinner. Dinner and a show, show and a dinner. Whatever you want, whatever order. You're in charge, Mazie.

I had no excuse not to, except maybe then I'll have to tell him the truth about what happened. But I told him I'd meet him tomorrow.

When I got home I told Rosie she'd have to stead me the next night at the theater. She can't deny me a thing right now.

Mazie's Diary, May 2, 1919

What a night! I can't figure out if I should have seen it coming or not. If I should blame myself for not knowing what was going on in my own home.

I met the Captain on the corner by the theater, far out

of Rosie's sight. We walked together to Little Italy. I didn't put my arm through his at first, but I did let him make me laugh. He took me to the Blue Grotto. I ate one of his meatballs. I nearly let him feed it to me, but then I took the fork from his hand. It felt too close, too fast. I liked how nervous he was. I was wearing my fuschia-colored silk dress I bought on Division Street last spring before I'd met him, before anything sad had happened. He tried hard not to stare down the front of it. After dinner he held my hand to his face. He wanted me to touch him. We could have been in love for all anyone knew.

I thought about telling him the truth, but I didn't know if he would care or not. He never saw my belly grow. He never held my hair back when I was sick in the mornings. He didn't bring me gumdrops from the candy shop when that was all I craved. That was Rosie, that was Jeanie. He didn't know about any of it. He didn't weep like a child, weep for me when I couldn't. That was Louis.

What did he have to do with any of it?

So I decided to pretend it was the first time all over again. I pretended I was just a flirt, a good-time girl. It's not a lie, anyway. I switched over. I felt myself doing it. I let myself be that person for the night. And it was a relief.

After dinner, we walked to the Thalia Theater. I'd been meaning to see Belle's show that we'd lost Jeanie to these past months, and it was closing night. Belle's leaving town, headlining her own national tour. I wanted the Captain to know that I was connected to a famous person. Oh how I wanted him to love me.

The show had already started. The theater was dark except for a light on the stage. A skinny magician was dangling silver hoops from his fingertips. There was a haze of smoke. The Captain pulled out a flask from his pocket.

He said: A little treat for you and me.

The tang of it was delicious. He put his hand on my knee, and it felt like it was supposed to be there, so I let it stay. I was dizzy with whiskey. Flames and fuel.

Next up were three tap-dancing sisters from Philly. It made me smile, thinking of me and Rosie and Jeanie, how we used to be thick as thieves, the Phillips girls. I started to forget for a second that our lives weren't perfect, that no tragedy had struck or would ever strike, and that we had everything we needed. Just as long as this man in uniform sitting next to me kept handing me his flask with one hand and tickling my knee with the other. As long as we didn't move, everything would be divine forever.

Then there was a tipsy juggler who kept dropping his pins, and then a comedian telling dirty jokes that didn't make either of us blush. The Captain's arm was draped around the side of me then, and then his other hand was clasped in mine. It was so comforting to be touched. I took another sip from the flask. The sting in the back of my throat was as perfect a pain as a girl could hope for.

The curtain opened again. Two white-blond men dressed in white sailor suits came out into the spotlight, a woman in a fluttery white gown hoisted on their fingertips. They threw her up in the air, and she spun in a circle once, twice, three times, her dress whirling all around her, and then she landed again in their hands. It was a goddamn sight. We all burst into applause.

The men lowered the dancer to the ground and spun her around again on her toes, passing her from one to another, the men spreading out farther apart on the floor. Eventually she was just whirling around everywhere. I worried she might pass out, but just when I thought she couldn't take it anymore, one of the men stopped her spinning and dipped her backward. The dancer's dark hair was wrapped up in a braid around her head, and her lips were brighter red than mine, but she looked like me. I rubbed my eyes and leaned forward in my seat. Well, I knew it wasn't me. It was Jeanie.

I watched the men flip her, back across back, to the next man. They tossed her through the air like she was nothing. I had seen her practice her ballet moves a thousand times but never knew she could move like this. Oh god, I thought. She's free. And there's no way she's coming home.

I couldn't spend the night with the Captain after that. I was too shocked. I asked him to walk me home instead. I kissed him only on the cheek. He grabbed me firmly at the end. He told me he'd be up late if I changed my mind.

He whispered in my ear: Why?

I didn't know him well enough to tell him the truth, and what would I have said anyway? My sister's a liar. And I am too.

George Flicker

If Mazie was the wild sister, then Jeanie was the free one. I couldn't forget either of them if I tried.

Mazie's Diary, May 5, 1919

It's been three days since we've seen her now.

Rosie says: Where's Jeanie?
Louis says: Where's Jeanie?
Ethan says: Where's Jeanie?
No one knows. But me.

PART TWO

Surf Avenue

4

So many of these lads came from chaos and tragedy. They didn't have a fair start in life. Your heart would have to be made of granite not to feel something for them, give them a nickel or a dime after you hear a story or two. Families who didn't care about them or beat them. Nothing to hold on to but the bottle. I never realized I was one of the lucky ones, having a family who loved like mine did. Maybe they held on too tightly, but they never let me fall into the gutter.

Mazie's Diary, November 15, 1919

I haven't written in all this time. We packed, we moved, we left Grand Street behind. Rosie said living by the ocean would heal us all. But what does she know about getting well?

And then I lost you in the move and it felt like I lost my life. All the things that happened till now, I'm not sure they were real unless I wrote them down. You held all the secrets. You're the most precious thing I own. I didn't know it till I lost you. I didn't know it till I found you.

You were in that last box, sealed off in Rosie's closet. I didn't know the box was in there and I didn't dare tell Rosie I was looking for you. I didn't want her to know all my secrets were kept in one place. But yesterday Louis was taking us to the track, and he told us both to get dolled up. We were looking for a pair of Rosie's high-heeled shoes for me to wear. They were midnight blue, and had an open toe and a heart-shaped jewel in the center. I remembered once I had worn them and felt like I was walking in the sky, alongside the stars. I kept on Rosie about them and finally she said she'd hunt them down. No one had seen them since we moved to Surf Avenue. Another treasure lost with the move. I was thinking about how we were leaving a trail behind us of our favorite things. Rosie was on her knees, digging through her closet. She ripped open the box with her bare hands, and there you were.

Rosie said: What's this?

I snatched at it, and she clutched it to herself, over her heart.

I said: It's mine. Give it now.

Rosie said: Still with this old thing?

I said: Why don't you worry about your own business?

She looked down at her hands. I was waiting for her to say one of a million things. You're my business, is what I was waiting for her to say. But she didn't.

She said: You're right. It's yours.

Our blood barely stirred in us, no yelling, no fighting. That's the way it's been for months. I feel sorry for her, losing Jeanie like that. She feels sorry for me, losing the baby. She thinks I'll never have love in my life. I can see it on her face. I never minded her pity before if it meant she would leave me alone. But some days I miss the spark of it. Fighting meant we were both still alive. Now I'm not so sure.

Still, she has her claws in me in one way. And Louis too. She makes Louis drive me to work and pick me up every damn day. I go from house to car to cage, then back again. No room to move. No shot at freedom.

Elio Ferrante, history teacher,
Abraham Lincoln High School, Coney Island, Brooklyn

Brooklyn is my passion, so I'm happy to help. Born and raised, Bay Ridge represent! [Laughs.] I'm impressed with your project, too. You got what, an essay and a few newspaper articles and that's it? And no pictures, right? Amazing. I should have you come talk to my classes. I don't think they get to meet too many writer-researcher types, let alone someone putting together a book. They don't even know what it means to do research. They just want to sit there and get all the information handed to them. Then they memorize it just long enough for the test and then poof! It's gone! Like it never even existed.

So all right, let me give you some information. Coney Island in the 1920s was mostly middle and upper class, and it really lived like its own separate entity from the rest of New York City—because there was no train there yet. Now you said Mazie was living on Surf Avenue, which was very different from one end to the other. The east end was where all the action was. Luna Park was there, for example. You know bumper cars and roller coasters and all of that. It's where people came to play.

But from what you've told me Mazie was living on the west end, which had a quieter neighborhood vibe—except in the summer, where there were these bungalow colonies. My grandfather actually grew up closer to that end, and in the summer his family used to charge fees to visitors who needed a place to change their clothes before a day at the beach. They had this locker setup in the backyard they hauled out every year. He said it was the best job he ever had, taking quarters from all the girls. Sometimes they changed right in front of him. My grandfather, he remembered it *fondly*. [Laughs.]

There's plenty of pictures of it, I can show you sometime. I've got all kinds of photo albums. My mother, she keeps everything, and so did her parents. She used to sit me down with albums filled with scraps of memorabilia—a hundred years of it. Not just pictures, but ticket stubs, napkins, menus, every little thing. She'd sit me down—imagine a little version of me, I was very serious then, thick glasses, a little nerd [Laughs.]—and we'd flip through them. "This is your history," she'd tell me. "History is important, there's lessons to be learned there."

I liked looking at the pictures the best, I guess. There's a lot of impressive facial hair in my family's history, twirling mustaches and all that. But I liked all the detritus too. And my mother was no fool. She knew if I felt connected to something it would help keep me on the straight and narrow. I'd be less likely to be looking for trouble out there on the streets and there was plenty of it to be found when I was growing up, right outside my front door. But I think most of all though she wanted to give me a sense of culture, that I was Italian, and I was American, and I was a New Yorker. All of these things at once. I come from a family of flag-wavers. For those of us who have learned how to work within the system, we love it.

Mazie's Diary, November 22, 1919

I'll admit I don't mind living in this house itself, even if I don't like Coney Island. There's a brand-new kitchen. The sink is white, the counters, the cabinets, too. Peppermint-pink flowers painted along the edge of the cabinets, little teacup roses. New matching dishes, all white, too, with green and pink flowers. The floors are white-and-black-checked tiles.

But Rosie can't stop cleaning it.

She said: Dirt's the enemy. Every little mark will show.

I said: A scuff here and there, that's what makes things lived in.

She said: That's what the table's for.

It's true, she hauled that same old wooden kitchen table all the way from the Lower East Side to Coney Island. Holding on to it thinking Jeanie will come back and we can all sit around it again. Holding on to air is what she's doing.

Elio Ferrante

I'm getting distracted here, talking about my family, when we're supposed to be talking about Surf Avenue. So yeah, in the summer, everyone wanted to go to the beach. But the rest of the year that end of Surf Avenue was a peaceful neighborhood, empty except for the people who lived there. When you walk out your front door and have the ocean right there? I guess you could feel like you're living in the safest place around. Either that, or that you're living in exile.

Mazie's Diary, December 1, 1919

This morning in the car with Louis.

I said: How's business?

He said: You tell me. You run my business.

I said: You got more businesses than that, Louis.

He said: Why you so worried about it?

I said: I'm making conversation.

He said: Let's think of something else we can talk about. Out of all the things in the world, Mazie, we got more to talk about besides business.

He sounded angry, so I didn't push.

He said: Look out the window. It's a beautiful winter day.

Some days he just doesn't want to talk to me. Some days I don't want to talk to him. But still we're together, no matter what, in the goddamn car.

Mazie's Diary, December 3, 1919

This morning there was Rosie at the sink again, rag in hand. How does she always have something to clean? Why does she need to clean this early in the morning?

I said: It's clean.

She didn't hear me. She never listens to anyone, especially not me.

I couldn't watch her scrub for another minute so I just kept on walking, past the lunatic in the kitchen, past the quiet man at the table, out the front door. The outside of the house is bright pink, like half the houses around us. I turned and stared. False cheer.

Then I walked to the end of the block, straight onto the sand. All before me was the ocean and the sky, gray clouds aswirl with violet air. I want to like it here, on Coney Island. I want to believe I'm living in the right place at the right time. A line of winter lightning cracked across the sky. There I was, at the end of the world. But out there, somewhere else, something was happening. Something was crackling in the distance, far away from me.

Mazie's Diary, December 13, 1919

Another postcard from Jeanie today at the theater. This one's from Cleveland. That makes three.

It said: All's well in Ohio. We're selling out every night. A big hit!

She drew a long vine of roses with sharp-looking thorns around the edge of the card. The front of it was a picture of downtown Cleveland.

It said: Welcome to the sixth city!

What's the fifth city, I thought. There's only one city that matters anyway, and that's New York City.

I put the postcard up in the cage next to the others she's sent and the postcards from the Captain too. A wall of places I'll never visit.

When I got home I told Rosie I'd gotten another postcard from Jeanie.

She said: I don't want to hear it. I don't want to hear it!

She went back to cleaning the kitchen. I've seen her scrub that sink a thousand times since we've moved.

I said: You can't get it any cleaner.

But she didn't hear a thing I said.

Mazie's Diary, December 15, 1919

Sister Tee visited me today. It's been an age since I've seen her. I'd been worried she was ignoring me. I decided to tease her. No reason, I wasn't being cruel, only having a laugh.

I said: You must be bored these days. No booze, no trouble.

She said: Funny how people always find a way to the trouble.

I said: Idle hands, idle minds, Sister Tee! Maybe you're finding your way to the trouble.

She said: Faith's where I put my energy.

I said: Fun's where I put mine.

She said: If you'd seen the things I see.

I said: I see exactly what you see.

I heard myself for a second. My voice sounded like the grind of the train on steel that I hear all day above my head. I didn't like it, neither did she. She looked more like a young girl than ever, soft and big-eyed. Baby Sister.

She said: How are you doing, Mazie? Are you feeling better?

I said: Better than what? What are you talking about?

She said: I didn't mean a thing, my friend. Only I heard you'd been sick.

I said: Look at me. I'm healthy as a goddamn horse.

And that was that. I don't tell anyone my secrets, especially no nun. I shut the cage, and didn't even say good-bye.

Mazie's Diary, January 4, 1920

Morning ride with Louis.

I said: Teach me about gambling.

He said: Never bet more than you have to lose.

I said: Boring.

He said: You should never gamble, Mazie. You're too hot-headed. You, your sisters, none of you would be any good at it. You'd bet it all on your gut. And you can't keep straight faces neither. You'd be out at the poker table in a heartbeat.

I said: We can't help it if we feel things.

He said: It's why I keep you around. You think I want to look at serious mugs all night long? Talk about boring.

I got good instincts, I don't care what he says.

He said: All right, all right. I got one tip. Losing streaks. If you get on one, you can't let it throw you off. You have to ride it out. We all go through them.

I said: Even you?

He said: Everyone. No one is so special in this life. We all lose sometimes. Life's plenty easy when you're winning. It's what you do when you're down. That's the real test.

I said: I used to think I was special.

He said: I know.

I wanted him to tell me I still was. I would have eaten my left pinky to hear it. Torn it off with my teeth. But you can't ask someone to tell you that.

Mazie's Diary, February 3, 1920

Our mother finally passed on to the next life, wherever that is. I'd like to say she lived a good life, but she didn't. I'd like to say she lived a long life, but that's not true either. I barely knew her. I won't miss her. You can't miss a thing you don't know. Still when I heard I wept like a baby fresh to this world. Rosie, too. We howled and held each other. Louis didn't know what to do. We just stood in that kitchen and cried.

Later I said: We should tell Jeanie. She'll want to know.

Rosie said: I'll have nothing to do with that.

I sent her a letter anyway. Care of a boardinghouse in Chicago. Last known address.

Mazie's Diary, February 4, 1920

Rosie left this morning. Drove herself and an empty trunk to Boston. I looked out the window and saw a gentle embrace between her and Louis at the car. He petted her hair, hunched over, and kissed the top of her head. Then he handed her a paper sack. Sweet that he made her lunch.

Later on Louis told me he'd be late picking me up, and I told him not to bother, I'd find my own way home. No words need to pass between us. He takes care of his business, I take care of mine.

After work I went to Finny's for a quick one. Knock twice, then knock three times, and then you're in. Lately I like it better than some of the noisier places, the ones with dancing and music. I don't need the gaiety. I ain't got nothing to celebrate, but I'm game for a laugh or two. Finny's is simple, clean, a place to drink and not much else. Old wood floors covered with sawdust, and chipped cement walls with a painting of a half-naked lady that everyone says is Finny's mom. I like to listen to the drunks talk. When I leave, my shoes are always a little dusty from the floor, like I'm taking a little bit of Finny's with me.

There were a bunch of old-timers there. George Flicker's uncle Al was there, head in a book, throwing them back. I remember him from the days he used to sleep below the staircase, when we lived in the first apartment on Grand Street. That bunched-up mattress. He built his own shelves beneath the stairs, stocked them with books. None I wanted to read but I liked looking at the covers.

For a bit I flirted with a young banker, William. He said he was going to own the world. He's been to a movie or two at the Venice, knew who I was when I walked in the door. I let him buy me a drink, then three more. He's sharp but he doesn't make me laugh. I just want a laugh! God, I'm desperate for it. All I could see was his desire. Stared at me like a dog waiting to be fed. I nearly barked at him. I thought he must be in some kind of pain between his legs so steady were his looks. I thought about telling him there's whores out there for that. But it's been too long since I've seen the Captain…

I've been bleeding for a few days though, so I only let him at my breasts. He nearly sucked my nipples raw.

Hungry William.

Mazie's Diary, February 5, 1920

I've just been taking cabs everywhere. No idea where Louis's been. Cash on the table this morning.

Finny's again last night. Al Flicker was there, in the corner talking to an Italian man. He was a real firecracker, this Italian. Dancing hands, dancing eyes. Looked over his shoulder a thousand times. I wanted him to look at me but he was looking at the door. Who you waiting for? I was thinking.

There was some grousing at the bar about the firecracker. They said he was an anarchist.

I said: You gotta be something I guess.

Oh, they howled at me.

I said: Politics is just a pose.

More howling. God bless America, what have you.

I said: Why don't you mind your own anyway? What are you, running for office? Gonna be mayor of Finny's?

Not a peep. These drunks.

George Flicker

I don't know if Al was exactly an anarchist in a political way, like a lot of those gentlemen were. Gentlemen, I don't know if they were gentlemen. Anyway, I think he just felt anarchic within himself. It was this spirit that he connected with. That word seemed to make sense to him. But the actual politics, what they stood for or didn't stand for, I can't say one way or another if he stood behind it. I think he believed in the right to believe, if that makes any sense at all. He felt it was his right as an American to be able to believe what he liked.

Mazie's Diary, February 8, 1920

Rosie's back home with us. Louis dragged the trunk in after her.

The first thing she said: That man's mad.

The second thing she said: The kitchen is a mess.

She looked at me when she said that.

I said: The kitchen is not a mess.

Louis said: Sit. Talk to us.

She gave the kitchen another look, paced around it, suspicious, running her hands all over everything. That woman needs a cage of her own. Finally we both yelled at her to sit and she did.

She said: I went to the hospital. They said her body was gone. I went to the funeral parlor. They said she was buried already. I went to the cemetery and they gave me a number. There's just a number on her grave. I put flowers on it. I thought someone should. Do you know what I mean, Mazie? Don't you think I should put flowers on our mother's grave?

I said: I'm glad you did.

She said: It was so cold I thought I would die right there. Then I'll be a number too, I thought.

Louis said: You'll never just be a number, I promise you that.

She said: That night I had dinner with Aunt Edith and she said there's nothing anyone could do about it. He hadn't talked to a soul. He makes his decisions, that's it. I went back to the house the next morning. It was nearly empty. Someone was hauling a table away when I got there. He'd sold it all. Anything worth selling, anyway. Not that any of it's worth much.

Louis said: Those are his possessions, the man's got a right to it.

She said: I just wanted whatever could have been ours. I thought maybe there was something she would have wanted us to have. Something from the past, I don't know what past. He was sitting on the back porch, still in his funeral suit. He had a bottle of something or other in his hand. I don't know what, it smelled foul. His eyes looked murderous. He was not of this earth.

She pulled out a paper sack and pushed it across the table to Louis.

She said: I didn't use it but I was glad I had it.

I reached out for it, I don't know why. But Louis just snatched it.

She said: I took whatever I could find that was hers. It looked like a bunch of junk. I was looking for our birth certificates, something that could have been about us. I got nothing. I never got anything from her. It's just trash. Old clothes. It's rotting. It's junk. Shoes. I don't think even half of them match. I don't know. I grabbed what I could from the bedroom. He followed me in the room. I said I'm taking it, old man. He said no one wanted it anyway just like no one wanted me or any of us or her. I said I will kill you if you don't keep quiet. I did pull it out of the bag, Louis, I'm sorry. I did wave it at him. I didn't mean to but the whole way there I was thinking I was glad I had it with me. But I wasn't going to use it. I wasn't going to be like him. The moment I saw him though I just wanted to wave it in his face. I wanted to scare him.

I think this is what she said. I'm trying to remember everything she said.

Louis said: It doesn't matter, you didn't do anything wrong, sweetheart. I gave it to you for a reason.

She said: I wouldn't have done it. I just showed it to him. I said, this is ours. I'm waving a gun in his face for a bunch of junk. I'm a fool. I don't know what I thought I would find.

I went to the trunk and opened it. It smelled horrible.

She said: Maybe I'm the mad one.

Louis told her she wasn't.

She said: There's nothing in there worth anything.

Louis shushed her gently.

She said: He pissed himself! Can you believe it? He was laughing at first, because my hand was shaking. Then it was steady and he wasn't laughing anymore. Nothing was funny anymore, I'll tell you. Then I heard it, and I looked down. We both did. There was a puddle at his feet.

Louis started laughing.

He said: You're one tough cookie, Rosie.

Rosie said: Oh my goodness, I'm so tired, husband.

I dug through all the holey, stained clothes, worn shoes, figurines snapped in two. Then I picked up a book. I nearly fainted. It was a diary.

I said: What about this?

Rosie shook her head.

She said: It's junk, I swear it.

Then she went upstairs to their bedroom. She's been asleep for a day now.

I've been trying to read the diary but it's impossible. Broken English, shaky handwriting. After all that time with him, she had a blurred brain. I can't read a damn thing. It's unfair.

I just wanted to know if she missed us when we were gone.

Mazie's Diary, February 10, 1920

Too quiet in the car this morning.

I said: Tell me about your family, Louis.

He said: Why you want to know about my family, Mazie?

I said: Because I can't bear to think of mine anymore. I can't stand it for another goddamn minute.

He coughed and then he was quiet for a long time.

He said: Well I had a father, and I didn't know him. He passed when I was young. My mother I remember. She passed when I was thirteen. She had a funny laugh, real deep, as deep as yours. She also had pretty skin. It was especially pale and soft. The thing I remember most, because as I get older things are fading a bit, is that she wrote beautiful letters. Every year for my birthday she'd write me a letter telling me all the things I had done in the last year, and all the things she wished for me the next year. I mean these are great letters, Mazie, for a kid to get. I still have them. It's a shame they stop so young. I had to make up the rest of my life all on my own.

I said: Where are the letters?

He said: Back at the house.

I said: Can I see them?

He said: Why?

I said: I just want to know how I'm supposed to be.

He said: Sure. You're doing fine though.

I said: How did your parents die?

He said: They got sick. People got sick a lot more then than they do now. They got sick, and they died, and it was sad, and then it was over. And now I have a new family. Now I have you.

Outside, the sky was white and gray and glittered like some kind of angel.

Then he said: You know maybe I don't show you the letters right away. It does make me sad to look at them. I like to look at what I have right in front of me, not what's behind me. I like to look at the good things.

Then he stopped talking. We were quiet all the way till we got to the city.

When I got home tonight I was praying I'd see Rosie in the kitchen but all that was there was that trunk. Together me and Louis moved it out back.

Out of sight, out of mind.

Mazie's Diary, February 11, 1920

She finally got out of bed today. Back in the kitchen when I left this morning.

Mazie's Diary, February 14, 1920

Not a love in my life, but a postcard from a captain will do. Postmarked San Francisco, but the picture was of a redwood tree, in a place called Eureka. A child stood next to it, dwarfed by the trunk.

It said: Don't change one goddamn thing about yourself before I see you again.

I tacked it to the wall. I stood very still for a moment and thought about staying exactly the same forever. That tree would grow, that child would grow, but I would stay just the same in my cage.

Mazie's Diary, March 15, 1920

The police shut down Finny's place last night, for good this time I think. Finny's in jail. I sent bail with one of his bartenders. Mack Walters stopped by, checking the temperature on the street I guess. We got into a tiff about Finny's arrest.

I said: I've seen you drunk there a thousand times.

He said: Finny can't be running booze like that anymore and he knows it.

I said: I notice you still have that flask of yours bulging in your pocket.

I pointed to his pants.

He said: Oh that? That's not a flask, Mazie.

He gave me the filthiest look. The lech! I flipped the Closed sign on my cage and turned my back on him. I was laughing though, and he knew it. He'd like to take me out, he's been asking. I keep telling him I live on Coney Island now, that's where he'll find me.

Mazie's Diary, March 16, 1920

I saw Sister Tee across the street this morning. In flight with her flock. Not a nod, not a wave.

I don't need her.

Louis stopped by later. A bag in the safe.

I don't bother asking because he won't tell me nothing anyway.

Mazie's Diary, March 19, 1920

I said: Do you worry about Rosie?

Louis said: What about Rosie?

I said: The way she's always cleaning the kitchen.

Louis said: Do you want to clean the kitchen? Because I sure don't.

And that's it for Louis I guess. We'll have the cleanest kitchen in Brooklyn.

Mazie's Diary, April 1, 1920

I got on the third train ever from Coney Island to the city this morning. I rode it and I waved good-bye to the ocean.

The train, I've been waiting on it forever. The train! Freedom. No more drop-offs or pickups from Louis, no more living on his schedule, on his time. The train! I'll be out in the world as I please. I can come and go, say hello and good night, whenever I like. My time becomes mine again.

The train!

Elio Ferrante

The completion of the Coney Island subway station was absolutely significant from a historical perspective. As I mentioned it was mostly an upper-middle-class population living on Coney Island, even if they weren't there full-time. But when they completed construction on the train, there was suddenly easy access to the beach and, thus, an explosion of the working class there on the weekends. So that's the thing we mainly study, the impact of the train on the class structure in New York City.

But you're right, it works in the reverse direction, too. Even if it's not the thing we study, that doesn't mean it's not important. If you lived on Coney Island, now you could travel to the city more easily. Trains changed everything. Trains, and also planes and cars, and while we're at it, the telephone, too. Radios! Color movies! Television! Computers! Medicine and weapons. Pollution. Skateboards. Condoms. Bikinis. Books. Magazines. Elections. Pornography. The lightbulb. I could keep going. Everything changes everything. Everything around us is a piece of history. Every invention, every reaction to it. Every war, every retreat. There is always a trail, Nadine.

Mazie's Diary, April 11, 1920

I adore every little thing about taking the train to work. I feel gentle, resting on the cushion of the straw cane seats, the ceiling fans above dusting me with air. The train rocks us all in sweet rhythm. Babies drop their heads on their mamas' chests. I keep catching myself smiling like a fool on the train. The smell of the burning oil even makes me feel a little lusty, though I know that's odd. No one around me knows what it means to me, what five cents a ride can do for a girl. Change her world forever.

Mazie's Diary, May 1, 1920

Another postcard from Jeanie today. A picture of White City. I liked all the sweet little trees around the edges of the park. Not so different from our Luna Park, I suppose, except we've got the ocean and all Chicago's got is some boring old lake. Phoenix Theatre, that's where she's playing these days.

The postcard said: Why didn't you tell me staying up late was this much fun?

A note like that, now she's just bragging. I hope she's having the time of her life. I hope she's breaking hearts and wearing out those heels on her dancing shoes. I hope someone's having fun somewhere.

Mazie's Diary, May 12, 1920

Sister Tee brought a peace offering, a bag of sweets, peppermint candies strong enough to knock you sober.

Sister Tee said: I didn't do anything wrong.

I said: It wasn't what you did. It was what you said.

Sister Tee: What did I say? I was only concerned for your welfare.

It makes me grind my teeth, her talking like she knows better than me how to take care of myself. She's no older than I am. Devotion to something doesn't make you any kind of expert on life. Life makes you an expert on life.

I forgave her though. I missed her when she was gone, and I adore her, it's true. No one I'd rather tease than my little Tee.

Mazie's Diary, July 1, 1920

Postcard from Jeanie.

It said: I'm in love with love.

I didn't like this postcard much. Michigan Boulevard, Looking North. Bunch of buildings and cars, no different than New York City. Cleaner, I suppose. Shoot anything from the right angle and it can look clean.

Mazie's Diary, July 15, 1920

Al Flicker was on the train this morning. He got on at Jay Street, with a plump, purple shiner.

I said: Hey, Al, I'd hate to see the other guy, right?

Just trying to make a joke, make things easy on the guy. But he didn't think it was funny. He didn't think it was much of anything. He just looked behind me, at the darkness of the station. He stared so hard I looked myself to see if there was anything there. But all I could see was pitch-black tunnel.

George Flicker

My mother didn't know where he was disappearing to, and I don't think he could have told you much either. He was a grown man though, and allowed to go where he pleased. I was still carousing in Europe myself, so I couldn't really disagree with how he spent his time. In my mother's letters and phone calls though, I could tell she was really worried. She used to say he'd be the death of her, and I'd say, "Ma, like anything could kill you."

Mazie's Diary, September 5, 1920

A postcard from the Captain.

It said: I'll be in New York City on October 4. I'd be honored if you'd join me for dinner. P.S. You look gorgeous in red.

Mazie's Diary, September 16, 1920

Devastating day. Ain't seen nothing like it before in my life, never hope to again.

A bomb went off down on Wall Street. I heard it at noon. A mile away and I could hear it, not like it was right next to me but close enough. No lines for another hour, so I shut the cage and stepped outside. I saw Mack running. Then more of the foot patrol. I watched them fly. I stopped breathing for a second. The whole city grew quiet, I swear it. And then I heard screaming. I hiked up my skirt and started running down Pearl Street. Don't know what I was thinking, don't know where I was heading. Just toward the noise. Just wanted to help.

After a few minutes a crowd was coming from the other direction. Some of them covered in yellow dust, like parchment, and then a few with some blood. Nobody was dying, but they were all scared and crying. Dazed creatures. I was pushing against them, I didn't mean to. I was going the wrong direction. I used to outrun all the boys. I still remember turning and seeing them all trailing behind me.

The farther downtown I got, the more dust I saw. All kinds of things flying through the air. The red of the blood against the yellow of the dust. I'd have liked to wash it all clean. Started praying for rain, thought that would help. Whatever's up there in the sky, let it rain. I looked up but all I saw was these clouds of smoke, yellow and green mixed together. Sirens screeching madness. Someone said it was the Morgan building, a bomb at the Morgan building.

I ran up Wall Street. Windows blown out in buildings along the way. I started seeing bodies. I saw some arms. I don't know why I didn't turn back. There was the leg of a horse. Blood on the streets. Then I saw Sister Tee on the ground, her hands pressed against a man's leg, a bleeding wound. I dropped to my knees. I took the scarf from my neck, and we tied it together around him. Police all around, everyone racing. There was another man bleeding next to him, and another, and another. We moved together. I ripped off the hem of my dress and we tied it on the next man's wound. Mack was in the distance, with other officers. The dust was all around us. We stayed until there was no one left to help, till all the bodies were gone.

Sister Tee and I walked up through Chinatown together, slow and dizzy. She stopped us in front of the Church of the Transfiguration.

She said: Look up.

There was a statue in the steeple, an old man, chipped white marble.

She said: Saint John Bosco.

I said: Well where were you today, Saint Bosco?

She said: Oh he was there.

She crossed herself and I would have laughed but today was no day for disrespect.

Finny's was open later. Funny how it opens and closes as it pleases. No one said a thing. I saw half the force in there I swear. Everyone needed a drink. The saddest day I've ever seen in New York City.

The anarchists, police were saying. Justice tomorrow, I thought. Tonight let's just sleep.

I got home a few minutes ago and Rosie said Louis was driving me to work in the morning.

Mazie's Diary, September 17, 1920

I rose at dawn and snuck out of my own home. I'd be damned if I didn't take that train with the rest of New York City today. I wondered if I'd be the only one riding, but sure enough, stop after stop, people got on. All dressed in dark colors, dark skirts, dark blouses, dark suits, dark hats. Their finest and saddest. The whole train hovered with gloom.

At Flatbush, a man boarded, hauling a crate of apples. They were small and bright green. I nodded at the man and he nodded at me. He was small too, short, with a dark, swirling mustache. An Italian I thought.

He said: I picked these in New Jersey yesterday. I was out of town all day. I missed everything because I was picking apples.

I said: Better to miss it.

He said: It's not the kind of thing you want to see but it's not the kind of thing you want to miss neither.

I said: I saw it. Believe you me.

He said: It just made me want to fight someone, anyone. Wished I could have helped.

I said: I know it.

He said: Hey, you want an apple?

I said: There's nothing more on this earth I want than one of those apples.

He handed me one. He asked a lady sitting next to me if she wanted one too, and then another, and then another.

Soon enough all his apples were gone. We all sat there eating them, our shiny green rewards for being alive. The train rocked us back and forth like we were babies. You couldn't hear nothing but the sound of people crunching on apples. It wasn't like we forgot the day before. It was just that those were some damn good apples.

Elio Ferrante

This city, as imperfect as it is, knows how to come together when things get rough.

Mazie's Diary, September 18, 1920

Louis drove me to the city this morning. Just because, said Rosie. Just because.

Louis said: You don't go any farther downtown today, you hear me. It's none of our business.

I said: It was working stiffs, just like me. Those are the people standing in my line, Louis.

He said: We ain't losing any more family members this year, Mazie.

Mazie's Diary, October 2, 1920

Rosie's on me about Louis driving me to work again every day. She wants me to go from cage to cage to cage. No way, no how. The train's the only time I have to myself.

Down on the floor scrubbing and she's calling out orders. That woman makes more rules on her knees than most kings do on thrones.

I said: I'm taking the train goddammit.

Rosie turned her back on me and started scrubbing again. But that didn't mean she agreed with me.

Mazie's Diary, October 3, 1920

Louis dropped by again, more money in the safe. I've been daydreaming about stealing it, not all of it, just enough. What's mine is yours, sis—he tells me that all the time. I could take it and go. But would I even know what to do if I ran? Where would I go? To White City to find Jeanie? I'd just end up working in another ticket booth. From one cage to another.

Mazie's Diary, October 4, 1920

I forgot about the Captain coming to town. How could I forget? I did, though. But there he was, at the cage. In his uniform.

I said: I forgot to wear red, sir.

He said: You're beautiful no matter what, miss.

He could bend me in two, that's how fragile I am these days. I'm made of paper, fold me at the edges.

We walked up the Bowery.

He said: It's cleaned up since the last time I was here.

I said: There's no more booze.

He said: There's always booze.

He pulled a flask from his pocket. Then he turned us down Hester Street, toward the park there. His hand on my elbow. He whispered something in my ear about loving my elbow and I nearly loathed him.

We sat in the park quietly. A gent and a lady, passing a flask back and forth.

He said: They take it away, it only makes you want it more.

I said: Abstinence makes the heart grow fonder.

I looked down at the ground, suddenly humbled. I had this feeling the whole time that seeing him was going to humble me.

A police officer turned a block up. The Captain slid the flask in his coat pocket, fast and easy. Like a thief on the street.

He said: What do you want to do on a night like tonight?

What I really wanted to do was get on the train with him to Coney Island so he could meet Rosie and Louis. Let's sit together on the train and be like people in love. Let's sit together in my kitchen with my family. Let's be like those other people.

He didn't wait for me to answer. He turned and kissed me, fingertips in my hair, wicked little pleasure points.

He said: What about that, beautiful? Do you want to do that?

My desire for him humbled me most of all. I went with him to his hotel. It was clean and quiet. In his room he kissed me at the door. Wretched and perfect. Oh he smelled like a man and I could have howled at the moon.

He said: I can't believe we'll have all night.

I watched as he undressed. He watched as I undressed.

I made him give me more of the flask and I drank it and he drank it till it was done. We spilled it on each other some too. We sipped it off each other's flesh. I got down on my knees. He said my name and told me I was beautiful as I sucked. Then we were on the bed. Then, at last, I howled at the moon.

It went on like that for a while. I'm raw today. Each step I take reminds me of him.

I'd love him if I could. But he's got a whole life out there, flying free wherever he likes, and I know nothing about what he does with his time. Except that I do know, I think. And I ain't a part of it.

Mazie's Diary, October 5, 1920

In my dream I tell him about the baby and he turns his back to me and I throw my arms around him and he says why are you telling me this now and I say I just thought you should know and he says what's the point of knowing and I say I'm just letting you know there was something there and now it's gone and he says I wish you hadn't told me I could have lived my whole life not knowing and I said me too and he said it would have been fine now I have to carry it with me forever and I say me too me too me too.

Mazie's Diary, October 8, 1920

Louis and me stood on the front porch and stared down at the ocean. Summer's gone, it's over. Nothing left to grasp at.

Louis said: You don't want to spend a little time with your old pal Louis?

I said: I don't want to be driven.

He said: I'll buy a new car, fresh off the lot. Your pick. And it'll be in your name.

I said: It's not fair.

I cried. He tried to hold me but I wouldn't let him. Let him go hold his wife instead.

Mazie's Diary, October 9, 1920

I'll move out, that's what I'll do. Back into the city. I got a job, I got money saved. I'll find a single apartment just right for a girl like me. Other girls do it, lots of them, all the time. I can find someone to rent to me. I won't even tell Rosie. I'll just move out in the middle of the night. I'll pack up my things and run in the night. If she wants to talk to me she can come and stand in line just like everyone else.

Mazie's Diary, October 11, 1920

Mack stopped by the cage.

I said: What's the good word?

He said: Nothing, not a peep.

I said: What about that thing that happened down on Wall Street?

He said: We're trying, we're trying.

I said: Truly nothing then?

He said: Not a lot of evidence to be found, unless you count a horse's head, and that horse ain't talking. But we've got our eye on some individuals. Just because we can't prove it doesn't mean they didn't do it.

I shuddered then. I don't like that kind of talk.

Elio Ferrante

But we have a little problem here in New York with authority. The cops are not afraid to use their fists or their weapons.

Mazie's Diary, October 13, 1920

Early morning, the coffee stinging more than most days.

Rosie down on the floor, washing away specks of nothing. Louis's eating eggs at the table, fork after fork, not breathing in between.

I said: The kitchen's clean.

Rosie kept scrubbing.

I said: Did you hear me? The kitchen's clean, Rosie.

Rosie said: It's clean when I say it's clean.

I got down on my knees next to her. I grabbed her hand and she slapped me away. Louis came behind me and lifted me up by my waist. All of this was done in silence, as if we were performing our own lunatic ballet.

I ran to the train in the rain. I ruined my new hat. I threw it on the ground in front of the theater, and watched it suck up the water from the skies until one of the ushers dashed out with an umbrella and threw it away.

Elio Ferrante

It goes both ways though, this problem with authority. You bear down too much, someone fights back.

Mazie's Diary, October 15, 1920

Oh my goodness! Oh my goodness.

This morning, we're sniping at each other, me and Rosie, like usual. She won't rest till she gets me off that train.

Louis said: Can't a man eat his breakfast in peace? The two of you are like children.

Rosie said: She's the child.

Louis said: Take it outside. I can't stand another minute of it.

We went to the porch. Rosie slammed the door behind her. I felt bad for Louis, that he'd be getting it later from her. He must have thought it was worth it. Every once in a while it must be.

The sky was that brilliant early-morning violet I've only seen since we moved to Coney Island. I swear the ocean has a different sky than the rest of the world.

I said: Could we look at the sky for just one moment, sister?

Rosie said: Why won't you do as I wish?

I said: Look at the sky. Look at it.

Rosie said: It's your safety I'm worried about more than anything.

She started to say something else, but then suddenly the fanciest car I've ever seen pulled up in front of the house. I don't give a rat's ass about cars, but this was something special. It was a Rolls-Royce, silver. The air changed around it. For a moment I believed Louis had bought me this car. I pictured myself being driven to and from the Venice in it. What kind of ticket taker has a car like that? Me, that's who. I felt this stir of arrogance. Even writing this now is making me laugh out loud. A-ha, I thought. My ride is here.

But it wasn't my ride at all. A driver got out of the car, a proper one, wearing a special cap and gloves. He opened the rear door of the car and leaned inside. Someone slid an arm around his neck. Finally he stood, a body in his arms. I saw the casted leg first, and then I saw her face.

Jeanie's back.

5

Some of these bums are singers—every morning outside my cage I could hear them singing their Irish folk songs, or even a sea shanty or two. There were others who liked to draw, sketches of the park where they're sleeping, that filthy noisy train overhead, or pictures of the other bums, just being bums. I've got hundreds of them, swapped for a nickel, swapped for a drink. There's real artistic souls out there on the streets. A passion for something vivid and beautiful, not everyone has that. The bottle dims the passion, though, ruins the talent, too. If you let it. But I think you have to want to ruin it in the first place.

Jeanie Phillips, October 21, 1920

Mazie said to write my story down, it's too long for her to tell, and that it'll be good for me, it'll clear my head, and I'm the one who lived it, not her, anyway. Then she said start at the beginning until you get to the end, tell the truth, no point in lying to the page, to the diary, to yourself, and then she handed me this diary and this pen, and away we go.

I skipped town a year and a half ago because I wanted to make my own fate, choose my future myself, rather than accept what Louis & Rosie wanted for me, what Ethan wanted for me, too. I would have been married by now, I would have been working at the candy shop or at the track or at Luna Park, or cooking and cleaning like Rosie, or making babies with Ethan. And it's not that I'm too good for any of that, or even that there's anything wrong with that. Only I wanted to dance, I wanted to use these legs, these arms, my body, my gifts, my weapons. I didn't want to waste them on sitting still, at least not yet.

So I started dancing with the Folsom brothers, Skip & Felix, two white-blond-haired boys from Pennsylvania, escaped from a milk farm, no teat squeezing for them, just throwing me around in the air instead. A better fate, they said, more fun to throw the pretty girls in the air than touch the cow's titties. They were tall and strong, strong enough to toss me and catch me, and make me feel like I could disappear forever. If they just kept spinning me, I'd turn into a whisper and I'd be gone.

Felix is the elder brother, older by a year, and he still reads the Bible every night, but says it's only a habit, and the stories put him to sleep. He's married to Belle's girl Elizabeth, who does all her hair and makeup and sits by her side. She's a cherub from Philly, round cheeks, big eyes, and a real pleaser, yes's rather than no's any day of the week. And Skip's the dreamboat that everyone else falls in love with, and so I did, too.

I didn't fall in love with Skip until we were out on the road together. I swear on my life, on the air that I breathe, I wouldn't treat Ethan like that, never lied to him, never cheated, only loved and respected that boy, him being my first sweetheart and all. But Belle says tour love's as common as the flu, highly contagious, and I caught it, sleepless nights and dizzy daydreams and all the rest. I fell in love with the world we built together, the nerves before the curtain opens and Skip squeezing my hand for luck, the applause at the end taking my breath away every single time, whiskey & wine after the show, me on Skip's knee, Elizabeth with her hands in Felix's hair, Belle barking at all of us to do as she bid. Belle's always telling me she's the one who gave me a shot, like she's twenty years older than me instead of two, and didn't grow up three streets away from me. I let her say what she wants though, because she's more right than wrong. Without her I'd have been nowhere at all, or at least in the same place as always.

We started our tour in Philly, where Belle's husband's from, and where his father has a theater of his own. We stayed there for a month, reworking our act for the road, testing it out on those audiences that already loved Belle, she could do no wrong. Then we went to Cleveland to see what they thought, and they liked us there, they liked us a lot, and we liked them too, Cleveland was a gas. The theater was brand new, and we had crowds every night, on and on, all the applause thrilling me, until suddenly it seemed like everyone in town had already seen us once, and once was enough. Belle said it was time to move on, and what Belle says goes, because Belle runs the show, because Belle is the show.

There was more money to be made in Chicago, bigger crowds, more Jews, Jews who wanted all the Yiddish songs as much as the English songs, more than the English songs, never tired of them, and they were always Belle's favorites too. Belle's husband left us there, back to Philly, back for the spring, a relief for Belle because the only one who barks more than Belle is her husband. She told us she got us to Chicago but now we were on our own. So we did two shows a night with her on the weekends but nothing during the week, and we were worried we'd go broke, but Skip, my baby, my talker, my charmer, got us work at White City. I loved White City, with its twinkling lights all over the place, crowds of jolly Chicagoans, clean streets, wide skies. Three nights a week there, plus two with Belle and we were set.

Oh, everything was such a laugh! Rushing to the theater, hustling in a cab, breathless, tumbling out the door, but never tripping, never falling, we were dancers and we would never fall. I could have kept going across America, I liked the driving, I liked the road life, I liked setting up house for a spell in a hotel or a boardinghouse and then taking everything apart again. I could have looped and looped around this great country of ours forever. I liked these people, these performers, and I liked being buddies on the road. Skip & Felix & Elizabeth & Belle & Jeanie, that's me, the girl in the air.

But if I had to stay in just one place, Chicago was as good as anywhere else. They got a mayor there who's a real hoot, puts on a good show, even if he's bad news. He makes his own rules, doesn't give a damn about Prohibition, lines his own pocket from booze money. I read the papers, and I spent enough time there to know, Chicago is one wild town.

I never met that mayor, but I met a lot of people who worked for him. It seemed like half the town was either coming or going from his office. One of his special assistants came backstage once, a man named Paul, a gentleman in a fine suit, tall and meaty but with long sweet eyelashes and enormous, plush lips. Paul was an American but the child of Italians, so he was Paulo once, he told me, that very moment we met, sharing a new secret between friends, we shook hands on it, and the minute we touched I thought only one word: Yes.

Paul loved our work, loved our show, all three of us, me & Skip & Felix, and he offered to show us the town. He was one of the mayor's special assistants in enforcing Prohibition, which made him an expert in exactly where you weren't supposed to go but sometimes could. There was a wink after that, a wink just for me. Yes, we will go with you, Paul, wherever you go, yes.

He had his own car, the fanciest I've ever seen, with a driver who tipped his hat at us once when we got inside, and then never spoke to us again, quiet as a ghost in the front seat, he might as well have been a puff of smoke. We went from speakeasy to speakeasy, Paul shaking hands with all the men in fancy suits hovering near doorways, surveying the scene, running the show. I'm in Skip's arms the whole night dancing, but I can see Paul watching me, burning a hole through Skip with his eyes like he's not even there, and I'm staring right back at him, and I know something's going to happen because I want it to and all I have to do is say yes.

So yes, I say, yes yes yes, I scream it. He's married, who cares, yes. He's a criminal maybe, yes yes yes. You're just a girl he tells me, I say yes yes yes. You're so skinny I could slip my hand right through you, he says. Oh I'll feel it, I say. A skinny pretty Yid from New York City, he said. Never did I know that was a thing that could be desired, but in fact it is a thing that he desired, and so he had it.

What about Skip? How did I get it past him? We shared a room, like a married couple, husband and wife, till the curtain closes for good, he used to say, but we were definitely not married. The answer is that I'm an excellent liar, I have lied for years, so long that it has become as easy as telling the truth.

It went on for a few weeks, me and Paul, sneaking around Chicago, seemed like he had keys to every door in town, hotels and warehouses and clubs, front rooms, back rooms, a key to my door too. He offered me money sometimes but I always said no, because I didn't need his money, and also I might be a liar and I might be a cheat, but I'm definitely not a whore.

Every day my hair was a mess, messy sex hair, and Elizabeth hadn't the time to get it right every day, the tight waves and curls, the two of us racing to get it done before Belle's set. She said she didn't know what to do with me, that the Chicago wind must be stronger than she knew, and I laughed, a dirty laugh, a good-time-girl laugh, and she gave me a look like maybe it wasn't the wind, maybe it was Skip, and then she sighed, "Oh those Folsom boys."

Then one day we were running later than usual and Belle was in a monstrous mood, her husband was in town and he was not a part of the road family, him being bossier than Belle herself, and there couldn't be two bosses of the show. Belle started griping that Elizabeth was her girl and not my girl, and we were wincing hearing her voice, so beautiful when she sang but intimidating when she spoke, and Belle was right, it's true, Elizabeth was hers and not mine. And Elizabeth said she'd rather just cut all my hair off and be done with it, and then I told her to do it and the very next day she did, it was a bob, and it was done.

Now the men in my life had even more ardor for me, this new me with the new hair. Paul liked it because it was different, spontaneous, a change of plans, and Skip liked it because it was smart and stylish and fresh. I liked my hair because it didn't slow me down. I was a twirling, racing, breathless, desirable woman. I felt like I had everything I needed for one perfect week.

But one morning I woke up with a pain in my stomach, serious and low, slow and steady, and along with that my undergarments were stained with a white mess, and that didn't seem right either. And I tried all the old wives' recipes I've heard, gypsy recipes too, but alas and alack, the pain would not stop, the undergarments continued to spoil, and I knew I was ruined in some way.

I didn't believe I could tell anyone in my road family about my pain, not Elizabeth or Belle or Felix and especially not Skip. This is the hard part when you're a liar and a cheat and you have secrets, because you're really alone when things are bad, then you're really invisible. So I found a doctor for ladies and he stared at me down there for a while and coughed and hemmed and hawed and then, without looking me in the eye, told me I had the clap. The clap! Here I was, living for applause all this time, and boy oh boy, did I get it.

Now I knew I could have gotten the disease from either Skip or Paul, but I had an idea it was from Paul because I was sure I wasn't his only girl on the side, that there were other girls, ones who took money from him, and those kinds of girls sometimes have the clap, although there I was with it too, so who was I to judge or say anything? I asked Paul about it, I asked him if he had a little something going on down there, and he said that when you lived a life like his, there was always a little something going on down there.

Then I had to tell Skip, and I didn't want to, but I knew I had to, so I raced to the theater to tell him, to the backstage dressing room, and he was sitting there with Elizabeth looking serious, and when I looked at his face I saw that he already knew he had it too. I said I was sorry, awful sorry for everything, and that it was all my fault, and he said my name and shook his head and couldn't look me in the eye, and then Elizabeth reached out and held his hand and I felt shame. And then I saw Elizabeth was crying and I realized that she had it too, and that she and Skip were lovers. Then I could really hear the crowds roaring in my head, an ocean of applause for me, Jeanie, the girl in the air, taking down everyone around me. It was only a few minutes later that Felix showed up, whistling, humming, ready for another show, and then we had to tell him, all of us, that our road family was sick, we had all given each other a case of something horrible, and the minute

we told him he walked out and didn't return until right before
the show.

Elizabeth left to do Belle's hair, I smoothed mine down
on my own, Skip sat next to me in the mirror, I put on my
lipstick, I kohled my eyes, I looked at him in the mirror and
I couldn't tell what he was feeling at all, who was this person next to me, this beautiful fair-haired boy, but he wouldn't
look back at me, somehow he was looking anywhere in the
room but at me, and then I knew he was just as much a liar
and a cheat as me, we were the same, me & Skip, and Skip &
Elizabeth were the same, and it was only poor Felix who got
the short end of it all, happy, whistling Felix, now on fire like
the rest of us. And then it was showtime.

It took about five minutes into our act, the first real spin of
the night, for me to fall. I can't say as to which one of them
dropped me, Skip or Felix, because when you're in the air like
me you lose track of who is supposed to be catching you. You
just close your eyes and hope everyone's doing their job, and
this time they weren't. Skip or Felix, Skip & Felix? I didn't get
a good look at their faces afterward, I was up in the air, and
then I was down, and I felt a crack in my leg, a very particular
crack, and I screamed, and all I saw was stars in my pain, stars
and theater lights and then blackness, and then I passed out.

I woke up in a hospital, a doctor telling me if I had landed
differently I would have broken my back. It's how you fall,
he said, that matters. Youth helps, fitness, and how you fall.
He's telling me how lucky I am, lucky with the cast up past
my knee. I told him I didn't believe in luck, I'd make my own
fate, thanks.

No one came to visit me the first day, not Skip or Elizabeth
or Felix, but then finally Belle, my old friend Belle, showed

up at my bedside. She told me that she was sorry but that I would have to leave town, or at least leave the show, and that as soon as I was recovered enough to travel she would be happy to buy me a train ticket back to New York City, back where I belonged, with my family. She said she had taken a chance on me and I had failed because I had upset the balance of the road family. But also she said that she loved me like a sister and she bore me no ill will, would hold no grudge, and would be happy to keep all of this a secret amongst our mutual friends and family as long as I would agree to do the same. And when I looked deeply into her eyes, those hooded soulful eyes, I knew that she had the clap too.

Paul came to the hospital in an elegant wool coat with black leather gloves that smelled like the woods, and I will never forget how handsome he looked, my married Italian man. There he was, kissing both of my cheeks, holding my hands, kissing them too. He said he was sorry that it had come to this and that I was a beautiful girl and I would someday recover and dance again like an angel, and he would remember our time together fondly, and that it was a crime to break a leg like mine, as graceful as it was, and with all the joy it offered the world with my fantastic performances. Then he offered to kill someone for me as an act of revenge and I said no. Then he asked me if I needed a ride home and I sobbed yes yes yes.

So last week I was driven from Chicago to Coney Island in Paul's fancy car, and he gave me some money and this time I took it, and I did not feel like a whore, I only felt like a person in need. Paul's driver, Mauro, is a friend of his father's from the old country, their old country anyway, and he is my friend now, too. I told him everything that happened, start to finish, from Chicago to here, and it felt so good to tell the whole truth to someone.

He said it's not the worst thing in the world the things that I did and that I had a little fun and there's nothing wrong with that. I said that yes I had had my fun. He told me it's fine to be young and entertain myself, but that I should stop lying so much because no one likes a liar and that I'll keep all my secrets stored inside and it'll show in my face, and I'll end up an ugly old woman that no one will want to touch or love. He said there was a woman like that back in his village in Italy and she was a witch, and all the young boys threw stones at her until she bled. He said don't be that way, don't let the boys throw stones at you. He told me to be nice, he told me to be good, I said I would try. But already it felt like another lie. I'll be good and bad, I'll be right and wrong. I'll be just like everyone else.

Lydia Wallach

Mazie was the hero to my family, but I'll admit I daydreamed about being Jeanie once or twice. Obviously there was absolutely no possibility I'd live her life. I'm not a risk taker. I seek no thrills. But still I thought about it. Jeanie, the dancer, traveling the country, fluttering in and out of everyone's life. It was a point of contrast more than a pleasant distraction. If I were not that kind of girl, what kind of girl was I?

Mazie's Diary, November 11, 1920

My life right now is back and forth on the train, home to work, work to home, not a moment free in between. Jeanie begged me to be with her as much as possible, and I'm living up to my promise. She's a cracked egg, a sticky mess on the ground before us all. Every day Rosie tries to clean it up.

She said: Don't leave me alone with her.

I said: I gotta work, sister.

She said: You don't know what it's like, being trapped with her all day long.

I said: Oh, I know.

Jeanie's got six more weeks left in the cast, and even then it'll be a while longer till she gets around on her own. Meantime, I'm counting the cash, shutting the cage, and rushing home every night so I can crawl into bed right next to her. And every night she asks me the same thing.

She says: Tell me the story of your day.

Some days are more interesting than others, but most of them are exactly the same. People stand in line, they slap some cash in front of me, I give them a ticket and tell them to enjoy the show. The line's not the interesting part. It's the people on the streets, just hanging around. Too much time on your hands means trouble. Good kind, bad kind, both. But the streets seem cleaner these days. Now that most of the bars are closed, some of these bums have cleared out. You need money to have a good time in this town right now. The kind of fun I'm thinking about anyway.

Last night she clung to my arm, nuzzled her face up against it, desperate for attention.

She said: Tell me that people are still having a good time out there.

I said: I wouldn't even know if they were. I'm right here with you in bed every night. You want me to have fun, let me go.

Mazie's Diary, December 1, 1920

Sister Tee came to the cage this morning and I was glad to see her. Jeanie spends all her time feeling sorry for herself, high and dreamy, and Rosie spends all her time indulging her every whim. It's no game I'll play. So it was nice to talk to Tee, a woman sincerely devoted to helping others. She was looking for some help for a few more women.

She said: These girls, they have bad husbands. It's not their fault.

She wanted more help than I had in my purse. I thought of the bag Louis had dropped off just a few hours before. I stuck my hand in and grabbed a fistful of bills. I tried not to look too close at how much was there. It was full, though.

I thrust the money at her. I said I didn't want to know. It makes me sting thinking about my own mother still. When does that sting die? Does it die when I die?

Mazie's Diary, December 5, 1920

Last night Jeanie was passed out on the couch, snoring, one arm flopped to the side. There was the tiniest line of drool sliding from her mouth. Rosie was sitting in front of the hearth, reading the paper. I saw a tin of whatever Rosie's been feeding Jeanie to keep her quiet. I pointed to it.

I said: You gotta stop with that business.

She said: I'll stop when she's better. She's in pain. Her legs itch. Her nerves tingle. You're not here all day. You don't know how she moans. I'm the one who's taking care of her, not you.

I put the back of my hand on Jeanie's forehead. She was cool. I said her name. She fluttered her eyelids open.

I leaned over her and whispered in her ear.

I said: Do you want to sleep forever? I don't think you do.

I rubbed her neck for a second.

I said: Did you hear me?

She mumbled that she did.

Rosie said: What did you say?

I said: I told her to wake up.

Mazie's Diary, December 29, 1920

Ethan's come courting again. I guess he forgives easily. Can't say I'd do the same. I could hear Jeanie tittering from up the street as I approached the house. Nice to hear her happy anyway. She was sprawled on the couch by the hearth, a bag of chocolates next to her, her casted leg balanced on a pile of pillows.

She said: Ethan brought me treats.

She held up a stack of gossip papers.

He said: She sounded so bored, I couldn't help myself. We can't have our Jeanie bored.

I said: Oh brother.

Rosie called me from the kitchen, and I left the two of them with their sweets and gossip. Louis was seated at the table, Rosie behind him rubbing his shoulders.

She said: Leave them be. Let them get reacquainted.

I said: He's a fool.

I repeated myself, said it louder.

I went out onto the porch, lit myself a cigarette. My throat's been sore lately from yelling at all the holiday crowds above the noise of the city. Is it possible the city is getting louder? Could it be that the streets are fuller? More cars, more trains, more people, more noise. I can't stop smoking to save my life though. Often it feels like it's the only joy I have.

Ethan soon joined me on the porch. So tall, yet somehow he still seems like the runt of the litter. A stretched-out baby face.

I said: I thought you were clever. Doctors are supposed to be clever.

He said: I'm an animal doctor.

I said: So you're not clever?

The both of us were trembling in the moonlight from the winter chill, made more deadly by the wind blasting off the ocean.

He said: My heart can't help it, Mazie. She's a rare breed.

I said: No she's not. She's a street cat, can't you see? The kind who'll only rub against your legs long enough till you feed her.

He said: I see an injured creature who needs my love and support.

I waved my hand in front of his eyes a few times.

I said: Just checking to make sure they work.

He thinks he can handle a Phillips girl, let him try.

Mazie's Diary, December 31, 1920

We closed the theater last night till the New Year. Gave everyone the day off, paid.

Louis said: Thank god this year is over, let's hope the next one is better.

He handed everyone bottles of this and that and a hundred-dollar bill each. One of the ushers wept and hugged him, and sweet Louis hugged him back.

In the car ride home I smiled at Louis.

I said: You could have given them a tenner and it would have been fine by them, more than they expected.

Louis said: I could have given them a hundred more and it wouldn't have been enough.

Now it's lunchtime and we're all lazing about the house. Rosie and Louis rose early and drove into the city and spent a fortune at Joel Russ's shop. There's an abundance of food before us. Jeanie's eyes are clear. She's got just a few days till the cast comes off, and she's counting them down. She swears she feels healed. We've been picking at the whitefish, slicing off chunks of sour pickle, too, for the last hour. I've been flipping through the pages of this diary, looking at how lousy the past year has been.

Jeanie said: Anything good in there?

I said: You were someone else for a while it seems.

She said: Who was that girl?

I said: I missed you while you were gone.

She said: I missed you too.

I didn't quite believe her though.

I said: So you and Ethan are back on, are you?

Jeanie said: It's the oddest thing. He's right where I left him.

I couldn't help but think of the Captain. I'm right where he left me.

Mazie's Diary, January 1, 1921
Jeanie said: This year's going to be your year.

I said: For what?

Mazie's Diary, January 5, 1921

Mack wants to take me out on a date. He's insisting on it.

He said: A proper date for a proper lady.

I laughed.

He said: I'm an officer of the law. If you can't trust me, who can you trust?

I said: Oh really, Mack Walters?

He said: I'm being a straightforward, honorable man.

I laughed some more. Mack, the biggest boozer I know, and that's a lot coming from this boozer. Mack, with his oversized head and that extra chin and that beard that changes colors all year round, red to yellow to gray lately, like it can't decide what looks best on his face. Maybe none of it does.

I said: Maybe.

He said: Mazie, Maybe's what I'll call you from now on. And I'm planning on calling.

Walked off whistling, like he knew something I didn't.

Mazie's Diary, January 9, 1921

Jeanie came back from the doctor's, still on crutches, Ethan and Rosie helping her through the door. She'll be hobbling for a while yet.

She said: I don't know why I thought I'd be better. I was dreaming the cast would be gone and I'd be leaping through the streets, dancing in circles beneath the sun, whirling and twirling.

She waved her arms so gracefully in the air that I could nearly see her dancing myself.

Ethan said: You're young and strong, you'll heal just fine. Just do those exercises the doctor told you about.

I looked to see if Ethan was telling the truth and I could see that he was. Then Jeanie showed us her leg, scrawny and yellow and bruised.

Jeanie said: I nearly passed out when I saw it.

Rosie said: If that were a chicken leg I wouldn't serve it for dinner.

All of Jeanie is thinner now, I noticed for the first time. Her dress was falling off her shoulders, her petticoat dragged on the ground. Bones poking from her neck. Her hair was limp and untidy. Somehow her hair has turned from black to brown.

I said: No point in feeling sorry for yourself now. You're on the way to well.

She said: I'm not, I can't do anything at all.

Ethan helped her to the living room, and there she began to weep. I could hear it from the kitchen. I could hear him comforting her. Nurse Ethan.

I could not bring myself to embrace her. I said I had to go to work. A train to catch. The wind was bitter off the ocean. By the time I arrived to the station my eyes were full of tears. On the train I had to assure several old nosy women nothing was wrong. I told them I only had a chill.

Mazie's Diary, February 18, 1921

He was four days late, missed Valentine's Day, and I don't care because I'm not thinking about him at all, because who needs to bother with a lousy skunk? I put the postcard up in the cage anyway because the picture was pretty. The ocean, the other ocean across America. Mountains in the distance. I don't know if I ever need to see a mountain in person, but I like knowing they're out there. I've been turning and looking at it all day. I don't know why, but it gave me a kind of faith in the world.

Doesn't matter what it said on the other side of it, though. His words are so slippery they might slide right off the paper.

Mazie's Diary, February 27, 1921

There was Jeanie in the living room this morning before I went to work, bending and stretching, trying to stand on her tippy toes. Desperate. Half squatting. Wobbly, leaning on the walls, breathing like a wretched old woman. I watched her from the doorway and she gave me a glance but kept huffing away. Then she fell backward and I rushed to her. There she was, tender in my arms. I kissed her forehead.

I said: You can do whatever you put your mind to.

She said: I want to be better right now, not later.

I said: You will. You're from a family of tough broads even if you think you're a fairy princess.

I hugged her, and she hugged me back.

I said: I didn't realize I was jealous of you until you came home.

I didn't even know where it came from, but now at last, there was a real truth hovering between us.

She said: I bet you're not jealous now.

I said: No, I'm not.

So we'll work on this for a while. We'll work on getting our Jeanie stronger. Whatever she needs, I'll give her.

Mazie's Diary, March 1, 1921

Told Mack he could pick me up tomorrow in the early evening just to get him to shut up already. Rudy said he'd stead me. Rudy wishes I'd fall in love more than I do, more than Rosie, more than anyone.

Lydia Wallach

She did not have the best of luck with men. Dating in New York City has apparently always been terrible throughout history. You know: A good man is hard to find, and all that jazz.

Mazie's Diary, March 3, 1921

Well, that was a flop.

First, the weather was cursed last night. Blustery spring wind, the kind that shakes up all the dirt and debris. I kept having to hold my skirt to my legs while waiting in front of the theater.

Then Mack showed up three sheets to the wind. He stumbled into a trash bin a half block away, and then struggled to right it. I laughed while I was watching him and then I remembered that was my date for the evening and it wasn't funny at all.

I said: Oh brother, here comes trouble.

For his one and only act of chivalry of the night he removed his hat, but then promptly dropped it, and the wind grabbed it. I watched him chase it down the block. I turned to Rudy in the cage. Rudy whistled and looked away.

Eventually he got ahold of his hat and ran back slowly, then stood in front of me, breathless for a moment.

I said: Are you completely sloshed, Mack Walters?

He said: I am, ma'am.

I said: I took a night off work for this?

He said: I got nervous.

I was fuming. I started flapping my hands around and giving him the what for. I can't even remember all that I said except for the last bit.

I said: And now Rudy's got to stay late. He's got a wife and children who'd like to see him one of these days.

He said: I didn't know what else to do. You're just so lovely, Mazie Phillips. You're a pretty, pretty girl. Look at your pretty hair.

He reached out and touched my hair, the creep. I swatted his hand away, and gave him a good shove to boot. His eyes got larger, and for a moment I was terrified. I had just hit a police officer. In or out of uniform those lads still rule the streets. But instead his eyes filled with tears.

He said: I've been waiting for years for this and now I've gone and messed everything up.

I said: All right, all right, don't go crying, especially not on your beat. You don't want anyone to see you like that.

He let out a sob.

I said: Come on, you fool.

I dragged him down the street and the spring wind soon cooled him off. Finny's was the only place I could take him. A drunk for a drunk's joint. When we walked in the door Finny raised his hands in the air and everyone in the bar slid their drinks behind their backs or in their coats. As if that would make a goddamn difference. I snorted at them.

I said: Put your hands down, Finny. He's off duty.

Finny said: I never know what to expect from the long arm of the law anymore.

I shoved Mack up to the bar and told him he'd better start buying, and he spilled some change on the counter, and paid into the wee hours. It wasn't all bad, last night. I stayed late, so I must have been having some kind of fun. There was a laugh or two, once he calmed down. I wouldn't let him touch me though. Funny, I'll let any old fella passing through for the night grab me and squeeze me, but the men who'd stick around, I won't let them near me.

Also he told me something that scared me—that they're looking at Al Flicker for the Wall Street bombing last year.

I said: Al Flicker wouldn't hurt a fly. He's an intellectual.

Mack said: What do you know of intellectuals?

I said: I know enough to know they're too caught up in their heads to worry about bombing J. P. Morgan. They'd rather just talk about it all day instead.

Mack said: Well Al Flicker's the one we're watching.

I said: If it was me and I killed all those people, I wouldn't stick around. Whoever did it is long gone.

At the end of the night Mack poured me into a cab. He had somehow drunk enough to be sober again, while I was finally as drunk as he'd been when he first arrived. I let him kiss my hand. I did let him do that. His lips were like cool jelly on my skin and I knew he was not the one for me.

Mazie's Diary, April 16, 1921

Sister Tee's been telling me about some of the saints. She says every kind of person has their own kind of saint to watch over them. I told her about my date with Mack and it made her titter.

She said: Saint Liberata, patron saint of unwanted suitors and marriages.

She stands at the cage and rattles off their life stories. Better than the gossip rags sometimes. Better than my life anyway. Some saints begin their lives imperfect and then turn into something special. Sister Tee says we are the sum of our imperfections. We sin and then we learn from our sins.

Sister Tee said: You can do wrong and then turn right.

I said: You believe that?

Because I truly needed to believe it, too.

I want saints for everything. Saint of Free Spirits. Saint of Dancing Fools. Saint of the Ocean. Saint of the Sky. Saint of the Moon. Saint of the Lovers. I want to feel watched over and safe, but from afar. I like to think about all the saints looking over me. They're above and I'm below.

I know they're not real. I'm no fool. Only it's sweet to have something to dream about in that cage of mine.

Mazie's Diary, April 20, 1921

Jeanie's health is much improved. She walked down to the ocean with me this morning. Scarves and hats and in the wind, wrapped so tight we could barely move our mouths. We stood together in the sand. It wasn't a far distance. But it was the end of the block. It was somewhere.

Mazie's Diary, April 25, 1921

A teacup overturned, the stain of leaves on the kitchen table. Rosie seemed excited when I got home. A visit from the gypsies. Rosie's probably trying to secure Jeanie's fate. Like a good life's something that can be paid for. Like our future's up for purchase.

Mazie's Diary, May 1, 1921

Sister Tee found Al Flicker in an alley today, down off Bayard Street. Beat up bad. She wasn't looking for him. She doesn't look to help the men. But she couldn't step over his body, couldn't just leave him there bleeding. I saw her walking him along on Park Row, his arm around her neck, her bending from the weight. I ran from my cage. I hollered that I knew him, and she stopped. I know him, I know him. Screaming like a loon. We walked him into the theater. Rudy grew pale from the blood. Rudy's useless sometimes. I told him to get some towels. We sat Al on the balcony stairs. There was a cut under his eye that was gushing, and his nose was off center, mushed up, and bloody. His long legs and arms were bunched up, still in fear, and I remembered him crammed into his bed beneath the stairs, surrounded by his books. I asked him who had done it and he said it was the police. Told me it wasn't a crime to speak or think or be aware of the world.

He said: I didn't bomb anything.

We pressed a towel against his wounds, and it soaked through, and then we pressed another and another, until finally he stopped bleeding. I sent one of the ushers to find his sister, and she came and took him away. I think she might have even said thank you, words I never thought I'd hear from that woman's mouth. Slighted me since childhood. We're all the same when our loved ones are injured though.

George Flicker

This is when my mother called me back, when Al started getting in trouble. I didn't want to come. In France the girls found me charming and they were free with their bodies in a way American girls would never be with me. In New York City I knew I'd be just another schmo from the Lower East Side. I had the same nose as everyone else and eventually people would forget I'd served my time; they'd forget that they were supposed to respect me. In France I was an exotic Jewish American soldier, an enemy and a savior at the same time, and I swung my cock like a champion.

I'm one hundred years old, and every morning I get up and read the paper and have coffee and a roll and then I take a walk through the garden here and then I come home and lie down in bed and I often spend the rest of the morning thinking about my time in France, which was one of the best times of my life. But my mother sounded scared in her letters, and there was one phone call in particular that rattled me. She cried the entire time. This was a woman who never cried, a tougher human you'll never meet, so when she cried, it meant something. All the French pussy in the world couldn't compete with my mother's tears.

Mazie's Diary, May 15, 1921

I always know Ethan's around before I even see him. Laughter and flowers, Ethan's around. There were the lilies, drooping in a vase in the kitchen, smelling faintly of piss, like a dog had gotten too friendly with them. Then there's Jeanie laughing over nothing, just to have a good time with him.

They were dancing in the living room. I stood and watched them, Louis and Rosie, too. Two left feet, Ethan has. Suppose that's why he fell in love with a dancer, admiring that which is not his. He nearly dropped her when he dipped her and we all gasped.

She said: It's all right. It doesn't matter really.

He said: I'll take lessons.

She said: You're sweet.

He said: Sweet on you.

She said: You don't need to take lessons.

He said: Do you think I'm getting better?

She said: You couldn't get any worse.

He stepped on her foot and she yelped. He was all apologies. Rosie nearly went to her. Those precious legs.

She said: It's fine, I promise.

He said: Truly it doesn't matter?

She said: Truly.

I think we were all watching her to see if she was telling the truth.

Mazie's Diary, May 31, 1921

Al Flicker got beat again last night, and it was bad. I heard it from Rudy who heard it from one of the ushers who heard it from a friend on the force who was there while it was happening.

I saw Mack in the afternoon, walking his beat. I yelled at him that I wanted to talk about Al. At first he ignored me, but people started looking at us and he couldn't dodge it. Lousy coward is what he is. He sauntered over to the cage, dragged his nightstick slowly across the bars. He didn't scare me. He'd never scare me.

He said: How about you show some respect?

I said: How about you and your thug friends respect the people in your neighborhood? And not pummel innocent men for no reason.

He said: I wasn't there and I don't know what you're talking about anyway.

I said: He's not a criminal.

He said: Mind your own, Mazie.

He doesn't understand a goddamn thing though. These streets are my business.

George Flicker

Al kept getting beat up, and we were pretty certain he had developed some kind of brain damage. Al started calling them "Bad luck nights." Poor guy would come home early in the morning, blood on his clothes and on his face, wobbling and dizzy. Half the time he'd tip over into the furniture. And then—always with a smile on his face—he'd say, "Had another bad luck night!" I don't know why he didn't just stay home but we couldn't stop him for nothing. He thought it was his right to walk the streets when he pleased. Which it was.

A few times I tried to talk to him about it and he shook me off. Finally my mother insisted I corner him, and so we took a walk to Washington Square Park where he liked to play chess on occasion. I said, "Al, we're all so worried." Then he very carefully explained to me that because of the color of his skin he was much better off than many people in this country, and if he had to take a little bit of beating he could survive it. Because in the morning he would wake up free to walk the streets again. He could sit where he wanted to sit, eat where he wanted to eat. He was free. He said, "None of it bothers me because I always remember it could be worse." Which was a beautiful notion in a way, but at the same time, something an impaired man would say too.

But then another time I asked him about it and he said, "George, I'm making a point." And I said, "What point?" And he said, "If you have to ask, you don't get it." And he waved his arms around at nothing. Now this was nonsense of course. Just tell me the point already. I want to know the damn point. It was hard not to write him off as damaged goods. My best guess is he was somewhere in the middle.

Mazie's Diary, June 4, 1921

Louis drove me to work today. No reason why. We just missed each other, our time alone together. We didn't even discuss it. He was up early and so was I and away we went.

He said: So what do you think about Ethan?

I said: I like him just fine.

He said: He's asked for Jeanie's hand in marriage.

I said: Quite the surprise.

He shifted a little bit in the seat, squeezed the wheel with his giant hands. His voice dipping down deeper than usual. A little bead of sweat emerged from his fedora.

He said: I'm not her father. She can do what she likes. But what do you think? He's good to her, yes?

I said: If she loves him too, she should marry the poor guy. It's obvious he's smitten for eternity.

He said: He'll provide for her.

I said: Yes! Oh, Louis, she means the world to him. He's got a good job. He's not going anywhere.

He said: All right, I was just checking. Rosie thinks so too. It's not that I don't trust her opinion. There's no one sharper than your sister. Only I know she'd rather see all of you married off sooner rather than later. And I'd just like for you girls to be happy.

We were quiet for a long time after that. My mind went somewhere dark, and I tried to pull myself out of it, but I was sunk with sadness.

I said: You know there's no hope for me. No husband in my future.

He said: You're better than all that anyway.

He said it without thinking, and it made me think that it was true, or at least that he believed it was true. That was good enough for me. Good enough for now.

Mazie's Diary, June 12, 1921

Walked down to the water this morning and Jeanie was already there. Not whole yet, but closer to who she used to be. Leaping and skipping. A tumble in the sand but she laughed as she fell. Still lean, always lean, but healthier. One leg matches the other now. She was nodding in the wind. Seagulls scattering. I waved at her and she waved back. We didn't join each other. But I was satisfied that we were both bearing witness to the same sunrise.

Jeanie Phillips, July 7, 1921

I know where Mazie hides this, but I swear I don't read it, only needed to write down one more thing, shed this skin, bleed this blood. No one wants to talk to me about Mama. She's dead, I know it, what's the point anyway? And it's true I've not thought much about Mama & Papa in my life, not knowing them, barely remembering even very much about them. But I have something to say.

Rosie & Mazie told me Papa was bad, and so I believe it to be true. He hit her, for years he hit her. Rosie says he's a bastard, I believe it. Mazie says I should be grateful to Rosie for saving us, and I believe that, too. Our mother was once beautiful, they've both told me that. I let that roll over in my imagination and accept it as fact even though my only memory of her was dark circle eyes and clumps of hair that came out in her hands. I squeeze my eyes shut and she becomes a whole woman again, because they say it, and I want it to be true.

But when I think of him, I only remember him dancing. He danced with me when I was a little one, held me high in his arms and swayed me around the room. And I remember once, only once, going to a fair, all of us as a family, and seeing him dance there. We were there for hours, we lost him, and I slept in my mother's lap while she stroked my hair. It was safe there, the comfort of her lap, her thighs, her hips I remember it all as soft and bounteous, and that's all I wanted was her touch. Stroke my hair, hold me close, dance me around the room.

And when we found him there was music like I had never heard and strings of lights everywhere. It seemed like millions of them, but only now I realize that wasn't true, it was only because I was little, and so everything seemed bigger. But oh it was dazzling! All those lights. And the crowds of people dancing. And there was our Papa, dancing with a stranger, and I looked at how happy he was. But Rosie stopped him, made him stop dancing with the woman. The last thing I remember about this was thinking: Why is Rosie making Papa stop when he's so happy?

Later I knew it to be true that it was bad that Papa left us all alone, and bad that he had his hand on this woman, and especially bad that later on he hit Mama and Rosie, I know all of that. But one of the most beautiful things in life is seeing someone else happy. Isn't that the most we can dream of?

Mazie's Diary, August 15, 1921

I only saw what she wrote just now. We all forgot about everything after she left again.

Life is full of lies just waiting to be told.

Mazie's Diary, September 1, 1921

Walking wounded, and we never even went to war.

Mazie's Diary, September 15, 1921

She had someone who loved her and it didn't even matter. She threw it all away like it didn't mean a goddamn thing to her. I want love. I want it, and I can't have it, and she throws it away.

Mazie's Diary, October 3, 1921

I got a postcard from Jeanie today, at last.

It said: I'm not done yet.

6

EXCERPT FROM THE UNPUBLISHED AUTOBIOGRAPHY OF
MAZIE PHILLIPS-GORDON

They're not criminals, they're just drunks. Still they spend half their time in jail. The police are always roughing them up. I've watched it with my own eyes, every day for decades. But rich folks, they commit all kinds of crimes and nobody ever blinks. Hell, I drank straight through Prohibition, and that's the least of my crimes. I knew the rules, and I knew how to break them without getting caught. No one ever threw me in jail.

Mazie's Diary, November 1, 1921

Twenty-four years old today, though I feel like I'm a hundred.

Louis requested my presence in the car this morning. I said yes because I say yes to everything they want lately. We didn't even drive anywhere. We just sat. The seagulls were screeching at the end of the block.

He said: Hey, sis.

I said: Yes, brother?

He said: I'm thinking you should become part of the family. Legally. Be a Gordon like your sister and me.

I said: I'm already your family. You raised me, you fed me, you took care of me.

He said: I want you to be blood. I've been watching over you forever, let me call you one of mine. That other one, there's no telling what she'll do, when she'll be here, even if she'll ever be here again. But you're here, you're our girl, you're not going anywhere. So be one of the Gordons.

I thought about what it meant to be a Gordon versus a Phillips. My father is a violent rat bastard. A man who hits women is the worst kind of man. Still I am part Phillips, always will be. There's no denying the truth of your blood. But

I'm a Gordon too. When Jeanie left, everything shifted again. Our family rejiggered.

I said: It's an honor that you ask me, Louis. But I don't know if I can give up my name.

I prayed he didn't take it as an insult.

He said: Maybe you could be both names. A Phillips and a Gordon. Make one of them your middle name.

I said: That sounds like something I could do.

He said: I'll adopt you like you were my own.

I said: I'm yours, Louis.

Then we hugged, me and the big guy, until we cried.

This is the safest I've felt in years, knowing I'll be his. Knowing he's claimed me for his own.

Mazie's Diary, April 16, 1922

Louis spoke to me yesterday about signing the theater over to me. He told me it'll make his life easier in taxes, and that I'll get more of a share of the money we bring in. He makes too much money, but not enough, whatever that means.

He said: It'll be good for you to have it in your name. You practically run the joint anyway. Someday it'll be yours for real.

I said: I'll do whatever you ask. Give me a pen, tell me where to sign.

Mazie's Diary, May 1, 1922

A postcard from the Captain, and I barely read it. Saw his name, looked at the lake, the mountain, somewhere in Oregon. Blue skies surrounding it all, a picture of a perfect day somewhere far away. He saw it, I didn't. What do I care? I put it up in the cage with the rest of them.

These people who come and go can just stay where they are.

Mazie's Diary, May 11, 1922

Saw Louis down the road from the theater with a dapper Jew. Nice suit, fine, narrow features, olive skin, doe eyes, thin. A tidy kippah pinned to his head. I could see how shiny his shoes were from half a block away. I don't generally go for the religious ones but this one might make me change my tune. I'd slice some challah for him any old time.

I was hoping Louis would bring him over so I could give him a closer look. I waved at the two of them, but if Louis saw me, he was ignoring me. Finally he nodded at my future husband, no handshake exchanged, and the two of them parted ways.

Louis made his way over to the cage, hands in his pockets, stooped over, whistling.

I said: Who was that young fella you were chatting with?

He said: I wasn't chatting with nobody.

I said: I just saw you. With that well-dressed Jew.

He said: That wasn't anyone you should be worried about.

He smiled when he said it, all casual-like, but I felt prickly and cold. I never got a chill from Louis before, not my entire life.

Elio Ferrante

Was Louis Gordon a criminal? I guess we should think about what it means to be a criminal. History teaches us that some of our most successful leaders engaged in illegal activities. Hell, all of our presidents are war criminals. And I got some tough guys in my family, even though I love them like crazy. I've seen fights. Growing up in Brooklyn, you see fights. But I don't mean Mafia, just, you know, big guys, tough guys. Some do time. But sometimes it's just people blowing off steam.

And then there's my cousin Joseph. He's a gambler, and he got himself in all kinds of trouble, fell in a hole he couldn't climb his way out of, but what he got caught for was credit card fraud. This is considered a victimless crime. He certainly felt that way, and for the most part, so did the judge. He's in a halfway house now. His wife left him, took the three kids with her, left the dog behind. It was *his* dog. But he can't keep it obviously, so guess who has the dog now? Me.

This is a beautiful dog, an Akita. Do you know about these dogs? They've got this soft, plush fur, and they're sort of like stuffed animals. They don't give a crap about anyone but their owners—they'll basically ignore anyone else, maybe at best have a lazy interest in them—but they are loyal to the core to the hand that feeds them.

My cousin's dog, she's in perfect condition. Her teeth are as white as yours, like polished stones. This dog has been loved and cared for her entire life. Beautiful fur, shiny eyes, great disposition. And she sits by the door every night waiting for him to come home—even if his wife doesn't. How bad could a person be if he took care of a dog this well? But he's a criminal, I know it. Everyone in my family knows it. Thanksgiving was the worst last year. You know when everyone's *not* saying someone's name but you're all hearing it anyway? It was like that.

There was a documentary that came out a few years ago on these guys, these Coney Island guys, not Louis specifically, though. I ordered it for the school library. Kids watch it sometimes for extra credit. I could get it from the school library and we could watch it together; I can fill in some of the blanks for you. A lot of these guys were heroes in their community. I think that's an important thing to remember. They were legends and saints. Even if they broke the law.

Mazie's Diary, June 15, 1922

Postcard from Jeanie. How'd she make it all the way to California?

Daydreamed about the Captain showing up one day at a performance of hers, just stumbling in there, an accident, maybe another girl on his arm. Jeanie and him never even knowing I loved them both.

Mazie's Diary, July 2, 1922

Saw that dapper Jew down the block today again.

Nobody knows Louis's business except Louis, not even Rosie I don't think.

Elio Ferrante

My cousin I was telling you about last week, the one on the force, he took a look and there's no record at all of any arrest of Louis Gordon, anytime before 1923. Now, if he had any aliases, it might be a different story. And that doesn't include other states obviously. And to be honest, my cousin says the paperwork system from eighty years ago, maybe it's not the most reliable in the world. But according to existing records, Louis Gordon was never arrested or convicted of any crime.

Mazie's Diary, August 3, 1922

In my cage, counting pennies, a smack of hands against my booth. I looked up, and there was the Captain, forehead pressed on the glass.

He said: There she is, the most beautiful lady in the world.

I raced from my cage and embraced him, a girlish fool. I pretended he was mine to keep.

What else can I do but love him?

I don't care if I'm supposed to care that he'll never be here when I need him. Fleeting as a fly. I only know that I have a good time when I see him, that he makes me feel like a good-time girl again, back when I knew nothing of the world, back when all I cared about was a laugh. And I need that right now. I need a laugh. Squeezing both my hands. The kisses all over me, and his sweat on my flesh. All the world contained between us. Even that grunt he makes when he's done that I know has nothing to do with me, it makes me laugh. He's just him, he's just a man. Weak and human and all it comes down to is a noise.

Mazie's Diary, August 5, 1922

Last night, damp in his hotel room. I threw away everything for two days just to lie there sweating with this man. He gave me a dozen dangling gold bracelets and they dripped down my arm. The fan blew overhead, an open window, the breeze coming off the river, and still we were just stuck in each other's sweat. I couldn't move away from him, neither he from me.

He said: Come back with me to California.

I laughed at him. Not being cruel, just amused. How funny to think about that. How funny it would be if I left, too. What would my world be like somewhere else? I hadn't thought about that in so long, being somewhere else, it felt almost like it was never. So I had all those thoughts at once, and his arms were around me and I was covered in his sweat, and so I laughed.

He said: Don't be mean.

I said: I'm not being mean. It's a lot to ask.

He said: It seems like nothing to ask. It seems like the simplest thing in the world. Marry me, Mazie.

I said: What would I do in California?

He said: This. Exactly this. Every day. For the rest of our lives.

I said: Life isn't made of just this.

But I didn't know what else it was made of either.

He said: This isn't how I thought it would go, proposing to a lady.

I said: We don't even know each other.

He put his fingers inside me, two of them, deeply.

He said: I know you.

Rosie would never get the kitchen clean enough if I left, is what I thought. If I'm so special to this man why don't I see him but once a year, is what I thought. I don't know how it works, that kind of love, is what I thought. I only know the temporary kind.

He said: The air is cleaner, the sky is bluer, and the trees are as tall as skyscrapers.

I said: That's not possible.

He said: I'm telling you, Mazie, you don't need skyscrapers when you have trees like these.

I told him no, but I was gentle and I kissed him and I whispered only that I was too scared to say yes. Which was not a lie, though not the whole truth. I have never been able to tell him the truth about anything though.

I know you, is what he whispered over and over in my ear all night. But this morning he seemed relieved I had said no. Or maybe I was just imagining it. Or maybe I wanted to imagine it. He told me I could change my mind if I liked. He said California would always be there, and so would he. A great big state far away, on the other side of the country. I gathered up my things and returned to my life. He went off on a ship. Tomorrow I'll explain to everyone in my life where I've been. Today I'll think about California.

Mazie's Diary, August 6, 1922

I found Rosie on the floor in the kitchen, sobbing, when I came home early this morning. Hysterics. I couldn't calm her. The sunlight lit up her face, those lines drawn in her forehead, her mustache untended to, eyes bulging and pink. I gave her a glass of water and she pushed it away. I tried to hold her and she shook beneath me. I shushed her, I stroked her hair, and it was no use at all, none of it. Finally I slapped her, and she looked as if she might murder me right there on the kitchen floor, but it was better than her sobbing like that.

She said: You can't just do that to me. You can't disappear on me.

I said: Rosie, I didn't mean it like that. I got caught up on something. It was just a man.

I should have just told her everything then, told her I loved him, told her who he is to me, who he was to me. But he's my secret goddammit. He's all mine.

I said: Where's Louis?

She said: He's gone, doing whatever it is he does out there.

I said: Who ever knows what Louis does?

She said: I was fine when he left. It's only when I'm left alone I get like this. I don't mean to get like this.

I said: You've been better lately.

She said: I haven't. Not truly.

She didn't know what I was doing all day and I didn't know what she was doing all day either. She could weep in the mornings and scream in the afternoons for all I knew.

She let me hold her then. Soon enough Louis got home. Maybe he could hear her howling from wherever he was. By then she had calmed. Still, we were slumped on the ground together. He whistled as he entered.

He said: The kitchen's really sparkling today, wife of mine.

He leaned over her, kissed her on her head. Gave her his hands and she took them, and then she was up, standing. Gave me his, and I was up, too.

I'm in bed now, a flask next to me. There was something I was supposed to be dreaming about but I forgot already what it was.

George Flicker

When I came home I moved right back into the apartment I grew up in on Grand Street. I was a world traveler! I had fought in a war. I had saved people's lives. I got a Bronze Star; do you see that over there on my mirror? [He points at a dresser.] A Bronze Star! And now I was crammed back into that same damn one-room apartment. It was not pleasant. My parents were older, and they were starting to smell like old people, just like I do now. With Al not being well, everyone's nerves were frayed, and we were stepping all over each other. My mother swore I was half a foot taller than when I'd left, like I'd had some sort of growth spurt in France.

And I had to start all over finding work, building a career. Girlie, I'm telling you, it's no fun to start over when you've already started over once or twice, and you're doing it right under the nose of your mother. But in France I had worked for a tie manufacturer, and he had taught me how to make ties, and how to sell them, too. When I moved to New York I got a job at a tie factory for fifteen cents an hour. I started to save enough money to buy my own ties, which I sold on the streets. But what I was really thinking about was real estate. It was not an original thought, of course. I don't know anyone in New York City who doesn't think about it. It's impossible to walk those streets and not think about real estate. Louis Gordon was in it, I remember. He owned a few buildings here and there, along with all his other...investments. You know, he was a dabbler.

Elio Ferrante

It's pretty unlikely that he was solely a gambler based on what you've told me. Money laundering, sure, that was a possibility. Could have been a loan shark. Could have run booze, could have run drugs. There are myriad possibilities.

Mazie's Diary, September 22, 1922

After breakfast this morning Louis asked us if we wanted to take a walk down to the ocean.

He said: Come on, nobody's out there. The street is all ours.

Louis opened the front door and the most delicious ocean air came in, cool and moist. A gentle slap in the face. Rosie stopped scrubbing. She rubbed the back of her neck with her hands.

Louis said: Let's pretend like we own it all. Like we're the king and queen of Coney Island.

I said: I'll play princess, Rosie. You're the queen.

Rosie said no, and there's no arguing with her after breakfast. All those dishes in the sink and everything. But I said yes.

I took his elbow, and we walked all the way to the end of the road. The seagulls in their loop de loops. When we got to the sand we stood quietly and I leaned against him. He took my hand and kissed it.

He said: What if we had a conversation about your sister? About her mental state.

I nearly keeled over. For years I've been waiting for him to want to talk about it. Rosie's madness.

I said: I worry sick about her sometimes.

He said: She worries about you, too.

I said: But we're not talking about me.

He said: No, we're not.

I said: Do you think she's crazy?

He said: You live with her, you know what I know. For weeks she'll be fine. Months and months even.

I nodded, this was true. All had been quiet until I went off with the Captain.

I said: What about behind closed doors? That I don't know.

He said: Behind closed doors, she sleeps like an angel.

He grimaced for a moment.

He said: Except when she doesn't sleep at all.

I said: What can we do?

He said: Be there for her when she needs us. Show up when we're supposed to. Schedules are important to her.

I said: But what about my life?

He didn't answer me, he just shrugged. A tiny airplane dragged over the ocean, and he pointed at it, but didn't say a damn thing. The wind that had felt so lovely before now stung my eyes.

I said: Haven't I done enough? Don't I do enough?

He walked off.

I said: But what about me?

George Flicker

Look, he was never arrested for anything, not that any of us knew of. In my book he was no worse than anyone else of his ilk. Likely he was much better.

I'll tell you this story though. I remember I saw him one last time, right when I got back in town from France. It must have been two in the morning. I'd have done anything not to be in that apartment. The streets were empty, and I was marveling at how much cleaner they were than when I had left. Less riffraff, for starters. But there was no garbage either. I remember just the fall leaves beneath my feet.

And then he sort of startled me, and I don't really startle easily. I'm small now, I've shrunk, my bones are tiny, but I was at my peak then. You know, I was this young, healthy, fit guy who'd served his country. I wasn't so far away from battle that I wasn't on my toes.

But Louis was an enormous man, and he tapped me on the shoulder and all I could see was this big figure behind me and I jumped. Well, he started laughing. He said, "It's me, Georgie, your old neighbor Louis." I said, "Louis! Of course!" My heart was racing, I had to bend over for a second. I was kind of half laughing, half breathing hard.

So he patted my back until I calmed down. He said, "Aw, I didn't mean to scare you." Then we just shot the breeze for a while, it was no big deal. He thanked me for my service. He'd heard about the medal from my mother, I guess. Then he offered me his card and said if I ever needed anything, some work, money, anything at all, he'd be happy to help me out. "Two pals from the neighborhood," is what he said.

And I remember thinking exactly this to myself at the time: George Flicker, no matter how bad it gets, you never call this man for a job. Because you are no criminal.

Elio Ferrante

I know it's killing you that you'll never know the real truth because it *seems* like he might be a criminal. You'll just have to accept the fact that you'll never really know. I mean there's just so many goddamn things we never get to know. We're not entitled to all the truth.

Mazie's Diary, November 11, 1922

Louis's in the hospital. He was at the track and he fell forward, his heart seized on him. He was talking to a trainer, one hand on the horse, and then down he slid. It scared the horse, who ran off to her stable, where she hid for the rest of the day. No one can get her out. This is what the trainer said to me in the hospital when he came to pay his respects. I made him tell me everything. Every last detail.

I said: What track was he at?

He said: The Empire City, miss.

I said: What color's the horse?

He said: Chocolate brown.

I said: What's her name?

He said: Santa Maria.

I said: Is she favored to win?

He said: Not anymore.

I'm only home to bathe because one of us should bathe, between me and Rosie. One of us should be presentable to talk to whoever needs talking to. Because it doesn't look good for Louis.

Mazie's Diary, November 13, 1922

Louis left us yesterday. We held hands with him, me and Rosie, one hand in each of ours. Ring Around the Rosie went through my head. Ashes, ashes, we all fall down. We didn't know what else to do but touch him for as long as we could before we couldn't touch him anymore. Rosie sang to him in Hebrew, a song I never heard before. She said it was about being between two worlds, ending a life here, beginning a life somewhere else. I didn't want him to go anywhere else. I held his hand against my cheek, felt his skin go from warm to cool to cold. All the wailing. A doctor, a nurse, another nurse, stuck their heads in the room, until finally they stopped looking and left us alone.

Mazie's Diary, November 14, 1922

There were four of us, and then there were three, and now it is just two.

Mazie's Diary, November 15, 1922

Rosie sits like a stone in the kitchen. Barely made of flesh. I nearly didn't get her to the funeral. I couldn't find Jeanie to tell her he was sick, let alone dying, now dead. She's just...somewhere in California. She will always be somewhere in California. Louis will always be dead now.

So it was just the two of us, and Louis's aunts and their husbands, wading through the fall leaves toward the grave site. All the Gordons weeping, and Rosie just stock-still, until she fell to her knees, the lower half of her collapsing where the top half of her could not. Her dress was covered with dirt and when she stood I dusted her off.

I said: You'll be all right.

I must have said that a dozen times until I realized I was still saying it out loud and not just in my head. Everyone looked at me as I chattered. I put my arm around Rosie and said it one more time.

Mazie's Diary, November 17, 1922

We sat shiva today. Neither of us wanted to, as we practice no faith, but Louis was a Jew, in his way. And so for Louis, we opened our doors to his aunts. They arrived like a squadron, a squat army of mourners. I was glad they were there for the help. One of his aunts had brought what looked like a wall of smoked fish. They were noisy and busy in their preparations. It was good to listen to their chatter, their huffing, the opening and slamming of cabinet doors as they found their way through an unfamiliar kitchen.

Rosie sat slumped in the living room. This morning I noticed whatever drugs Jeanie left behind in the medicine cabinet were gone. I've been keeping an eye on it this week. Thought I might have suggested it to her myself as a way to get through these trying days, but it looks like she figured it all out on her own. I left her alone, only once I asked she move from the couch to the armchair. In my mind I thought she should be alone on a throne. The visitors in our home should pay their respects to the queen. Also I thought it might keep her propped up, because she looked as if she'd tip over at any moment.

I spent a good deal of the morning dodging any real conversation with these strangers. Some of them were familiar. I knew them from the track, and from Grand Street. But the rest of them were a mystery to me. Who were these men, where did they crawl from? They weren't like bugs, they weren't like rats, they weren't like cats, but there was something feral and wild about them. Creatures of the dark corners. Dark suits, dark hats, pitted skin. A stench of cigars and booze, a smell I've never minded before, but on them they wore it like spilled cologne. They were rough trade. All of them introduced themselves to me as Louis's business partner. Every last one. All these men in a room and none of them for me.

Then the well-dressed Jew walked through the door, shaking hands with everyone until finally he arrived at me. Up close he was handsome, sinewy, with slick, shiny hair, and a clever expression on his face. He murmured something in Hebrew I didn't understand, and then he took my hand.

He said: Miss Mazie, how are you doing?

I said: I'll be fine. He was family, but he wasn't my husband. That's a greater tragedy.

We both looked at Rosie, her head lolled to one side, her arms splayed on the chair, her legs uncrossed.

He said: I'll wait to meet her. It's you I'd like to have a word with.

Together we stepped into Jeanie's old room. He said his name and I realized I'd read it before in the paper, though no photo of him had ever been printed, as none exist.

He said: I was in business with Louis.

I said: He sure did a lot of business.

He said: And I'd like to buy out his end of it from you.

I said: What kind of business was it?

He smiled but his face turned into something sharper. Like he might snap his jaw at me. His teeth would be in me before I knew it. I was too weary to be scared of him, though.

He said: Now a smart girl wouldn't ask a question like that. Louis always said how smart you were.

I said: I am smart.

He said: And you're the money girl, right? Louis said you handled the money. And I'm here to buy out Louis's end of the business. I'm here to make things even.

I said: All right. Go on then.

Then he handed me an envelope.

He said: Count it.

I said: I don't need to count it. I don't know what the business was, and I don't know how much it's worth, and I don't know if you're cheating me or being fair or even being generous. The number means nothing to me.

He didn't like what I said but he couldn't argue with it, either. So he left. I stood there with the envelope in my hand. The money girl holding the money. Then there was a knock at the door. One of the vermin from the living room. He, too, wanted to buy out a dead man. He handed me another envelope. Then there was another, and another, and this went on for quite some time, the men with the envelopes. After they were gone, I didn't know what else to do but count the money. When I was done counting, I came out of the bedroom. The living room was empty. Rosie was up in the kitchen, cleaning, the last of Louis's aunts hustling out the door. It made me think she was going to be fine again someday. She couldn't have those women cleaning her kitchen. Only Rosie cleans the kitchen.

I said: We got a lot of money today.

Rosie said: I'd burn it all if it would bring him back.

Then together we ate the wall of fish until nothing remained.

George Flicker

I will tell you this one last thing about Louis Gordon. I heard when he passed a cheer went up in the stands at Aqueduct. Not because he was a bad man or a cruel man, but because when he died, half the men there had their debts wiped out.

Mazie's Diary, November 20, 1922

We met with a lawyer today. Now Rosie owns our house on Surf Avenue and two apartment buildings and half of four racehorses and a quarter of a dozen more and a bumper car ride. I own a movie theater, which I suppose I have for a while now, but something about him saying it made it seem more real. And I had never truly thought of it as my own anyway. I had signed some paperwork but all the money still went to Louis. Now there's no Louis. Also Rosie has everything he had in the bank, which was not a lot because Louis was not a fan of the banks.

And there is more, somewhere, I'm sure of it. In a safe, maybe, or in a closet. There's gold and there's diamonds and there's bills. I saw things sometimes. I saw the glint. But it's hers, not mine.

We went home and stood, dizzy, outside Jeanie's room. The money in the envelopes was still there, stacked on Jeanie's bed. Neither one of us had been able to touch it. It was a thing that we didn't need, this money, but we couldn't throw it away neither.

I said: Should we hide it?

She said: Get it out of my sight.

I put each envelope underneath the mattress, one by one.

The mattress was higher in the air when I was done and wobbled a bit. But no one would be sleeping there anyway. No one would ever know.

Mazie's Diary, November 23, 1922

At last I went back to the cage today. Rudy told me he'd handle the tickets as long as I needed. But Rosie told me to go, it was our business and we needed to be looking after it. She believed Rudy was to be trusted, he was a good man, but he was only human and had many mouths to feed in that family of his, and leave a man alone with money long enough he just might want to put it in his pocket. I'm thinking her sharpness might be a sign of a return to health so I did not argue. But Louis would give Rudy whatever he needed whenever he needed it. Rudy wouldn't have ever had to steal from him. Nor would he have to steal from me.

It was a relief to be back there in the cage, surrounded by all my postcards from Jeanie and the Captain. California. Might as well be the moon. I counted my cash. The regulars started lining up before eleven. The mothers with their children, the gentlemen with no place better to be. These are my people, is what I was thinking, and it made me laugh. Bitter and sweet, these tastes I know.

And then one by one, after I gave them their ticket, they gave me a gift. A flower, a card, some sweets from the truck around the corner. Offerings of sympathy, offerings of regret.

They said: Sorry for your loss.

They said: Our condolences, Miss Mazie.

They said: We missed you while you were gone.

I tried not to cry. I didn't want them to see me that way.

But I failed. I can't blame myself though for feeling it all so deeply. These people all woke up this morning and reminded themselves to be human beings. Not everyone knows how to do that. No vermin, my people. Real human beings.

In the afternoon Sister Tee came to the cage. She marched straight to the door and rapped on it with her tiny fist. I'd never opened my door for anyone like that before, not one person. But for her I did. Because she asked. She wrapped her arms around me. Our cheeks touched. Her skin was soft, and she smelled like the soap I used that one weekend I spent in the Captain's hotel. Then she pressed something into my hand—a medallion.

She said: It's Saint John the Evangelist. He's the patron saint of grief. He'll look out for you now.

I needed no saints though, not today anyway. I had all of Park Row with me.

Mazie's Diary, January 1, 1923

Sweet Jesus is this house empty.

Mazie's Diary, January 10, 1923

Last night I came in and I found Rosie standing at Jeanie's door, her arms crossed, back hunched, face all twisted up into something I didn't recognize. I touched her real gently on her back and she jumped, spooked. I stroked her back and calmed her.

I said: What are you thinking about?

She said: That money's no good.

I said: It isn't, but it's ours anyway. And we're good.

She said: Do you really think we're good?

A year ago or maybe two or three I would have said we weren't good, or at least that I wasn't. But I know a little more these days.

I said: Well, we're not bad. We're definitely not bad people, Rosie. And that will have to do for now.

Mazie's Diary, January 15, 1923

This morning, Rosie came into the city with me. First time she'd left the neighborhood since Louis died and we went to see the lawyer. She said she needed to check on the buildings in Chinatown, that she'd been hearing all kinds of stories about them being run into the ground. We might need a new superintendent. She wore a tidy suit. There was a new hat too, violet colored with a jewel on it, and some lace netting she drew around the edges of her face. There was some color on her cheeks. Where it came from I'll never know. I only see it as a sign of life.

Mazie's Diary, February 10, 1923

Sister Tee needed to buy some winter coats for some girls she knew so I took some money from the envelopes in Jeanie's room. Not even an entire envelope, just a few bills was all it took. I don't know what else it's there for if not that.

Mazie's Diary, March 13, 1923

Rosie took the train again with me this morning.

I said: More business in the city?

She said: I'm getting my hair done.

I said: Your hair looks fine.

She said: You got a problem with me going to the city, miss?

I said: I'm just asking what your business is, is all.

It went on like that for another stop, us having a not-conversation. Everything felt flipped around, me wondering what she was doing, her not answering me straight.

I said: Do what you like.

She said: I don't need your permission.

The subway door opened just then and she got off. Her back to me on the platform. She didn't even turn and wave.

Mazie's Diary, April 3, 1923

There were forty-six envelopes in Jeanie's room and now there are forty-one. I'm not crazy. I counted them myself. There were forty-six in February when I took money for Sister Tee. It's not mine to wonder but wonder I will.

Mazie's Diary, April 20, 1923

A postcard from Jeanie, Los Angeles. The sign that says HOLLYWOODLAND in the hills. I've been seeing pictures of that sign in my magazines forever. I got a little excited, I couldn't help myself. But then I flipped it over.

It said: What happened to you just happened to me & it is terrible, Mazie.

A lot of things have happened to me in this life but I knew exactly what it was she was talking about.

As much as I wanted to add this postcard to my wall, I

threw it away. I know it's bad juju to have bad news floating all around you. Same as that money too, still sitting in our house. Thirty-nine envelopes left.

Mazie's Diary, May 1, 1923

Tea leaves in a saucer, a haze of incense in the house. Dishes in the sink. Rosie's nowhere. The house stinks of gypsies. I could not bring myself to count the envelopes.

Elio Ferrante

My grandmother on my father's side was part Romany, but she was not the kind of gypsy who conned, and anyway, even if she was, she married out of it. Her skin was colored so that she could pass for Italian, like Sicilian Italians, the real Mediterranean Italians. You should see me in the summer, my skin gets so dark, I can pass for all kinds of ethnicities, Latino, African-American. I'm a citizen of the world come June. Anyway, my grandmother knew grifters, and there were stories passed around our family, cautionary tales more than anything. One of them was about being a single person, a lonely person looking for companionship or comfort. Widows were easy targets. There was one con where they'd tell these widows, Oh, you give us X amount of dollars, ten dollars, a hundred dollars, a thousand dollars, whatever, and we'll burn it, we'll burn your loss away, we'll burn your pain away. And then it's just this sleight-of-hand trick—they take the money during these sessions and they slip it into the linings of their skirts. They kept everything in these skirts. Coins, jewels, and cash. Gypsy skirts were like Fort freaking Knox.

Mazie's Diary, July 9, 1923

I know that it was wrong when all Rosie did was clean, but now the house is pure filth. Worse, the summer heat is roasting the dirt. A trail of tea leaves across the kitchen table. A line of ants following. A march. I'm at the theater all day and night, holding everything together while Rudy's out again. I can't do it all. I can't. I need help.

Lydia Wallach

Rudy had five heart attacks in his lifetime. I'd guess in 1923 it was probably his third heart attack? Some of them were smaller than others. Each one he bounced back from within a few weeks, until the last one, from which he did not bounce back at all. He was this calm, loving, supportive man who took on the pain and stress of others without flinching, and his heart attacks were his moment of flinching. And when he was in the hospital, everything collapsed around him. My great-grandmother, their children, the theater. He held all these worlds in his head. I understand this. If you let go for a second, it all unravels. The loose threads of the universe.

Mazie's Diary, July 15, 1923

I told Sister Tee everything about Rosie. It felt so good to tell someone even one little thing about my life, and this feels like the only thing in my life now. That and the theater.

Tee hates the gypsies as much as Tee is capable of hating anyone. She thinks they're godless. I told her I'd known some kind ones but she's come up against them too many times to forgive or at least to forget.

She said: They'll rob you blind then leave you standing on the corner in the cold and the dark.

I said: I don't think she thinks she's being robbed.

She said: I think that money could be better spent else-where.

I said: But what if it soothes her?

She said: A con's a con. Those gypsies should be punished.

When Tee turns to tough talk I have to laugh and kid her.

I said: Where's your forgiveness, Tee? I thought everyone had a saint.

She stopped her ranting and thought about it.

She said: Saint Dismas watches over criminals. But it's the ones who are seeking pentinence that he cares for.

I said: And these gypsies don't care.

She said: They don't care one bit.

Mazie's Diary, August 28, 1923

I took the money. I took it and I put it somewhere she can't find it. There were just twenty envelopes when I did so. More than enough money to last us a long time, yet it seemed like not very much at all considering what we started with. It's not hers, it's not mine. It belongs to strangers now.

Isabel Kaller, bookkeeper, Church of the Transfiguration, Chinatown

We've got archives dating back to the late 1800s. They're treasures, really. All of the bookkeepers over the years have had the most darling handwriting. These teeny tiny letters and numbers in perfectly straight rows. It's very sweet to me. I like the way the ledgers feel too. They have a real heft to them.

I found the ledger from 1929, and it indicates there was a fund set up by Miss Phillips-Gordon in honor of her mother, Ada Phillips. The money was earmarked to help women and children. It was blind on the part of Miss Phillips-Gordon, meaning she gave the church the money, but had made a request to never know what was done with it, or rather, who was helped with it. The fund was used to establish battered women in new homes, pay for doctors' bills for them and their children. At the time we worked in tandem with churches in Montreal and Buffalo, and so these women from New York were set up with new lives in those communities. I wouldn't be able to tell you how many women she helped. Hundreds? Thousands? I've no idea. Many, many women. There was a substantial initial deposit, and then this fund was maintained annually until Miss Phillips's death in 1964.

I don't know what we'd do if we got a comparable donation now. Gosh, we could do so much good with it. I don't even want to think about it, but I do, you know? What a dream it would be.

Mazie's Diary, September 2, 1923

She's lost her mind. Tore the room apart looking for the envelopes. Bed up, sheets off, curtains down. Rug on sidewalk. I think she threw it out the window, but can't be sure.

George Flicker

There was some bad blood between Mazie and Rosie for a while but no one knew why.

Mazie's Diary, September 3, 1923

A screaming match at the cage. She was trying to claw me at the window. I didn't even recognize her at first. The eyes confused me. The cruelty of her gaze. Then her hands were up against the cage, trying to shake it, shake me out of there. No blood of mine, is what I was thinking. She's not my sister.

She said: Where is it?

I said: It's gone and that's all you need to know.

Rosie said: Give it to me. I need it.

I said: You're being a fool, Rosie.

She said: You don't know anything about anything.

Rudy came running and held her back as best he could with those tiny hands of his. She shook him off and ran.

Mazie's Diary, September 4, 1923

Tee said: Wait it out. It's all you can do.

What I want to say to Rosie is that I know her pain is like no other, but also that it is no worse or better than anyone else's. We do not get to suffer forever.

Mazie's Diary, October 1, 1923

She's out there somewhere. I stopped by the Bayard Street building to collect this month's rent, and the tenants said she'd been there already and taken their money. Likely handed it straight to the gypsies.

Mazie's Diary, November 1, 1923

Happy Birthday to me. Twenty-six years old and my life's chaos.

Sister Tee brought me some daisies, and later I threw one back with Mack. I haven't forgiven him one thing. But I was lonely. Surrounded by people all day long yet as lonely as can be.

Mazie's Diary, November 2, 1923

The rent's gone again, in her pocket, in their pockets.

Mazie's Diary, November 5, 1923

Saw her on the street, grabbed at her arm, and she ran. I chased her, chased her through Chinatown, we ran and ran.

I said: Please, Rosie, please.

I said: Please come home.

I said: Please, I love you.

I lost her on Canal Street.

I don't even know if it really happened or if it was just a dream I had this morning. Or if it was even her, even Rosie at all.

Mazie's Diary, December 4, 1923

Rosie's home. I found her last night on the couch. Thin and gray and snoring. I just covered her with a quilt a moment ago. I was afraid to touch her, I thought she might disappear.

I'll forgive her anything if only she'll forgive herself too.

Elio Ferrante

The thing about these gypsies is eventually they leave. There's no long con in their world. Get in and get out. Change your look, and hit the road.

Mazie's Diary, January 3, 1924

I found her in the ocean last night. The door was open when I came home from work. I walked the street calling her name like she was a lost dog. Then I saw her standing in the ocean, nearly waist high in it. Not close enough to drowning herself. I write this so that it will be true. That she does not want to drown herself.

The moonlight was all around her. The ghost of my sister. I waded my way in, pulled her back toward the sand. We stumbled a bit. The surf crashing around our ankles, both of us shivering. She was white and blue at the same time. I threw my whole self around her to warm her but she shook me off.

She said: It's been a hard year, Mazie.

I said: I know.

She said: It's been a hard life. Thirty-four, and I've nothing to show for it. A dead husband. No baby. What do I have left?

I said: You have me. I'm here. I'll never leave you.

I'm not going to leave her. It's not a lie.

I said: Come on, Rosie, it's cold as a witch's tit out here. You'll catch your death. And if you die, I'll murder you. I'll do it with my own two hands.

I wanted her to be beautiful in the moonlight—everyone looks beautiful in the moonlight—but all of Rosie's collapsed now. Been falling apart for years, Rosie has. More of her hair is gray now than not. It flew all about her, nearly purple in the moonlight. The lines around her eyes and lips jagged and deep in her skin. The chin, sunken and wobbling. Once it falls like that it never rises again. Those are the rules of life. Only the pale cream color of her skin remains. That reminds me of young Rosie.

Slow steps to the grave. I won't be the one to bury her though.

I said: I'll kill you if you die.

I put my arms around her throat. It was and wasn't a joke. We just stood there like fools, our teeth clacking, our lips turning blue, two corpses in the ocean, only one of us more alive than the other.

Finally she fell on me, and held me for warmth. I don't know if it was her body or mind that gave in first. I will take what I can get from her.

I said: At least you had a love.

Then we both started crying. I wept into my brokenhearted sister, and she wept into heartless me.

Mazie's Diary, April 2, 1924

Postcard from the Captain. Niagara Falls. A place not so far away from New York City. A day trip, a train ride away. I can see it on a map in my head.

I read the back of it once and that was enough. But I liked the picture, so I put it up on my wall. I can hear the crash of the waves when I look at it. I can feel the spit from the falls on my face. I bet it's cold up there near the water. I bet the air stings your skin red. Like a man slapped you hard and meant to leave a mark.

Mazie's Diary, April 15, 1924

We'll move again, is what I decided. Back to the city, where I can keep a better eye on her between work and home.

She said: But I can't go through his things.

I said: We'll leave them then. We don't need any of it.

She said: This house is a mess.

I said: Leave it. Let the next person worry about it.

She said: Where will we live?

I said: Anywhere we want.

Finally I convinced her to agree to the move. Agree to living, that's the most I'm asking from her right now.

PART THREE

Knickerbocker Village

7

EXCERPT FROM THE UNPUBLISHED AUTOBIOGRAPHY OF
MAZIE PHILLIPS-GORDON

I think of all the misfortunes I've had through the years, but none of them landed me on the street—not unless I chose to walk it myself.

Do I have to? [Groans.] I have to. All right.

How did I find the diary? Well, I keep my head down a lot; I'm always looking at the ground, because I find things. Sometimes I find stuff I can sell, or I can use in the shop. For a long time the best thing I ever found was thirty-two Polaroids of this middle-aged Chinese lady stripping. They looked like they were taken in the eighties. They were all washed out, and there was something about her skirt that looked kind of eighties, maybe my mom had one like it? God, I don't want to think about my mom stripping. [Laughs uncomfortably.]

Anyway, there was an order to the photos, like shirt on, shirt off, bra off, skirt off. There was definitely a little act to it, although I don't know how sexy it was. I kept the pictures for a while. I couldn't stop thinking about who she was undressing for. Whoever was taking the pictures, or if there was someone else in the room, too. For a year or so, I guess, she was on my mind. But then I stopped thinking about her. I just gave up trying to figure it out. I was never going to know, and then I stopped caring. I didn't need to know how the story ended. It was sort of enough that I had seen the pictures in the first place, you know?

Now, the diary was a whole different game. I found it two years ago, give or take. It was in the fall. I was over near the Navy Yard walking to work. This was just a few months before I opened the shop, and I was still working at a studio there. I saw a big box over by where they used to have the used car auction. Most of the stuff in the box, I couldn't use it or sell it. It was like, old lightbulbs and a roll of movie tickets and a flask. I opened the flask and it still smelled like booze. I mean old booze, but still.

But also in there was the diary with the postcards. Everything was pretty ratty. The diary was leather-bound once, but most of the cover was coming off in strips. The pages were loose—I had to be careful or they would slip out and blow away. All the paper was yellow, everything was crumbling in my hands. But all of it was like, chattering at me, asking to be read. I know that sounds kind of nuts. It looked like junk, but it was actually the exact opposite of that. So I stashed it all in my backpack and took it to work.

During my lunch break I started reading everything and then I was late getting back to work, and then after work I went to a bar and sat there and read them all the way through. Her handwriting wasn't the greatest, you know that, but I made it through. I didn't know anything about her, except that she sounded like a saint, the closest thing I've ever heard of anyway. I went to Catholic school, I studied them, but I never believed any of them were real people. She was definitely real. Because I saw the words in front of my own eyes.

There were parts of it that felt pretty personal to me. This person who felt like she had been bad but didn't want to give in to it entirely. She thought maybe she had a shot at being a better person but she couldn't shake who she had been. We all live with our pasts. I live with mine. You live with yours. I don't even think she did anything wrong. She had just lived a big life, even though it was mostly in this confined space. And when you live big you fall big.

Near the end I started reading really slowly because I didn't want it to be over, I just wanted it to go on and on. I wanted her to live forever. At the very end I cried. Then I put the flask in my pocket, close to my heart, which is where I still keep it. I fell in love with her a little bit, and I wanted a piece of her right next to me.

Mazie's Diary, October 1, 1924

We're back on Grand Street, six doors down from where we once lived, the home where I was raised. Now we're in a two-bedroom flat, one room for Rosie, one for me. We've given up on Jeanie coming home. The only thing that feels familiar anymore is our table and our couch. Those things we brought with us. A table to eat on and a couch to faint on.

I've been walking to work again, through the throngs of the Lower East Side, the Jews, the Russians, the Italians, the Germans, the Chinese, the Gypsies, the cops, the children, the lads, the broads. The swirl of people, it's heaven.

I miss taking the train sometimes, though, and the time I had to gather my thoughts before the day began. I always had a seat. I could watch the people get on and collect themselves. A tidy and a tug. I'll miss seeing the people from across Brooklyn heading to work. I'll try to remember what they looked like. I won't have cause to return to Brooklyn again anytime soon. Once you cross the river you stay there.

But it'll be nice to stay here, I think. I'm still trying to understand what here means. All our things are still in boxes. Rosie's promised to unpack but it's been weeks and she still hasn't touched a thing but what she needed for the kitchen, a few dresses, some pairs of shoes. I kept you for myself, though. A book of secrets. Mine, and Jeanie's.

Mazie's Diary, October 11, 1924

Rosie hates the kitchen now, says there's mold, can't get rid of it, no matter how much she scrubs. I can't see it, but she swears it's there.

She says: There! There!

I say: Where?

She says: There.

Mazie's Diary, November 1, 1924

I'm twenty-seven years old today. Rosie served me ice cream with raspberries and chocolate sauce when I came home, and there was a chocolate bar on my bed, as well. Sweets for the sweet. A quiet birthday, I didn't mind it. She was calm for a moment. Not a word about the kitchen.

Mazie's Diary, November 14, 1924

A postcard from Jeanie, birthday greetings, two weeks late.

It said:

You'll always be older than me & wiser too. I hear you in my head when I least expect it.

Like she'd listen to a thing I have to say.

Pete Sorensen

Oh yeah, all the postcards are pretty special. All the places she saw but never went to. Oh California! [Clutches heart.] You and I disagreed about that Niagara Falls postcard, and what it meant exactly. "It could have been you." You think it's romantic but I think it's ice cold. The Captain was spitting in her face. Why would you tell someone something like that? That you've married someone else but you had your shot. I'd rather not know. I think it's disrespectful.

Mazie's Diary, January 4, 1925

We're moving again and there's nothing to be done about it. I can't argue with her any longer. I can't listen to her yelling. I can't bear the neighbors knocking on the wall. I can't bear the tears. The pointing at the floors, the ceiling, the corners, the crevices, the mold, the germs that don't exist. I don't see a damn thing and she sees everything. I have dreams about her pointing at things.

Mazie's Diary, March 1, 1925

234 Elizabeth Street, second floor, new kitchen. Scrubbed clean. Sparkles. Sunlight through the window, hands in front of our squinting eyes.

I said: Can you argue with this?

Rosie said: I cannot.

Mazie's Diary, July 31, 1925

Rosie hates all our neighbors. Let's see, what's her list of complaints. Hershel downstairs reeks of fish, she hates passing him in the hallway, especially when it's hot, and lately it's hot. Menachem on the third floor is too religious and she swears he's judging her for not going to services every Friday night. But that Russian seamstress next door with the newborn, it's her she hates the most. Says the baby's too loud, and that I don't even know the half of it because I'm gone all day.

I said: Then take a walk.

She said: All day? I can't walk all day.

I'd kill to take a walk all day but that's not what she wants to hear.

I said: It's a baby. How can you hate a baby?

She said: Well it's no blood of mine.

I said: It's a helpless human being.

She said: It's rattling me.

Rattle's a word I don't like her using. When she gets shook there's no unshaking her.

Mazie's Diary, August 3, 1925

Mack Walters passed. His heart gave. Tee and I went to his funeral in Queens this morning. I hadn't seen him in a long time, a year, maybe more. We'd stopped talking, stopped flirting, and then he transferred uptown. After that it was like we hadn't even known each other in the first place. Still I remembered that day we all ran downtown when the bomb went off. Tee did, too. A day when you witness something terrible together, you don't forget a day like that. You can't unsee what you saw. So I'd give him tribute.

Mack was Catholic, and Tee knew every single prayer before the priest said it out loud. I liked the church, the cool wooden pews, the stained-glass windows dividing the sun, the statues of Jesus and Mary all around us. A mother and her son. It meant nothing to me, none of it, but it meant everything to Tee.

There was no family at his funeral, just other police officers. He was an orphan from a young age, is what I learned. These officers were the only family he had, and I noticed a few of them pawing away their tears. I was an orphan in a way but I've always had Rosie steady in my life, even if she's unsteady herself. Poor Mack didn't even have a lunatic sister to call his own.

Afterward someone asked me if I was Mazie and I told him I was and then a few other officers came to greet me and suddenly a whole crowd of them was around me. The famous Mazie, is what they were saying. You're the one. They told me Mack talked about me all the time, that I was a heartbreaker. I forgot I could do that, break a heart.

Tee and I held hands the whole time. She told me later she could tell I was nervous. My whole life I handled attention from strangers just fine. It's just lately I'm used to the bronze bars of a cage between us. When the rush stopped I remembered that some of these men could have been the ones beating up on Al Flicker. I wished that I could humble them instead of being so humbled myself. But I was there to pay respects, and that's what I did.

Mazie's Diary, August 15, 1925

A postcard from the Captain. Washington, DC.

He wanted me to know he's back east now.

The picture on the front is of the Washington Monument. A giant prick.

Pete Sorensen

I'll be honest, I like a girl with a little seasoning, a little special sauce. I'm not interested in the helpless young virgin type, I guess partially because I'm not so innocent myself. And women that have had some experiences in their lives, there's some kind of wisdom that comes with that. Also they're less likely to make certain kinds of demands, particularly of, say, a permanent nature. I just never wanted to settle down or anything like that. Opening my shop was about as settled as I was going to get. But I swear to god, reading this diary made me want to settle down. I actually found myself wanting to marry her! I know it's nuts. I just heard her in my head so clearly and thought I *know* her. I mean I didn't know every little thing about her. But I knew that she liked to walk the streets of New York, and that I love more than anything. And I knew the quality of her character, which made me think I could spend the rest of my life with her.

Mazie's Diary, September 1, 1925

112 Delancey Street. Only elderly women reside in this building, polite old Catholic ladies. Tee told us there was a room for rent—she'd heard it through the grapevine. They're all her favorite tithers. Quiet mice with hair like snow. They've even

got a knitting circle every evening at sunset. Dolores with the bad knee one floor down has already offered to make us a quilt. We're on the fourth floor in three rooms. There's no street noise. Kitchen's clean, I made Rosie run her finger on the counter and show it to me. Here we sit, here we stay.

George Flicker

So that was a thing that was very strange for a long time with these two ladies. They could not stop moving. Six months max, that's how long they lasted in each apartment, and it went on for years, this moving-around business. This was when I was just starting to investigate a career in real estate. It seemed like the only economy that never changed in New York. People always needed a place to live, and you didn't have to have much of an education to get started in it. So I started circling everyone. I got to know a lot of the building owners on the Lower East Side. A few of them, I had grown up with their families, or I'd seen them around. So I was just schmoozing with them. The good ones and the bad ones, both. I wanted to know what they knew. And one of the things I kept hearing about, just as part of everyday gossip, was that the Gordon girls were on the move. Who knows why, but they had turned themselves into gypsies.

Mazie's Diary, November 1, 1925

Twenty-eight. My waist is still trim, but my breasts have gotten bigger this year, maybe it was last year and I didn't notice. As if they weren't already big enough. My back aches, sitting there, hunched over those tickets, counting cash, head in my stories. The lines are longer at the theater. We make money. Good money, legal money. I give Sister Tee a fistful every month. I'm a good businesswoman. This is what I learned this year. This is what I know.

Dolores prayed for me, she told me. Sister Tee said she did too, and she gave me a box of peppermints. Rudy hugged me and gave me a new scarf. Rosie rubbed my shoulders when I got home, she's seen me hunching, knows my posture's gone.

She said: It hurts for you now the same way it hurts for me.

I don't think she knows my pain, though. Just like I don't know hers.

Mazie's Diary, November 8, 1925

He was here again. How long has it been, one year, two, three, and there he was, and I was not surprised. He came to me, and I went with him. Didn't blink, didn't pause, just went. He stood in line with all my regulars, the last show of the night, at the very end of the line, and he bought a ticket like everyone, and when I handed him the change, he held my hand. I sat there, burning, both of us burning, stupidly burning, looking at each other, and holding hands. I rested my head forward on the cage, and he put his hand against my other cheek. His hand was cold, and my face was warm. Burning, burning, burning.

I said: You're late.

He said: For what?

I said: You just missed my birthday.

He said: Oh, Mazie, I'm always going to miss your birthday.

I said: I'm going to think of you as my present anyway.

He said: You can if you like. But I think you're mine instead.

Later, in the hotel room, he held his prick against my cunt for a while, and he commented on the size of my lips, the way his prick looked up against them, all of those swollen things next to each other. It looked beautiful and I became fascinated with it, I couldn't look away, and he couldn't either, and together we did that, we looked at our parts touching, while he moved everything around slowly with his prick.

I'll never be more intimate with any man than I am with him.

He's married now. I knew it, but he showed me his ring anyway, which he had in his breast pocket.

He said: I want to speak the truth to you, Mazie.

I told him that it didn't matter, and it doesn't. Our union is our union, and theirs is theirs. This bride in Connecticut means nothing to me. I had him first. I chose not to keep him because I knew he couldn't be kept. Him standing before me at that very moment last night proved it.

Mazie's Diary, November 9, 1925

I smoked and smoked all day today, and licked my flask clean. An early snow for the season. I watched my customers dust the flakes off their coats, smiling. When it was all over, there were peach-colored clouds gliding through the sky. I thought: No one else can see this sky like I can. No one else sits here and watches it change all day except for me. I see the snow and I see the clouds and it is all a show for me. Everything is for me.

Pete Sorensen

I loved her because she was tough and knew what she wanted. It wasn't like she always knew, but by the end of the diary I think she did. I mean she spent all this time trying to acquire her exact purpose in life. Maybe she didn't mean to, but she did. And how many of us get to know that? I'm pretty sure I'm doing what I'm supposed to be doing with my shop, but what if I'm supposed to be a painter? Or build houses? I know I'm not supposed to be in a band anymore. No one would give a shit about our reunion tour. But what if I'm supposed to move back to Saint Paul to take care of my mother in her old age? Like that is actually a thing it would make sense to do. That is what people do; they take care of their family. She knew that! She did it. She knew how to be a human being.

I wasn't jealous of her, but it did make me a little angry with myself that I don't know exactly everything yet. But being a little angry with yourself is all right. That's how shit gets accomplished. You know what I mean. I know you do.

Mazie's Diary, January 15, 1926

Dolores died, and it took two days for anyone to find her. We all thought there was an animal trapped somewhere, a dead rat in the floorboards. Her hair went white during that time. It happened over the weekend. No knitting circle on the weekends, so it took till Monday to realize the poor woman was gone.

Rosie says she can smell the body still.

She said: You can't smell it? I know you can smell it.

I said: I ain't moving again, Rosie.

She said: Who said anything about moving?

I asked Tee to teach me a prayer Dolores would have liked. All that she did for me I could do for her.

I said: It's tragic, lying there like that for days.

Tee said: She lived a long life, and there is that to remember.

I said: Rosie's kicking up a storm now. She'll say the place is haunted in no time.

Tee said: That's our Rosie.

I said: I'm tired of looking for apartments.

Tee said: The wandering Jews.

Mazie's Diary, February 13, 1926

Postcard from the Captain. Just a sailboat in the water and his name with love, and nothing else.

Every morning I stand at the sink, I wash my face, I brush my teeth, I brush my hair, and then, when I'm ready, I look down at myself, and I think of him.

Filthy, awful, beautiful man.

Mazie's Diary, February 18, 1926

Tee's truly my best girlfriend, a good friend to have. She stops by the cage now nearly every day, even in the rain. Sometimes she comes home with me for tea after work. Rosie coddles her. She loves any sort of spiritual type, no matter what they believe in, as long as they believe. And though Tee's not our Jeanie she feels like family. But I've never seen her home, after all these years.

I said: Tee, why don't you invite me over?

She said: I've got the smallest room. The two of us could barely fit at the table.

I said: Aw, Tee, I'd squeeze in for you.

I like to have a little fun with her. I like to grab at her belly through her habit and try to tickle her. Little Tee. Today she said I could come by sometime though. After we move again.

George Flicker

These landlords said they paid first and last, and when they moved out the apartments were cleaner than when they got there, so there were no complaints. It was just kooky behavior. How could they have been happy doing that? You had to wonder. They were always the kind of family that circled the wagons, but now, with all the moving, that circle was closed shut. So who knows why? No one could keep track of their business.

The only thing you could count on when it came to them was seeing Mazie in her ticket booth on Park Row. Sometimes I'd swing by Chinatown for lunch, my office not being too far from there, and I'd see her there, and that was a nice way to pass the time. My crush on her hadn't withered, I'll be honest with you. We were both young people. Her bosom grew every year, and she wore the most flattering dresses. That girl just had a really enjoyable figure.

I was always waving to her from the street corner. If she didn't have a line or her head in one of her magazines—she loved all those *True Romance* type of magazines—she'd wave back too, even blow me a kiss sometimes. She'd yell, "George Flicker, there he is, ladies and gentlemen, a real-life war hero!" She was the only one who didn't forget.

Mazie's Diary, April 1, 1926

416 Mulberry Street. Our neighbors are young, single ladies, most of them in nursing school. Top floor. On Friday nights they go to the movies together. They stand in my line and I sell them tickets and they all greet me with respect. They're not so much younger than myself, but it feels ages between us. They're just starting out and most days I feel like I'm already done.

Mazie's Diary, May 3, 1926

Rosie said: Why are they having so much fun? Why are they so goddamned happy all the time? What's with the tittering?

I said: They're young and full of life! Look, lady, we wanted young. And none of them are going to die on us.

Rosie said: Not unless I kill them.

Mazie's Diary, May 15, 1926

Tee lives down near the water, in a narrow but tall building filled with all the other extra Theresas from her settlement. Her building is quiet, whispers all around us, the lobby barely lit. We came in off the street and it was as if Manhattan disappeared behind us. So different from all the homes I've had in the city, where I've always heard the streets below calling up to me.

The elevator was out, so we climbed the stairs to get to her apartment on the top floor. Round and round. A maiden high in a castle, was what I was thinking. As soon as we entered her apartment, she took off her headpiece. She looks so young without it. That blond hair hanging about her shoulders. A real blonde, not a fake one like me.

The room is as small as she promised. Dark gray walls, two square windows, one with a view of the Woolworth Building. I asked her if the lights kept her up at night and she said she didn't need much sleep.

I said: That's right. Who needs sleep?

She said: When there's so much to be done.

There was a hot plate in the room, and a small card table for dining. One giant painting of Jesus, and a few smaller ones. A single bed, a wooden frame, one small pillow, a wool blanket. A bookshelf, books in Latin. A Bible on a nightstand. I realized Tee doesn't have much more than the people she helps.

Next to the Bible there was a framed photograph of Tee with her parents, standing in front of a waterfall, somewhere upstate I imagined, where her people are from. Her hair was all around her shoulders, and she was young and smiling. Tee, before sisterhood.

She cracked a window and put on some stew. I bought some bread at the market yesterday morning, and we barely used our spoons as we ate, just hunks of bread soaked in stew. We sucked our fingers. It was salty and I liked it. When we were done, we pushed the bowls to the center of the table.

I noticed the ring on her wedding finger. Married to Christ. I took her hand in mine and twirled the ring. I asked her if she always knew she had her calling.

She said: I think my parents wanted something else for me. I'm an only child. They dreamed of me getting married, and giving them a grandchild or two to dote upon.

I said: You never wanted that?

She said: I always dreamed of the stars and the heavens, and that someone was looking down on me, watching over me. My daydreams were about God.

I said: Do you really love him?

She said: I do. I truly do. My heart feels full when I think of him.

I had no response. My heart was full of so many things and yet not one thing at all.

She said: Who do you love?

I thought of the Captain.

I said: No one. Or no one like that.

Now she was holding my hand.

She said: I'm not trying to convert you. I accept you for who you are. But I would like to help you.

Instantly I was angry. She's always making me angry. Whenever she tries to help me I can't stand it. I don't want anyone to help me. I don't want her to think she knows better than me. I pulled my hand away from her.

She said: I'm not trying to change you. I swear to you, Mazie. I only care for you. I know you have secrets. You don't have to tell them to me. You never have to tell me anything you don't want to. I'm not your confessor. I'm your friend.

I said: Yes, you're my friend. Not my parent, not my god. Nothing like that.

She said: I said I'm not. I know I'm not.

I said: Fine. You're not.

I started to calm down. It was quiet there in her apartment. Just the moon and the Woolworth Building. What was I going to do with all my anger anyway? Was I gonna strike her? No. I love her.

She said: But you could tell your secrets to someone else. No one would have to know. It might make you feel better. Just to talk to someone.

I told her I'd think about it. That's all she was looking for.

Just so she knew I heard her. I'll never do it, though. Trust a stranger? What a hoot. Plus, that's what this diary's for.

Before I left I gave her a gift, a stack of *True Romances*. She laughed at me.

She said: What am I going to do with these?

I said: For when you get bored with Jesus.

She said: Never will I tire of my savior.

I said: Boy oh boy, you and your savior.

She took them anyway. I know she likes them. I saw that juicy gleam in her eye. Who doesn't love a little dirt? Surely she can't dream only of him at night.

Mazie's Diary, June 18, 1926

A postcard from Jeanie.

I'll be in the Bay Area for the foreseeable future, darling. There's money to be made here. Big crowds every night. Come visit if you please.

California's on the bottom of my list of things to do, right after jumping off the Brooklyn Bridge for a nice swim. Wish she'd give us a ring though. I'd like to hear her voice.

George Flicker

This is something I never mentioned to Mazie or Rosie at the time because it all had seemed rather delicate, and I don't like to get into anybody's personal family business unless it's offered to me or asked of me or they're my own blood or what have you. But I had a cousin named Morrie who saw Jeanie perform in San Francisco, at a place called the Capri. It was maybe not a nice club, is what Morrie said. I said, "Well then

what were you doing there?" "Ohhhh, I got dragged there."
Okay. Whatever you say, Morrie. She danced with a fan, and
then she danced without a fan. It could have been worse. I'll
give her the benefit of the doubt. Live long enough, you'll
give everyone the benefit of the doubt. It costs you nothing.

And who really cares what kind of dancing she did? Who
cares, I say. Do you care? I didn't think so.

Mazie's Diary, July 1, 1926

I don't believe in hell but I'm probably going there anyway.

Just to make Tee happy I went to confession. I said all that
forgive me father nonsense she taught me.

It's hard to believe the man listening on the other side
won't run and blab all my secrets to any bum on the street. So
I only told him a few. Just to see how it felt. I told him about
some of the lovers I've had around town.

But if I'm really going to be confessing here, I was bragging
more than anything else.

I tried not to laugh. I tried! Heard him grumbling. Finally
he asked me if there was anything else.

I said: So much more. So many more.

I hustled out of there and straight to Finny's. I gave it a
shot anyway.

I know there are other things Tee thinks I should be talking
about. But I ain't ready yet, might never be. I still can't tell
if they're a burden or a comfort, these secrets of mine. Is it
going to make me feel better or worse if someone knows the
truth about me?

George Flicker

It was a strange thing, this being Catholic all of a sudden. Look, I don't think she was 100 percent Catholic, whatever that means anyway. But she was always palling around with that nun, you'd see them walking in the streets, arm in arm, whispering in each other's ear. And she definitely went to church, here and there. She prayed to *that guy*. I don't know if she went all the way and converted, or anything like that. The strangest part of all of it was Mazie believing in any sort of organized anything, because that family had not stepped foot inside a synagogue in years, if ever.

But you know, whatever works. I believe in that. Whatever works, whatever gives you hope.

Mazie's Diary, November 1, 1926

Twenty-nine now.

New home. Always a new home. There's nothing new about a new home. What would be new is if we stayed somewhere.

Pete Sorensen

So after her twenty-ninth birthday, this is right about when the diary starts to drop off for a while. I had one theory, which was Mazie was sad the Captain didn't show up again, and so she just got real quiet. She was hoping for it but didn't want to say it out loud. Maybe it's something she prayed for, but just couldn't tell anyone about it.

I had this other theory that all the excitement happens when we're younger. Everything feels so big then because you're learning all the important lessons. When I toured with my band, I was twenty-two and twenty-three and it was, like, every day my mind got blown with a new experience. Mostly it was a new girl, but that counts, right? [Laughs.] Then I was twenty-four and it started to feel familiar, and then I was twenty-five and none of it felt new anymore. My brain slowed, the world slowed. I stopped seeing things with fresh eyes. I started to realize what I knew.

After that, we really only see her checking in three or four times a year for a while. But she doesn't miss her birthday too often. I'm not big on them myself; I don't like all the fuss. You know, maybe knock back a beer with your buddies. But I get it; it's a way to mark time. When your life's too busy, it forces you to check in with yourself. Or when it feels all the same all the time, maybe it can make you feel special. I'm not knocking Mazie for caring about her birthday.

But I really started missing that time, those days of hers that were gone that I was never going to know about. I wanted to see everything she saw. Also I was worried about everyone. I was like, how's Rosie, how's Jeanie, how's Tee? I felt a little greedy, like why couldn't I know everything about their time. How would you like it if someone you cared about just disappeared on you?

Mazie's Diary, April 4, 1927

6 Clinton Street. A married couple beneath us, older than us, no children. He's a librarian, and she's a teacher. Jews. Quiet, smart Jews. They seem kind.

She said: Maybe I'll borrow some books.

I said: Maybe you'll learn something from them.

She said: What do they know that I don't? You think they're smarter than me?

I don't care what she thinks. There's a bakery next door, and when we open our windows every morning, in comes the smell of bread. I wear the scent all over me, and it lasts for hours.

Mazie's Diary, May 1, 1927

Tee showed up late at the cage. I hadn't seen her in weeks. Rapped her wee knuckles on the cage. Her skin was pink.

I said: To what do I owe the pleasure?

She said: No reason. It's just a nice night. Walk me home. Talk to me about the world.

She was coming from a shelter. She seemed down. I knew I should go home to Rosie, but it cost me nothing to give a little of my love to Tee.

So we walked downtown, through Park Row, past City Hall, down Broadway. We talked about all the money in this town lately, more than usual it seemed. Everyone's so giddy but it can't last. The city's pregnant with hope, but only that. New construction everywhere we looked. It's made of air, this money, this wealth. It's not real.

I told her about this new film Rudy's talking about, coming out this fall. A talking movie. He thinks everything's going to change. Tee told me nothing will change for those less fortunate, the poor and the hungry. She never lets up, that Tee. But I couldn't argue with her.

She asked about the new apartment, if we'd be staying awhile. I told her Rosie's fine for now, but I'm never sure of anything with her. I don't think she sleeps anymore at all, but I can't be certain.

I said: I never unpack all my boxes.

She said: And how does that make you feel?

I said: I'm used to it now. I miss some of my shoes though.
That made her laugh. My vanity entertains her.

We stopped in front of the Seton Shrine. Her favorite of all
the saints. Tee loves her because she started an entire school
system, and she helped poor children, too.

I said: You're as good as she is.

Then we were at her house.

She said: Come up, I've got chocolates.

I said: Slow down, slow down. Chocolates? You're a wild
one, Sister Tee.

It's been a long time since I've slept there, and only twice
before. Rosie doesn't like it when I don't come home at night.
We sleep together not as sisters, but not as lovers, either. She
could never give in to that. She's not as bold as me. Although
there is love. And we hold each other. What comfort it is to
be held, and to hold. So tiny beneath me, our chests pressed
tight. We are silent, and we hold each other. I said but one
thing, and I don't know where it came from. I just sighed it
out of me.

I said: You're divine.

And then she wept.

She said: I'm not sad, I promise. It's just the pleasure of it all.

Pete Sorensen

I kept wishing a nice guy would show up. But then I realized
she had Tee.

Mazie's Diary, November 1, 1927

Thirty. How? Thirty.

Mazie's Diary, February 2, 1928

Rosie says she can't breathe the same anymore. Bad air. The wheat from the bakery, it's in her lungs. It's been building up for months and now it's trapped in there. She claims.

I said: You liar.

She said: Listen. Listen to me wheeze.

I begged her. Please let me stay here. Let me stay near the fresh loaves of bread in the morning and the kind and quiet Jews with their heads in books and the Bowery up the road.

I said: We were getting comfortable. Don't you feel it? Don't you feel calm?

She said: I can't breathe.

Mazie's Diary, April 1, 1928

The hustling I do. 14 Division Street. Over Louis's aunt Josie's dress shop. The only apartment in the building. Just us and Josie. A kitchen cut from diamonds. A window out onto the markets. New dresses for Rosie every day if she likes. New dresses for me as well.

I said: We will stay here, Rosie.

She said: We'll see.

Am I allowed to unpack? Can we look inside these boxes at last?

Mazie's Diary, November 1, 1928

Jeanie called! Jeanie. Happy Birthday to me.

I said: Sister, how are you?

She said: Sister, all is well. Things are just dreamy and easy out here in California. I dance and play all day.

I said: That's living.

She said: I miss you though. I always miss you.

We both started crying like crazy. A fella came up to get a ticket for the two o'clock show and I shut the curtain on him, yelled at him to come back later. He knocked on the window and I growled at him.

I said: Don't make me come out there. I will smite you.

Jeanie said: You're still working too hard.

I said: Someone's got to pay the bills around here.

She said: How's Rosie?

I said: Why don't you call her and find out?

She said: I might do that.

I know she won't. It's foolish, the two of them not talking like that. Jeanie's scared, I know it. You don't get to break someone's heart twice like that and get off scot-free. You have to walk through a little fire first.

Mazie's Diary, January 1, 1929

I thought I'd see Tee, wish her the best for a New Year, but she's nowhere, disappeared. It's been weeks. No Christmas either. I had a gift for her. A small scented pillow for her head. I'll keep it in the cage. She'll show up someday.

Mazie's Diary, February 9, 1929

I took my lunch break in Chinatown, I wanted to see the parade for the Chinese New Year. I'd heard the men banging their drums all the way from Park Row. The brash clash of the cymbals made me feel proud, and I don't even have anything to brag about. But their pride was enough to buoy me.

It was snowing, but that didn't stop anything. The gold and red dragon stomping down Canal Street, the white flakes dripping down like crisp tears. Year of the Snake, someone told me. Snakes mean wisdom. I'm going to take that as a good sign. I'll be smarter this year. I'll wise up this time around.

Then there was Tee at my elbow. I threw my arms around her, and nearly wouldn't let her go. She laughed at me. She said we should keep moving, it was cold, we'd catch our death. So we walked arm in arm through Chinatown, following the parade, schoolchildren all around us, the rattle of their laughter, chattering, chasing the dragon.

I said: Where have you been?

She said: I've been run-down.

I said: You're not avoiding me then?

She said: Why would I avoid you? I've been tired. Those moments when I'm not caring for others I'm sleeping. It's winter. It's cold.

I said: That's a lot of reasons why.

She said: I wouldn't lie to you.

I said: I know that. It was only that I wondered where you were.

She said: This is not about you. This is about those children, and the abuse that they suffer. And the tenements are a disgrace. Everything is a disgrace. I feel as if I plug one hole and another starts to leak and it is all I can do to keep myself dry, let alone those smaller or weaker than myself.

We stopped walking and the crowds following the parade passed around us. Tee looked devastated and exhausted, and I thought thinner, and older, like a withering piece of straw, and not like my sweet Tee anymore, but someone else, another girl, a sad one, one that I would pass on the street and worry if she were all right.

I said: All right, Tee, I understand.

She said: Sometimes I feel like I only have so many prayers in me.

She gasped and grabbed my arm.

She said: Don't ever tell anyone I said that.

I said: Who would I tell?

Mazie's Diary, February 14, 1929

A postcard from the Captain.

It said: I'm a father now.

I'll be sure and send a present.

Pete Sorensen

Even though I wanted to know what happened, I still didn't want to show the diaries to anyone, because it seemed like she wanted them to be a secret. I was cool with that; I respected that. It was like we would have a secret together, Mazie and me.

But then I met you, and my first thought was that you would appreciate it just because you're such a special lady. For sure I thought you would know what to do with it, if it even made sense to do anything with it. You said you thought you could fill in the blanks, you could try to anyway, and that you could make it a project, like a professional project for yourself. I'm all about making projects for yourself.

Also we talked about how you hadn't been passionate about anything in a while. Me, I'm passionate all the time. I'm always busy, the shop's going well, I've got people working for me that I care about. Even if I'm not being hands-on all the time, I like doing the design work. Also being a good boss is a thing I care about. There are a lot of things I care about in my life, and there are people who need me just to show up every day and be me.

But all of your film projects had been a dead end. You couldn't find funding for anything, like, arty. And even though this wasn't a film project, you said it felt akin to what you had done in the past. You were looking for a passion project. So I said you could have the diary for a while if you thought it would help. And now here you are traipsing all over the place, tracking down anyone who has any little bit of information about Mazie.

It's funny, isn't it? How we can treat the same fascination so differently. I'd have daydreamed forever about her.

Mazie's Diary, March 1, 1929

Tee's sicker than I thought.

I hadn't seen her in a month, longer, two, I lost count. I thought she disappeared on me. I thought I'd done something wrong. I thought I'd never see her face again, and that she didn't care to see mine either. I stopped my clean living. I dug my flask out.

Rosie said: What's wrong with you? Why you mooning about?

I thought I saw her yesterday morning from far away, another nun on a corner, talking to a wicked-looking girl. Lipstick on fire. Me, I thought. That should be me. I'm your wicked-looking girl. I waved, but she wasn't Tee after all. She was old, much older, and she didn't smile at me, she didn't wave back. Where's Tee? I was thinking it all day. I drank more than I should have. I dropped in on Finny's after work. I hadn't stayed out late in so long. I decided to find her, to climb up her castle.

I walked downtown, past her beloved Seton Shrine. I crossed myself in front of it even though I didn't know what it meant to do that, but I knew it meant something. Praying she'd never abandon me, Tee wouldn't. Not by choice. Not my Tee.

The dark lobby, the elevator down, the elevator always down. Up the stairs, my head swirling as I walked, drunk as I was. A huddle of nuns outside her room, silent but for one.

I said: Where is she, where's Tee, where's my friend?

And no one answered.

I said: Is it TB? I don't care, I'll see her anyway.

They shook their heads.

It's not TB. Her breast is sick. The right one.

I said: Let me see her.

They didn't stop me, I'd like to have seen them try.

She's skin and bones, bones and skin. She'd been losing weight for a while and I hadn't noticed. No one had noticed. Tee hadn't told a soul she wasn't feeling well. She'd had too much to do, is what she told me. I touched her cheek with my hand, I said her name. I leaned in close.

She said: You're drunk.

I said: I am.

She said: Now I have to pray for you tonight all over again. Just when I thought I was done with all that.

I said: Stop it. I'm praying for you, I'm praying for you!

She said: I'll take your prayers, Mazie. Bless you.

Then she put her hand to my cheek.

She said: But you absolutely must brush your teeth first.

I was up all night with her, now I'm home. Rosie made me breakfast, and I ate it only so I won't be sick at work all day. Because I don't feel like I want to eat ever again. After she fed me, she made a noise for a moment, a heartbeat of a complaint about street vendors blocking the door in the morning.

I said: We have to stop moving for a while.

Rosie said: Do you think I'm making this up? I can barely get out the front door when I need to.

I said: My friend is dying, Rosie. Tee is dying. I need to sit still for just a moment. I'm exhausted. Let me sit still. You can do whatever you want when she's done dying. When she's dead.

Rosie said: What if there's a fire and I can't get out?

I slammed my fist on the table, the only thing we've held on to after all those moves.

I said: Goddammit, Rosie. Goddammit. Let me sit still.

Pete Sorensen

I mean, yes, obviously, I wanted to impress you. I wanted you to see something more than just this guy who works with his hands all day. I'm an actual community college dropout, have you ever met one of me before? I'm like a total joke in the intellectual department. And you're smart. And fancy. You look fancy. You feel fancy. You smell fancy. I thought maybe showing you this would make you feel the way about me that I felt about you. It was like an offering. It was one of the most precious things I owned, as much as anyone can own something like this. And I didn't realize how precious it was to me until I handed it to you and never saw it again. I thought, well I'll give it to her, and maybe I'll have a shot. I'll give it to her and maybe she'll love me for it.

Mazie's Diary, October 24, 1929

I walked down through Wall Street before I went to visit Tee. Today, I had to see today on the streets, the day Wall Street fell. People were weeping on the corners. Why is this city so beautiful when it mourns? I pretended it was all for Tee.

I said: Tee, don't leave me.

She said: What if you don't think about it as me leaving you? And just that I'm going to him instead?

That's of comfort only to her.

I wrapped my arms around her. I asked her for the hundredth time if she wanted to go to the hospital and she said no, that she would die there, in her own bed.

I said: We could get you a better blanket at least. You deserve a thick blanket.

She said: I'm not better or worse than anyone else. We're all the same.

I said: We could get you silk sheets. You should be covered in silk. You should be swimming in it.

She said: It's all the same. It feels the same if you let it. Don't you see that yet? It's all the same.

I got under the blanket with her.

I said: Silk sheets, fit for a princess.

I stayed the night there. I held her and she moaned sometimes with pain and I tried not to cry. When I walked back through Wall Street this morning, the sidewalks were littered with garbage, and men in fine suits were passed out on the street, and I thought something felt different in the city, but maybe it was just me that was different, having slept on silk for the first time in my life.

Lydia Wallach

My great-grandfather ran the movie theater nearly single-handedly for a good six months while Mazie tended to a sick friend. This was noted as part of our family history because it was during this time the first of my great-uncles got sick and passed away. This would have been my great-uncle Gilbert. My great-grandfather was away from home, working at the theater, so sadly he wasn't there when his son passed away. It happened very quickly, he got sick and died within a week. No one was to blame. But it was devastating for everyone, Rudy in particular because he felt so helpless, so absent, although I suppose no one can judge who mourns the most. But it hit him hard, harder than one of his heart attacks. My mother told me that her father told her that he was the one to run all the way to the theater to tell Rudy about it, and when he told him he watched the color drain from his face. It went from peach to yellow to white. It was the opposite of blushing, is what he told her. And he never got it back; the color never came back to his cheeks. He became a pale man, and he stayed that way for the rest of his life.

Elio Ferrante

Without Sister Tee's last name it's impossible to find out any information, and even with it I kind of suspect it would be tricky because the place where she worked closed in 1960. I found out a few things about this place, the Mercy House. It was a settlement house on Cherry Street, not far from Knickerbocker Village, and it was founded in the late 1800s to help immigrants. Basically they fed and clothed poor families, housed the homeless, took care of sick people in their homes. The usual good works. I wish I could have found a record of her. Sometimes I guess we just forget people. Even if their work isn't forgotten or at least *felt* in some way.

Mazie's Diary, January 5, 1930

The Captain came back.

I thought I didn't want to see him anymore. I'd written him out of the story of my life. He's gone, he had a baby. He's not coming to New York City ever again, or if he is it's with his new family. Good-bye, good riddance, good night. That was how I wanted the story to end. But I can't lie to myself, at least not here. I was glad to see him in that line. I've known him for so many years. We've lain in each other's arms, we've shared our flesh with each other. He knew me when I was but a girl, and I knew him when he was the handsomest man in the world.

He's not a Captain anymore, not sailing the seas anyway. Now he's a businessman, working for his wife's father. No uniform. Just a regular Joe, even if he's a rich one.

I said: How's business?

He said: We'll survive this mess. People need cars.

I said: Can't we just walk instead?

He said: You've lived in Manhattan your whole life. You don't know what the rest of the country is like. Even if they don't need cars, people want cars.

He asked me to dinner, and I said yes. We ate steak. He insisted upon it. He told me I needed the vitamins.

He said: You look pale and thin.

I said: I've been in mourning.

He said: For whom?

I said: For everyone.

He said: I'm sorry.

I couldn't eat any more after that.

He said: Come back with me to my hotel. I'm worried about you. Let me comfort you.

I said: You're a father now.

He said: So?

I said: I don't know why that makes a difference to me, but it does.

He said: We don't have to do anything. We could just hold each other.

I laughed so hard at that the entire restaurant turned and looked at me, and then I waved at the lot of them.

He said: All right, all right. You don't need to cause a scene.

I said: I'll come back with you.

He said: Are you sure?

Once I told him I was mourning, I knew I couldn't go home, not right away. I've been sad for so long there. All of my sadness is wrapped up in that bed, that kitchen, that woman in the other bedroom. This diary.

And worse comes to worst, I'd have a roll in the hay with a handsome man.

So I went with him to his hotel, a nicer one than usual, nicer than when he was just a seaman. Uptown, a bellman with shiny buttons and downcast eyes. Deferring to the rich man.

There was whiskey on the table, and the room smelled of fruit. We sat next to each other, and he kissed me on my cheek and neck. I didn't mean to, but I tittered anyway.

He said: You're still a beauty.

I sighed, and then I held his hands for a moment.

I said: Could we do what you said? Would you just hold me?

He said: Mazie, what's wrong? What happened to my good-time girl?

I said: I'm sad.

I started to cry and he told me not to and he kissed me again and I said there was no way to stop, that I must cry, I must.

He said: Then if you must, I am going to have to insist you tell me everything. You can't go halfway. Let's just finish this. Tell me now or forever hold your peace. Just get rid of it, and then we'll be done.

So I told him about Louis dying, and how he had been a criminal, and how he had made me a criminal too, in one way or another, but that I had not fought too hard against it. And it started to feel good, to say these things, even as sad and awful as they were. I told him that my sister had gone mad years ago and I tried to help her as much as I could, but also that I hated her, too, I hated her for making me suffer as much as she did. I told him that Tee had died, and that I had loved her, and now that love was gone, and that I had tried so hard to be the person she wanted me to be and it hadn't mattered in the end, she died anyway, and what was the point in being your very best if all love dies?

He said: Not all love dies. Here I am with you now. Here we are together, Mazie.

It didn't feel real to me when he said that. He was listening but he wasn't hearing me, or he was saying the thing he thought I wanted to hear, but that wasn't it at all. It was not the right thing. And so I told him finally about the baby I had lost, nearly eight years ago, the baby that had been his. I told him how I had kept the baby a secret except from my family, and that I would have given it to Rosie and Louis to keep as their own, and he started to say something but then he stopped himself because I saw him working it out in his head, that there was a baby, and then there wasn't, and I told him that the baby had died, died inside of me while I slept, and I told him about the mattress, how it was suddenly soaked with blood, how it turned red, I woke up, and it was red and sticky and I was wet with my blood, the insides of me turned out, and I had bled so much I nearly died, but also it wasn't just losing all the blood that was killing me, it was the sadness, and the guilt, and the broken heart.

This was when he started to cry. He asked if it had been a boy or a girl and I told him a boy. He told me that he was sorry I had gone through that and if he had known I was with child he would have done the right thing by me and I told him that we had only met once, there was no right thing or wrong thing, and it was a good thing he hadn't because he'd probably be sitting in a hotel room with a different woman now, being the kind of man he was. That stung him, and I didn't mean to sting him, only I suppose I did. He told me there was no need for that, and I apologized.

He said: It was my child too.

I said: It's nobody's baby anymore.

The next part came from a place of sadness and us both being animals like we are. We removed just enough clothing for us to put all our parts together. I wasn't even wet enough for him to fit inside me easily but then very suddenly I was. I didn't look at him and he didn't look at me. I stared out over his shoulder, my legs wrapped around the small of his back. I couldn't tell if it was making me feel better or worse. Better, worse, worse, better. It didn't seem possible that I could feel either.

After, I couldn't stay there with him. I didn't want to wake up in his arms. I didn't want to talk to him anymore about the things I had just told him. I told him I had to leave, and he didn't argue, because he was thinking his own thoughts, about his lost son, probably, and the son he had now. I told him I'd see him around and he said the same and it was like a good-bye only more like a lie.

And then I walked home from his hotel, all the way downtown, and it was cold, and it tasted bitter, and I liked it. And then I saw it, truly, for the first time, the way this city has changed. It's lost its pride. There's bums everywhere, and there's drunks everywhere, and it's filthy, and people are hungry. It's not just in the tenements, it's everywhere. I ain't never seen anything like it. I was lifting my skirt up over the men in the gutters, but there were children there too, and women, and they were spread out all over the island. Maybe I've been blind because I've been mourning, or maybe I've just been trapped in my little cage for too long, because it is only just now that I am seeing how much trouble this city of mine is in.

I thought of Tee walking next to me, and what she would have thought about it all. Her habit gathered up around her as she bent to help. We never would have made it home, she would have stopped and helped each person. She couldn't turn down a soul.

I fished in my pocket, and I squatted down next to a man on the sidewalk. There was a cut on his cheek. Stubble, dirt, dried blood. Blood on his collar and coat. He was shivering. Everyone on the streets was shivering.

I handed him a quarter.

I said: This is for a bed to sleep in.

I handed him another quarter.

I said: This is for a meal.

I handed him a final quarter.

I said: And this is for a drink or two.

That last part Tee wouldn't have approved of, but Tee never knew how to have a good time.

8

The younger ones still have a chance to change their lives, and I'll lend them a hand if they like. But too many of the older men, they've been on the road so long they wouldn't know what to do with a proper home if they had one. The concrete feels right under their bodies. Their discomfort has become their comfort.

Elio Ferrante

Is it weird that I love teaching the Depression the most out of all the eras? I think part of it has to do with it being *the most*. Like it was the longest and the worst and it was global and terrible, and these kids only know how to pay attention to superlatives. Also the idea of businessmen jumping out of buildings freaks them out. Breadlines freak them out, too. A lot of these kids have had experience with food stamps, and then I get to tell them it was because of the Depression that food stamps were even created in the first place. This speaks to them. The image of New York City in trouble, with so many people down on their luck, that genuinely speaks to them also. They weren't here for the seventies and eighties, which is when I was a kid, and when New York City was still, pardon my language, a shit show. But the idea that it exists, that so much of New York City was in trouble that there were breadlines everywhere, it freaks them out, it makes them pay attention, and more than anything I like it when I have a classroom of eyeballs facing forward. All those heads up, listening to what I have to say, I love it. I wish I could teach the Depression all year long.

Mazie's Diary, February 1, 1930

Now I'm back regular at the theater, and Rudy and I met this morning about business. He said it's no good. First, people were coming to the theater to forget their worries, but now the money's run out. He thinks it'll be bad for a while. Gloom and doom on that poor man's face. Pale-faced Rudy, he is. The faintest sliver of a man.

I said to Rudy: We'll run it at a loss for a while if we have to. We're not closing this theater down. We won't put the people who've worked here out on their behinds like everybody else.

I talked to Rosie about it all over dinner tonight.

I said: Who knows when it will pick up?

She said: We won't close it.

I said: No, of course we won't.

She said: I'll sell all my jewelry, and whatever else I need to. Louis loved that theater.

I said: And those people are our family.

She said: I don't even understand why we're having this discussion.

I said: I only wanted to make sure. We choose this, there's no unchoosing it.

She said: You and I disagree about a lot of things, Mazie, but I think we can both agree we will not send our people out on the streets until the last dime is gone.

Ah, I loved her then. I loved my Rosie.

Lydia Wallach

They kept the theater running for two years at a loss, paying people out of their own savings. Supposedly they had plenty of money, she and her sister. Secret stashes of cash here and there. But still, to support an entire staff like that.

Mazie's Diary, February 15, 1930

There was no line at the theater today, we sold three tickets in the morning, and that's it. Same as yesterday, and the week before, and the week before that. I decided to check out the competition. Everyone was standing in line instead at the Bowery Mission.

I wrapped myself up in my warm cloak, and brought an extra pack of smokes with me, thought I'd hand them out if anyone was craving one. I hadn't seen the lines up close yet, or maybe I've seen them and just wasn't paying attention. I wore gloves and a scarf and a hat and the new wool winter cloak Rosie gave me in December, and I walked briskly, I swung my arms, and still I felt the chill. And I was thinking if I'm cold, how are those fellas doing?

I walked the line, nodding at the gents. So many of them had suitcases with them and if I didn't know any better I would have thought they were heading on a trip. But instead they were just carrying whatever they had left, what little remained in their lives.

I knew I'd seen some of them around before. Some of them were hustlers, but some of them were just regular old Joes from the neighborhood, working stiffs without any work, just stiff now. I couldn't name them, I couldn't place them exactly, and I thought maybe I was even making it up, them being familiar. But then a couple of them tipped their hats at me, and a few of them said my name. How do, Miss Mazie. So I knew I was right. These were my customers, starving on the streets. I offered out cigarettes to the fellas, and some of them took more than one and I didn't say a thing.

One of them touched my arm and I turned to him, offered him the pack.

He said: It's me, Mazie. It's William. From Finny's. Do you remember me? It's been a while, I know.

It was Hungry William, who had savaged my breasts a few years ago. The bites and the bruises, how could I forget him?

I said: Oh, William, of course. I'd know you anywhere.

I was girlish and flirtatious. I wanted to make him feel special right then. He took a smoke, told me that he was down on his luck like everyone else.

I said: Even the bankers have fallen.

He said: Especially the bankers. But I was not so much a banker as a bank clerk, I must admit to you. And now I'm nothing.

He started to cry, standing right there in the line. I felt all hot and teary too. I touched his face. I remembered him as so rough and arrogant, I couldn't stand to see him as anything but that. There's not much I ask for in this world anymore, but I want my memories to remain intact.

I said: William, don't be sad. We had such a good time together, think about that.

He said: There's no more good times left for me.

I pulled my flask from my coat.

I said: Drink this, it'll warm you up.

He sipped from it but then other lads yelled for it, and it was gone in a flash. Everyone was sipping. I couldn't deny them a thing. After the flurry of cigarettes and booze there was nothing left for them to do but stand there in the cold, some of them jumping up and down to keep warm, others hunched over, arms wrapped around themselves. I started to feel it, too, the cold to the bone.

I said: Listen, when you're done here, you come see me at the theater, I'll let you in for free. All of you lads, you come in, warm up, see a show, it'll take your mind off your problems. In no time you'll feel better. It's on me, you hear?

They all let out a cheer. I know it's just temporary, a temporary gift for them. I can't have them in there every day. I'll never get another decent customer in if I do. But for one day, I can let these fellas warm themselves under my roof.

Later on Rudy told me half of them slept through the entire movie.

Mazie's Diary, February 16, 1930

I don't know if we've ever had a fight before, Rudy and me, but letting the bums on the outside in, he isn't having it. Early this morning, before I opened up the cage, he asked me inside. We sat in the balcony. I hadn't been in the theater for nearly ten years. I'd forgotten what it looked like. Some theater owner I am. The screen was dark, and the lights were dim, and I was thinking that was for the best, that I wouldn't want to look too close at anything. The air felt thick and dusty, like maybe I could hold it in my hand. But I could be wrong about everything. It smelled fine in there, not moldy, not boozy. And the chairs were still plush beneath me. Nice seats, high-class seats. Those seats were good enough for me and anyone else who walked through that door. Which was the point I was about to make.

Rudy said: We're not a shelter or a flophouse, Mazie.

I said: I know we're not. But they were the same as you

and me six months ago. They had jobs and homes and money in their pockets. We're no better than them. This city is just stricken.

Rudy said: People think we're letting the bums run the place they'll never come back again, even when they do have money.

I said: You know what the movies mean to you. Now think what it will mean to these fellas, too broke to have any kind of treat for themselves.

He said: You want to talk about what the movies mean to people? I don't want to be rude but a lot of them, they're not clean. It's not their fault, but would you want to sit next to someone who doesn't smell so great? You've saved up your pennies, some fella's taking a girl he wants to impress, or this is your birthday present from your husband, say, and it's a big night out on the town and, Mazie, you're sitting in a theater filled with guys who haven't washed in a week or two because they're sleeping on the streets. I mean, who's coming back for that? What's going to happen to our business?

I heard him. I heard everything he said. It's his business too, he's put his whole self into it for so long. Front of the house is me, back of the house is Rudy. I know it. It's the deal we made. But I'm breaking the rules.

I said: I'll remind you it's my business, Rudy.

He said: Mazie, please.

I said: It won't be forever. And it won't be all of them. Only the ones that can behave themselves.

He said: And how will you know?

I said: I've been looking at these lines of people for ten years. I know.

Mazie's Diary, April 7, 1930

William's been showing up every day to the Venice. Filching smokes off me, sometimes I'll hand him change, and once I brought him a tiny bar of soap from home, didn't say nothing, just slid it over to him. He nods, I nod. Rudy told me he snoozes quietly in the balcony for a show or two. I never even see him leave.

Sometimes I can't tell if he's drunk or just sad. It's not a mystery I want to solve. I've no judgment either way, only I just want to know how to help him, if I can even help him. I know some of these lads you just have to give up on. But how can I give up on the one who sucked at my tit?

Mazie's Diary, April 15, 1930

Haven't seen William in a week. Asked around, nothing. Now he's not even showing up in the mornings. I think I'll walk the street tonight, see if I can find him. I don't want him to get lost in the shuffle.

Mazie's Diary, April 16, 1930

No William, but oh those streets, they're good for no one at night. The bodies all around, not dead, but some of them seemed barely alive. Passed out, skin and bones beneath their filthy clothes. I gave them all I had in my pockets and kept digging to see if I could find more.

Mazie's Diary, May 1, 1930

I found him tonight, in an alley off the Bowery, bleeding from his lip, a torn shirt, bleeding from there too. Some vomit down the front of him. He said he'd had work on a train and then he'd spent every cent he made, and what he didn't spend a buddy of his had stolen from him the night before. And now here he was, bleeding in an alley. I waited with him till the ambulance came, and then I had a drink at Finny's and then another, and then another, and I let a man walk me home and kiss me good night and touch my behind but I'd seen too much blood tonight to do any more than that.

Mazie's Diary, May 4, 1930

Went to Tee's church early this morning because I missed her. I sat through mass, and thought about her believing in those words. I confessed, and I did it with sincerity, and it felt good to speak some truth. Then I crossed myself in front of the shrine to see what the air felt like under my fingertips, if it changed, but it did not. The air is always the same. And I remembered I was still me.

Mazie's Diary, July 8, 1930

Rosie's back at her old tricks. It's been months of it. I can't move again. I can't I can't I can't.

Oh, this block is dangerous now. Oh, that mission around the corner is bringing all the riffraff here. Oh, we should leave the city, move to Boston, move back to Coney Island, move uptown, move to Brooklyn, move where it's safe and nobody's hungry.

I said: Rosie, people are hungry all over this country.

She said: I know, I know! But that doesn't mean I have to live among them.

I said: We used to live in a house with dirt on the floor. We ain't no better than them.

She said: I don't feel safe on this here block.

I said: You crazy old broad, you're tougher than I am. Nothing scares you.

She said: If you were home more I'd feel safer. Especially at night.

I said: I can't be home any more than I already am.

She said: I know where you go at night. I know where you go!

But how do I say to her that I need a drink at the end of the day? That a little hooch warms me, like I'm velvet on the inside and out. And that I need the company of men, that flirting feeds me better than her beef stew. Jesus, I need to remember what it's like to be a woman and not just a bird in a cage. Tee's gone now. Can I have this one thing? This one part of the day to be mine.

Mazie's Diary, August 1, 1930

No one's asking for change for a flop, it's too hot. In the winter it's all they dream of, getting warm. In the summer I'm noticing they don't mind sleeping on the streets. It's cooler outside than in one of those airless flops. They'll take the dirt, they'll take the sweat, over choking on the bad air. They'd rather pass out in the night breeze. Change for a meal, change for a drink, but no change for a home, not tonight anyway.

Mazie's Diary, September 2, 1930

Jeanie called, said she's been sick, hasn't been able to dance, and crowds have been dying down. She's in Chicago again, and that leg of hers is aching from the chill that rises off the big lake. I said I'd send her some money.

She said: That's not why I called. I'm not begging for money.

I said: No one said you're a beggar. I'm just offering. I have it. There doesn't need to be a fuss about it.

She said: I don't want you to think I can't take care of myself.

I said: You've been away long enough that's not even a question.

She said: I worry what you think of me.

I said: That's a first.

I got sharp with her. I knew she was just playing a game with me. She'd called for money, plain and simple. I told her not to kid a kidder and she asked for a hundred and I sent it her way.

George Flicker

What happened was my father died very suddenly—this was in the summer of 1930—and it was devastating for everyone because he was such a good man, though he was not a young man, so at least we could all say, "Oh, he led a good life," that sort of thing. Still, it was just awful, because he was so beloved. And then my mother died soon after that because she couldn't live without him, and this was another devastation, because say what you will about my mother—and people had said plenty—she was a real force in the universe. Although no one was walking around saying, "Oh, she lived a good life," because she never seemed particularly happy.

So then it was just me and Uncle Al in that tiny apartment. Even with less people in it, it still felt full. One day I asked Al if he thought it was haunted by my parents. I was just kidding around with him. And he said, "Of course. Where else would they go?" I don't think I had fully recognized what was going on with Al, how bad he had gotten, because my mother was the one monitoring the situation; it was her full-time job. I'd been sent out more than a few times to pick him up if he was sleeping in a park somewhere, and I know that it made my mother feel more secure with me being back home, but I wasn't home enough to know the complete reality. So when they passed, I found my whole life turned on its head. I had to watch my uncle Al. Now, he was lucid most days, very smart with his head in the books, always the intellectual, but also he was sleeping on the streets half the time. He was too skinny and he had awful bruises. And I just didn't feel comfortable letting the man wither, especially after my parents had just passed. I'm a human being. We're all human beings. We look after each other.

It was either I had to watch him, or I had to check him into a mental institution of some sort, and I wasn't in the financial position to do that, not yet anyway. It would have had to be somewhere sort of high class, not some awful state institution. I knew Al would never survive in a place like that; I'd heard those operations were miserable, real torture chambers. No way, not for my uncle Al.

What I was doing was, I was working all day for Frederick French, who was a very famous and successful developer at the time, but of course someone you have never heard of before because you are a child. This was just before he started on Knickerbocker Village, but he had numerous other properties in development. I was at the bottom of the totem pole but that was fine, I just wanted to get my foot in the door. I didn't want to work in ties for the rest of my life. How far can you really go with ties? So I'd work from very early in the morning till early evening, and then I'd go home, and if all was well in the world, Al'd be sitting there waiting for me. And we'd have dinner, and maybe we'd go for a stroll through the neighborhood, us bachelors, and maybe we'd have a drink. Also on nice nights we'd go to Washington Square Park so Al could play chess, and I'd smoke a cigar and watch him destroy those poor schmoes who dared to take him on. These were the best nights, and I had sort of resigned myself to this kind of life, at least as long as Al was alive.

But if all was not well with the world, I would come home, and there'd be no Al. And I'd have to hunt the streets looking for him. If I got lucky, he was down the block, or he was playing chess, or he was at the library. If I wasn't lucky, it could take hours and hours, or I wouldn't find him at all, and then I'd just be sleepless. It wasn't that the cops were beating him up anymore, they'd sort of forgotten why they were even mad at him in the first place; they'd found someone new to pick on I guess. It was just that he was damaged goods. He was an easy target. Someone else could beat him up or rob him and he wouldn't fight them off. And the streets were getting rougher. People were desperate. I lived in fear for Al.

One of the places I'd look for Al was Finny's, which no longer exists of course. The last time I checked, and this was more than a few years ago, it was a head shop. But at the time Finny's was one of those untouchable joints. Prohibition or not, there was always Finny's. The cops liked it; I think that helped. I wasn't much of a drinker before then, and I wasn't after, but for that period of time, those darkest days with Al, I can admit I sought some relief in a glass of beer. Oh, I was depressed, I guess. I had work, I was one of the lucky ones, but it seemed like no one else did. People were starving on the streets. We were all sad.

On top of that it seemed like my youth was passing me by in service of this man who did not seem to want to be helped. Of course he wanted his freedom. Of course he did! Who among us would want to have to sit at home and wait for someone? But I'd had this dream that eventually I would settle down, I'd get married, I'd have kids, I'd build this life that wasn't expected of me but that I expected of myself. But instead I was just chasing Al around every night.

Now the other person walking the streets checking on the lost souls, as you know, was Mazie. The early thirties, she was just starting to become the person she was going to be, if that makes any sense. I guess she was a bit of an eccentric too. I mean what kind of woman wanders the streets like that? At least that's what everyone used to talk about at Finny's. Sure, there was a hypocrisy there. Why was I allowed to and she wasn't? Well she was doing it anyway, so it doesn't matter what any of us thought.

Mazie's Diary, October 5, 1930

The lads at Finny's like to tease me about walking the streets. Like I'm a streetwalker, a real one. Oh Mazie's got a new part-time job, ho ho ho. Last night I twisted one of their ears, and I saw tears in his eyes, though he wouldn't admit it.

I said: I'm a queen, and don't you ever forget it.

He said he wouldn't.

George Flicker was there, too. I've always liked him fine, even though he spends half the conversation staring at my bosom. Once in a while I take his face in my hand and lift it up to meet my eyes. I don't think it's funny, and neither does he, but we both laugh anyway. I'd get mad at anyone else, but I've known him too long. I know he's not a bad sort. I think he's a good sort, actually. Except for the wandering eye.

Last night I sat with him after I twisted that man's ear.

He said: I know why I'm walking the streets but what about you? It's not safe out there for a lady. I don't listen to these jokers over here. I know you're a real lady.

I started talking and I didn't stop till I was done. I wish I could remember what I said! I was in a frenzy.

George Flicker

She gave me this speech once and I'll never forget it. It was this especially rough night at Finny's, the guys were teasing her. These were the days they still teased her. She was still young and pretty enough that they cared to bother. Isn't that an awful thing to say? Well I'm old now, and I know the truth, so I can say it. So they're teasing her, saying she's a street-walker, getting customers, whatnot. And she socked some guy in the ear I think. She said, "I'm the queen!" And everyone started laughing. So I offered her this safe haven with me at a corner table. But I'd been drinking and I couldn't leave it alone. I asked her why she did what she did when she could have just stayed home safe.

And she said, "These are dark days, Georgie. The city's lost its pride. And what does it cost me to buy these fellas a drink or two? Or to give them some soap to clean up with, or to buy them a place to rest their heads for the night? It's change that I already got in my pocket. What else am I going to do with it? Buy another dress? I got a whole closet full. Go on vacation? Where would I go? I live in the best city in the world. Buy myself a fancy dinner? Give me my sister's cooking any old time. No, my change goes to these fellas on the streets. I used to give my money away to strangers, I didn't want to look them in the face, I didn't want to know where it went. Now I want to know where it's going. I want to make sure it's making some kind of difference. I walk these streets because I want to help. Why is that so hard to understand?"

She got pretty emotional. She wiped some tears from her eyes. I handed her my kerchief. Then she said, "Is it so hard to believe I could be a good person?"

Mazie's Diary, November 1, 1930

I'm thirty-three now.

Rosie gave me a walking stick for my birthday.

I said: What's this for?

She said: I know your back bothers you, and it doesn't look like you'll stop walking those streets anytime soon. This'll help.

I held the stick in my hand. It's a fine, lacquered dark wood.

She said: I know what you do.

I said: Do you now.

She said: Everyone knows you're out there helping those bums.

I stood and practiced with it. I stood up straighter immediately.

She said: You're a good girl, Mazie.

I said: I'm no girl any longer.

She said: Well you're my girl, and you always will be.

George Flicker

Another time I remember her telling me about Rosie. I strolled into Finny's and there she was, and I tipped my hat at her, and she patted the seat next to her, and it made me feel special, and a little tight in the pants if I must be honest here. I don't mean to make you blush, honey. Those early sexual desires inform everything. This is what Freud said. I don't know much about psychology but I do know what Freud said, doesn't everyone? And that little boy in me, he liked having Mazie ask him to sit next to her. I asked her what the good word was, and she said, "I got nothing good. The streets are dire and my sister's a loon as usual." I said, "What's the problem, Mazie? Moving day again?" She looked shocked that I knew about it. Maybe a little embarrassed too, I guess. I said, "Not to make a joke out of it." She said, "I just didn't know it was common knowledge." I said, "I work in the business. I'm sorry. Plus I worry about you girls. No man to look out for you." I thought I'd give it a shot, show a little bravado, see what I could get out of it. "A man to look after us isn't what we need," she said. "A man for her to look after is what she needs. Just so she can leave me alone already. I'd marry her off in a second if I could, but she'd never go for it. She'll love Louis till the day she dies."

Mazie's Diary, December 3, 1930

Called an ambulance tonight, and both the attendants were cold to the poor bum. There was a bigger one, an enormous man, who was strong enough to carry the bum in his arms, but he was just flipping him around, dragging him a bit on the ground.

I said: He's blue in the lips, how about some respect already?

He said: He can't feel it anyway. Look at him, he's passed out cold.

I said: Be humane.

I growled it really, and then he listened, took a more tender turn, straightened the bum's coat for him. I think it was my voice that did it. Lately I've noticed it's as deep as a man's. All those years under the train tracks, yelling at the folks in my line just to be heard. I know I'm all woman. But I'll just catch myself here and there, and I'll forget it's me talking. It's good to have this voice on the streets though. It's good to feel tough. I gotta be at my boldest on the streets.

Mazie's Diary, January 8, 1931

Walked a young fella with a limp to the flophouse on the corner. Said his name was Winky, and that gave me a laugh. I should write down all these bum names I hear sometime. It'd be quite a list.

Mazie's Diary, February 6, 1931

William showed up today just long enough to filch some money off me at the cage. His coat was so worn it was barely more than buttons and some loose threads. He wandered off down the street whistling. Well at least he's happy enough to whistle.

Mazie's Diary, March 2, 1931

Ambulance tonight for Winky. He showed me his ankle and it was a blue so pale it was nearly gray and swollen, and a little green around the toes.

He said: I don't want to go to Bellevue.

I said: You gotta.

He said: Come visit me, promise you will.

I said I would but I won't. I'm only good on the streets.

Mazie's Diary, April 1, 1931

18 Mott Street, heart of Chinatown, blocks away from the theater so that's fine by me. Seems like a crazy move, crazier than usual. I don't know why Rosie thinks it will be any better here but she says she doesn't mind the noise as much when she can't understand what anyone's saying. It's a new building, across the street from one of our own, and we've got the top floor all to ourselves. I give her a month till she gets sick of the smell of food different than her own. She promises she won't. Says she loves chow mein, could eat it all day. I know my Rosie though. She'll get her fill.

Mazie's Diary, April 19, 1931

Saw an old fella stealing another's suitcase. First bum was too drunk to notice it was gone, the second fella was too drunk to run with it. Then he banged into a wall. He dropped it and the clasp flopped open. All that was in it was old clothes, and they fell in a pile, stink rising. Then a moth flew out.

I rapped him with my walking stick.

I said: This is your comrade. Don't steal his possessions.

He said: Ain't nobody my friend on the streets.

I pushed my walking stick farther into him.

I said: If you don't have any friends, then all you got is enemies.

I made him pick up the clothes and give the suitcase back. First fella didn't wake up the entire time.

Second fella spit at my feet and I told him to scram. I whacked him in the leg before he left. Wish I'd whacked him harder. All I'm doing right now is sitting here and wishing I'd left a mark and hating myself for feeling that way, too.

Mazie's Diary, May 4, 1931

Two ambulances this week, got twelve fellas beds for the night, and paid one hospital bill. Also I bought a big box of hotel soaps for the dirtiest of these bums. I figured I should carry them with me wherever I go. If I give it to them, I know they'll use it. Clean up the filth, one bum at a time.

Mazie's Diary, May 14, 1931

Winky's foot is gone, and they gave him some crutches and that's it. I gave him everything in my pocket.

I said: What'll we do with you, Winky?

He said: At least it's getting warm again, Miss Mazie. At least there's that.

I sat next to him for a spell on the bench. I asked him why they called him Winky and he told me it was short for Winklemans. I said that I used to know some Winklemans on Grand Street when I was growing up and he told me they were his cousins, that he'd come to visit from Philadelphia and never left and he'd had work, and then he hadn't had work, and neither had his cousins, and then he was too ashamed to go home, and then all of this had happened, and he smelled like rot, and his foot was rot, and his gut was rot, and it was more shame on top of shame. I asked him if he'd rather rot out of pride on a bench or swallow it all and go home. He said he was worried if they'd even want him like this, not being able to earn his keep. I asked him if he had a mother and if she loved him and he answered that yes, he did, and I told him that she'd love him no matter what shape he was in, and this story ends with me hailing a taxi and taking him to Grand Central Station and buying him a train ticket home, and him thanking me and then crying and waving good-bye to me from the window as the train left the station, one of his crutches resting up against the window.

Mazie's Diary, July 15, 1931

One ambulance last night. And he didn't even last till they got there. His hand in mine. The stench in the heat already rising, like dirt, like animal, like shit. And I smelled it on me all today.

I can't tell if it's making me feel better or worse anymore, writing all of this down. It's like I have to live through it one more time when I'd rather just forget at the end of the night.

Mazie's Diary, August 3, 1931

This morning, at the table, I'm eating, she's pushing the eggs around with the fork, and I can hear the fork scraping against the plate, that tinny sound in my ear.

I said: What?

She said: Nothing.

I said: Say it.

She said: The smell.

I said: I don't smell a goddamn thing.

Mazie's Diary, September 11, 1931

There's an artist named Ray who's been trading me sketches for change for weeks now. All he does is draw the Brooklyn Bridge, but I don't say a peep. They're beautiful anyway. He tells me he's selling me the Brooklyn Bridge and we both have a laugh. I put one of them up in the cage, next to all the postcards.

Last night I saw him in an alley. I'd thought he was just broke, not on the streets. He told me his lady had left him and time had run out on his rent. A friend came over and gave him a few bills for what he had left, some books, some art. The rest he'd sold a long time ago, or it was garbage anyway. He blamed himself for everything.

He said: I don't need to be down on my luck. I choose to be here. I've lost the fight. I'm no good at the other thing.

I said: What other thing?

He said: You know, life.

He's handsome, this Ray. He's long-legged, and his suit fits him well. He has a stylish bowler he wears and his blond curls flop around his ears. His face is long and drawn but a week or two of good eating and he'd be gorgeous again.

He pulled out his notebook and offered to trade another drawing for some change.

I told him he didn't need to sell his work to me any longer, that I'd give him change no matter what.

I said: I see how thirsty you are.

He said: I'm no beggar. I'm an artist.

He took his hat off and held it to his heart and focused all his attention upon me where I stood and I nearly desired him.

And then he said: But I am indeed thirsty.

So I took the drawing and he took the change and I put it where I've put all the rest of them. In the pages of this diary.

Pete Sorensen

I had all the Brooklyn Bridge sketches individually framed. There's twenty-two in all. I couldn't help myself. I hung them in my shop and I get so many compliments on them. A wall of nearly identical Brooklyn Bridges, signed by one Ray Frieburg. I looked him up. He was nobody special.

Mazie's Diary, November 1, 1931

Thirty-four. I took myself shopping on Division Street. I bought dresses, three of them, one violet and two blue ones, all in deep jewel tones, all of them silk. I looked real sharp in all of them. Afterward I walked along the Bowery and felt bad, indulgent and spoiled, because so many people are suffering on the streets. But then I felt fine when I got back to work because I need to feel pretty, even if no one can see what I'm wearing in that cage all day. I need it. Me. Mine.

I showed Rosie the dresses when I got home tonight and

she touched the fabric, looked closely at the seams, held the violet one up against her in the mirror. She declared them immaculate and stylish and the best quality. She grew sad for a moment, and said she wished she could fit in a dress with such a small waist.

She's become a big woman, it's true. In particular her arms are enormous, like an ape's arms. She's on that downward slope toward being an old woman. Her hair is nearly all gray, battle lines drawn around her lips. Just last week I suggested ever so gently she dye her hair.

She said: For who?

And I said: For you.

Mazie's Diary, February 6, 1932

William passed. A pal of his told me, this fella Gerard who was looking for money to crash in a flophouse tonight. Hit up old Mazie at the cage, that's what they all do. I didn't know his face at first. The street's aged him. He was a pink-cheeked cherub and now he's got bags under his eyes and chunks of hair gone and there's no color left in his face.

I said: Do I know you?

He said: Sure you do.

I said: From where?

He said: I met you with William, that day you let us all in the theater. It was a long time ago, but not too long.

I said: Two years ago nearly, I think.

He said: A lot's changed.

I said: You were just a kid then. Look at you now.

He said: The cold wind changes a man.

I felt bad. What does he need me insulting his looks for?

I said: You look fine, just fine.

He said: I'll take your word for it. I haven't looked in a mirror in a long time.

I said: Hey, where's that buddy William of yours?

He didn't say anything, just pointed to the sky. I looked up, not understanding right away.

I said: Oh.

He said: Yes.

It was months ago, and I didn't even know it.

Mazie's Diary, February 27, 1932

Called four ambulances this month and checked six fellas into flophouses. Feel like I'm just getting started here, like I could do this forever. Just keep helping them. Because someone's always going to need help.

Mazie's Diary, May 8, 1932

I looked up just before close yesterday and there was the Captain. Ben, now. I'm going to call him Ben. He hasn't been a captain in a long time. He's not the Captain I used to know either.

It was raining, and we ducked into a diner and sat at the counter. I'd promised Rosie I'd be home for dinner for once, and I felt anxious about that, but on the other hand I knew we needed to talk. About what I didn't know exactly. Only that there were things left to be said.

We both ordered coffee, and I realized it would be the first time the two of us were together without any booze in us. And the lights in the diner were bright. It was just the two of us. We could only be ourselves.

He showed me pictures of his son, his namesake. He was a cute kid, bright eyes, his hair slicked down and parted to the side, a tiny suit coat. A bow tie. I nearly choked up but I didn't and I'm goddamn proud of myself.

I asked him what his boy was like and he shifted around on his stool. He didn't seem too happy talking about it.

He said: He's angry already and he's not old enough to be angry at the world yet. And we've got a fine life there. Anything going on that might tick him off, he doesn't know about it.

I said: Kids are smart. He looks pretty smart in that picture.

He said: He's a good kid. I'm not complaining about him. I feel bad. Ah, I don't know.

I said: You could change your ways. You can be whatever kind of person you like.

He said: I've been this way so long I don't know how else to be.

I said: All you have to do is choose it. It's up to you.

He said: You sound like my wife.

I said: The last thing I want to sound like is your wife.

We both waited to laugh but then we did and everything melted between us. I let him hold my hand for a while though I knew I wouldn't go back to his hotel with him. But I felt like I could talk to him, more than I can ever talk to that priest I visit. Ben's not anonymous exactly, but it feels safe to tell him everything. He's a real friend now, and he doesn't want anything from me except maybe to have someone to talk to. And I found myself telling him things I hadn't even realized until the moment it came out of my mouth.

I told him about walking the streets at night, helping out the fellas. He told me it worried him, me walking alone out there. I told him I'd been getting to know them all, getting to know their true stories. I didn't think a one of them would hurt me. They were just alone out there, and I understood that. And then this one thing occurred to me.

I said: I'll tell you the real truth of why I do it, or part of it anyway. There ain't nothing wrong with being alone, which is what I am, or what I have been. It's when it turns to loneliness, when you get to feeling blue about it all, that you're in trouble. There's the problem, loneliness. And now I'm never really alone anymore, day or night. Even if I walk the streets by myself, I'm always surrounded by people. It's like being in the cage, only inside out.

He told me he was sorry I felt lonely. He told me to be careful, that I was precious. He held both of my hands in his. He comes into town every few months on business and he'd like to have coffee with me every so often. Would I like that, is what he asked me. Would I.

Mazie's Diary, June 1, 1932

A postcard from Winky, thanking me.

It said: Safe & sound & loved.

Mazie's Diary, November 2, 1932

Thirty-five years old. I wound up at Finny's, no surprise there. George Flicker was at the bar and I got looped enough that I didn't mind him looking at my bosom the way that he always does. Happy Birthday to me, why not have some fun? He walked me home and we kissed and kissed and kissed, and I let him put his hands on me for a minute or two or three. He's an all right kisser. He said he learned everything he knows from French girls.

George Flicker

She said that? She did. Well, I suppose it was true then. I wasn't trying to hide anything from you. I've told you everything else I know so far, haven't I? I was just being respectful of the lady. My generation, we showed some respect. It feels good to show respect. It makes you feel like a man. I wasn't going to kiss and tell unless I had to. And now I suppose I have to.

Mazie's Diary, December 1, 1932

It's cold now again, it won't warm up for a long time. I'm worried about the fellas. I collect nickels and dimes and quarters. I line my pockets with them. I hand them out freely. I pray every night they won't freeze to death.

Mazie's Diary, December 15, 1932

Last night she stayed up cleaning the apartment, every inch of it, not just the kitchen but the toilet, too, and her bedroom, and my bedroom, too. She came in while I was sleeping. She was possessed by a cleaning demon. I thought maybe she was walking in her sleep. I tried to rouse her. I shook her by her shoulders. I said her name and I begged and then I gave up. I put the pillow over my head and waited until she left.

I would give anything to make this stop. I'm used to this

pain—it feels so familiar, it's like it's my little pinky. But still I dare to dream of a life without it.

George Flicker

The month I can't remember so well, but I believe it was early 1933. It was freezing out, just a bitter, bitter cold, and she'd been on the streets, and she came into Finny's. Her cheeks were flushed and she looked very pretty. She'd been avoiding me since we kissed, or maybe I'd been avoiding her. But that night we were both exhausted, and we truly were so fond of each other that we gave in to it. We just liked each other and wanted to talk! And I think she needed to talk about Rosie with someone. It was this burden she carried with her. I had my burden; she had hers. And there are times when you need other people to witness your pain. Not anymore, I'm done with that. All my little aches and pains I've lived with long enough now, why bother? I'm one hundred years old. Guess what? I'm falling apart. But then we were young and we still felt entitled to some kind of relief. We believed in the possibility of relief. That we deserved a break. So we shared our problems. And then I knew all about Rosie, with the cleaning and the complaining and the in general obsessive behavior. And then we very naturally came up with this solution to both of our problems. Oh, we thought we were so smart. We were even a little smug about the whole thing. We thought we knew our family so well. Our people, they were our people. But we never could have predicted how it was going to turn out in the end.

Mazie's Diary, February 14, 1933

Well George Flicker and I had an interesting talk tonight. Who knew George Flicker could be interesting?

He's working for this developer, and there's going to be a new building downtown. It's going to be the finest building in the neighborhood, with a beautiful garden in a private courtyard. He told me that when I sit in that garden I'll feel like I left New York City behind.

It'll be difficult to get into the building. Everyone wants in. But he thought he could do it, could secure a small apartment for himself and his uncle. He could barely afford it but he thought he could make it happen. A chance to get out of the tenements, he'd make it happen. And he could secure another one for me and Rosie, we could be neighbors in this new building. And then he said the very interesting part, which was that maybe when we moved in there, Rosie could watch over Al.

He said: She just needs someone to worry about is what it sounds like to me.

I could not argue with him on that matter.

He said: And Al, he just needs someone to look after him. I can't do it forever, Mazie. I need to have a life of my own. And you do, too.

I said: When can we move?

He said the building wouldn't be ready till next year. That they had to tear down all these filthy tenements there first, then build the new one. They're going to build fast though, he told me.

He said: Hold on, Mazie. Just hold on.

Elio Ferrante

Lung Block, yea, Lung Block. I don't teach it anymore. I taught it a few times, and honestly? It grosses the kids out. Breadlines, they get, they nod their heads. Lung Block, it's gross, it's terrifying, and it doesn't really educate them about anything new. They kind of already know about mold and bad air, and if they really want to learn about the specifics of mold, I'll trust their health or science instructors to educate them on the particular details. But, just to explain here, these apartments had maybe one or two tiny windows and no ventilation, and they were packed with people. And they got sick.

There were more than a few Lung Blocks in New York City. So many of the tenements were terrible for air quality, germs, mold, but this one particular block, down by the water—north of the South Street Seaport, like southeast of Chinatown—a good percentage of the tenants there got sick with respiratory illnesses. Tuberculosis for one, which is highly contagious, so once it started, they all fell down. There were just germs everywhere. And hundreds of families lived there; everyone crammed into these small spaces. On top of that there were bunch of bars and brothels. It was just a seedy, germy block. Hundreds of people died. This was in the late 1920s. And New York being New York, instead of fixing the buildings, they just decided to tear them down and start over. And that is how Knickerbocker Village came into being.

Lydia Wallach

I should have had two more great-uncles, but they died from tuberculosis. They lived in a bad building. It wasn't a bad building when they moved in, but it became one. By the time they figured out they should move somewhere else, it was too late. They were no longer in control of their destiny, or the destiny of their children. And so my mother's father grew up with tragedy, and then my mother grew up in the shadow of tragedy, and then I suppose I grew up in whatever shade was left behind. Rudy with his heart attacks, two dead great-uncles. These stories that people pass on. You feel them. They haunt you.

Pete Sorensen

A thing you and I talked about for a while is how she starts to disappear into these men. Like we felt like *we* lost her to them. Like she became so obsessed with them that the other parts of her started to disappear. Or maybe those parts were visible to someone else? But the diary totally changes. It's just about these men; that's all she cares about. And you were like, "I get it. I get the obsession." And I was like, "I get it, but I reject it. Because there's more to life than just that. You have to care about more than one thing."

Mazie's Diary, February 26, 1933

One more body in the late-night frost. I tried to rouse him but his skin turned my skin cold.

I thought: We're both the same color. We're both blue.

But then I realized he was bluer than I'll be in a long time.

Mazie's Diary, March 15, 1933

Called six ambulances this month and they're sick of my voice and my face and I don't care.

Mazie's Diary, June 1, 1933

Lately I've been noticing that the bums are waiting for me to get to work. Just a few of them, same fellas, sometimes a bigger group of them. Waiting for their morning handouts so they can get a little of this or that and move on through their day. What's it hurt? Tee'd tsk tsk me, but what did Tee know about fun?

All of it makes me feel needed. And that I can help them. I can't help Rosie, but I can help them.

Mazie's Diary, June 5, 1933

A guy named Wilson died and I didn't know him but all the fellas were reeling this morning. He'd been good to them. They said he'd looked out for them. Someone stabbed him in his sleep, and he'd been sleeping on an old mattress in an alley and the mattress was all red when they found him. I was shuddering when they told me this and I didn't even know it till Rudy came out and shooed them all way. Ghost white I was, that's what Rudy told me.

Mazie's Diary, June 13, 1933

A boy with blond hair in my line, sixteen, seventeen, everything about him ragged and worn, his clothes, some scars, a sad, dazed squint. Willowy and breakable. Too young to be in line with those other fellas, and I told him so. Too young to be that battered is what I thought. He deepened his voice, swore he'd been working on the trains for a few years already. I asked his name. Rufus. It couldn't be, I thought. Not the same. I asked if he had a mother named Nance. He told me it was the name of the woman who bore him but that he barely remembered her.

I said: Who raised you?

He said: A hundred kind people and a hundred mean people and no one in particular.

I couldn't stand to see his face in my line. He told me he'd been working on the rails here and there, but that he dreamed of working on an apple farm in New Jersey. It seemed safer than the rails, where it was nothing but drunks and trouble. He'd heard it was all sunshine and fresh air on the apple farm. I gave him a few big bills. I told him to go to New Jersey now, get a head start on apple-picking season.

I said: I don't want to see you around here again, you hear?

He promised he'd never come back. Who knows if he was telling the truth or not? It wouldn't be the first time I've been conned. Only I needed to know I tried.

Mazie's Diary, August 9, 1933

Here she goes with the smell again. Chinatown in the summertime, it isn't pretty I agree. I finally told her about George Flicker's building.

She said: That's a terrible block.

I said: I told you they're tearing down those buildings.

She said: It'll be as if we're living on a cemetery.

I said: It'll be as if we're living in a brand-new apartment building. Rosie, it's built from scratch. There will be a garden. It'll be the fanciest in the neighborhood. We could live high up in the air, look at the bridge from our window. Look at the water. No bad smells, no street noises.

She was staring at me across the table, maybe for the first

time understanding my desperation although I thought I'd been plenty desperate already.

I said: It's a chance at a fresh start.

I said: It's the best we can do.

I said: It's the best I can do.

Elio Ferrante

I dated a girl who lived in Knickerbocker Village once. This Chinese girl I went out with junior year at Hunter. Her name was Ella, which was not her real name but just what she wanted to be called. It's weird but I don't even know what her real name was, or maybe I did once and I can't remember anymore. It's not important, I know, my ex-girlfriends.

Anyway there's lots of Chinese there. Chinese and Italians. The families get in there, and then they bring all their extended family members in, or sometimes the kids grow up and get their own apartment. People move in and just stay. It's not totally impossible to get in the building otherwise, but it's hard. The wait list is long. It's like Stuy Town, only smaller, and with way more soul.

Ella took me on a tour of it once after a big night out on the town so yes that's code for we were wasted. [Laughs.] There were two courts, an east court and a west court, and the buildings looked over these big courtyards. I don't remember much more about it physically. The things I do remember have to do with the history. Of course. Like the Rosenbergs lived there before they were executed and there were all kinds of Mafia connections and of course the whole Lung Block thing. That's the information my brain traps. You know what I mean; you get it. You've got a one-track mind, too.

I slept over that night actually. It was pretty dumb of me, her mother was in the next room. I snuck out early in the morning so I can barely tell you what the place looked like. But I could hear birds chirping in the courtyard from her window and I thought when I woke up, before I remembered where I was, that maybe I was in the country somewhere. It was quiet, it was early, and there were birds. And the ceilings were high. I don't know why I remember that. Oh, and when I walked out the front gate I smelled bread. I followed the scent to an Italian bakery across the street. I bought a loaf of bread and ate hunks of it while I walked to City Hall to catch a train to Brooklyn. Ha! That was a night. Her mother found out and wouldn't let her see me anymore. Maybe there was another guy involved, a long-term boyfriend. She thought I was a bad influence on her daughter. Me, can you imagine?

Pete Sorensen

We walked by there, you and me, last summer, do you remember? We went to Chinatown for dumplings. You had just cut off all your hair and you asked me a hundred times if it looked good and I told you that you'd look good without any hair at all and then we were standing in front of it, looking inside the garden, and you wondered if we could just walk in... and you tried but the security guard stopped you. "Just a peek," you said. And he said, "No peeking." And you tried all your wiles on him and it didn't work and then when we left I tried to make you feel better about it all and you said, "If I hadn't cut my hair he would have let me in." I told you you were so beautiful and you didn't hear a word I said. Why do you never hear a word I say?

Mazie's Diary, September 29, 1933

This morning's crew came, scuffling feet, filthy overcoats. Then the lineup, hands out, wishing me a good morning. I was busy thinking about the move, hoping Rosie can hold out a little longer, so I wasn't even looking in their faces, in their eyes. Here's a dime for you, a nickel for you. Told them to get a move on, and I got in my cage. Then one more man said my name while I was pulling out the tickets and the cash box.

I said: Hold on, hold on, buddy.

He said: Mazie, it's me.

I looked up and up and up because there was the tallest man I'd known in my life, Ethan Fallow.

I was confused for a second, thought he was looking for a handout like the rest of them.

I said: Not you, too!

He said: Not me, too, what?

I eyed him. His overcoat was clean, not a tear, not a tatter. He smelled like fresh soap and his hair was still damp and slickly parted to the side.

I said: You're not looking for some change?

He thought that was funny.

He said: Change I got plenty of. I just came to talk to you about Jeanie.

I said: What about her?

He said: I'm worried about her.

I didn't know he was talking to her. As far as I knew I was the only one from New York City she still kept in touch with. I asked him why he was worried and he gave me this long story, the short of it being that he's been giving her money for a few years to help her out, which I found awful funny because I've been doing the exact same thing.

Anyhow he said she sounded sad lately, sad and lonely, and he wondered if he should try to get her a train ticket home, and if he did would I be willing to take her in? I told him she was my sister and I loved her and she'd always have a home with me but if he was going to go to the trouble of bringing her home he might as well just keep her for himself.

Mazie's Diary, November 1, 1933

Well I'm over twenty-one, that much I know.

Mazie's Diary, November 13, 1933

Today a truck pulled up in front of the Venice, just before the sunset. The driver left the car running and dashed over to my cage with a big sack of something. He dumped it on my counter.

I said: What's this?

He said: A fella named Rufus sent it to you. He said to say thanks.

I peeked into the sack. Green apples.

Bums came out of nowhere all of a sudden, like they could smell the fresh air and sunshine on it. I handed them out, one by one, and then saved the last for myself.

Mazie's Diary, December 5, 1933

Prohibition's over, and this city's yawning. We've been making our own rules for years. Someone announced it at Finny's and there were a few cheers and one fella applauded until he realized he was the only one clapping.

Somebody said: I liked being illegal. It helped pass the time.

George Flicker

So the time came for us to move and I set everything up, and I was pretty chuffed about the whole thing, that I had maneuvered us in there. We were living on the twelfth floor, East Court. They had a two-bedroom corner apartment, Al and I had a one-bedroom next door. We both had great views of the bridge. I think there was a little talk at the last minute about trying to get a three-bedroom. Jeanie was supposed to come home. They didn't really want her there though. Well Mazie did but Rosie didn't. Or maybe Rosie did but Mazie didn't. There was tension around her. I told them I didn't think I could get them a three-bedroom and they backed down. Oh you know what? It was Rosie after all. Rosie was the angry one. Because now I remember her saying, "She'll have to crawl back on her knees, she should know something about that."

Mazie's Diary, January 10, 1934

Jeanie's back. She took a train from Chicago, no chauffeur this time around. We had coffee at the diner. Her hair's down to her waist, and her eyes still glitter, and she's still slender, all tree boughs bending in the wind. But her skin is off. It's dull and yellow, porridge that's been sitting out for too long. She's not the same girl she was, but still she'll always be beautiful to me. I told her if she didn't feel like staying with Ethan she didn't have to. He wanted to throw all that money at her for all that time, it was his problem, not hers. I said the minute she wanted out I'd find her somewhere to go.

She said: I don't mind one bit. He's been better to me than any of the rest of them.

I said: I don't know any of the rest of them.

She said: And trust me you don't want to.

I laughed. It was a joke I would make.

I said: Are you truly done now?

She said: I believe so. I can't think of anything else I feel like I have to do. This might be the problem though. I can't think of anything I even want to do.

I said: You haven't sat still yet. You oughtta try that on for size.

I told her she could come and work for me whenever she liked. I told her not to worry, she'd find a way to survive on her own. And I would help her.

George Flicker

So we move in to the Knickerbocker Village in 1934. We didn't have much, me and Al. We had our beds, some clothes, all of Uncle Al's books. Those ladies showed up with an army of Russian movers carrying steamer trunks of clothes, boxes and boxes of tchotchkes, beds, lamps, desks, bookshelves, rugs, and paintings. And there's Rosie barking at all of them, move this here, move that there. Al and I are standing there watching all this. He probably hadn't seen her in five years, ten, I don't know how long. I mean maybe he had but he wasn't acting like it. He's watching her boss all these people around and then he just lets out this whistle. Not a wolf whistle but something like it. You could not have mistaken that sound for something innocent. I said, "Al, calm yourself down, man, these are our new neighbors." He said, "I must have done something right to deserve this." I said, "Al, it's Rosie Gordon! You remember her. She used to live upstairs. What are you doing here? You can't hassle this lady." He said, "How did I miss that? How did I ever miss this woman before."

Mazie's Diary, March 1, 1934

I dug you out of this box just to write this down so that I never forget this moment. I came home last night to find Rosie sitting on Al Flicker's lap at our kitchen table.

I said: Well.

She said: Well.

I said: What have we here?

She said: Mazie, you remember Al Flicker, don't you?

I am cackling as I write this. Cackling at how dainty and ladylike she acted all the while she was sitting on his lap, her bottom on who knows what although I know what. And I am cackling at the two loons who are now singing little songs to each other in the next room. Every once in a while they clink glasses and toast each other and I just start laughing all over again. I am cackling at life. You're funny, life. Real funny.

George Flicker

And then the thing we could never have predicted in a million years happened almost immediately after we moved in. Rosie and Al fell in love. Can you believe it? The two craziest people we knew fell for each other. Like someone knocked them over the head with it. Like someone knocked them over the head with love.

9

EXCERPT FROM THE UNPUBLISHED AUTOBIOGRAPHY OF
MAZIE PHILLIPS-GORDON

What kills me about these bums is that they die, they're gone, and it's like they never even existed on God's green earth. Someone knew them once. A mother, a father, a doctor, a pal, somebody knew their name. But now they're only known by each other, and then bit by bit, they're forgotten. Quicker than they'd like, probably. And everybody wants to be remembered, don't they? Everybody wants one little piece of them to be left behind. Well, I remember them. I remember them all. They were nobody to nearly everybody, but they were somebody to me. I knew all their names. Everyone's names. I knew them.

Phillip Tekverk, publisher emeritus, Tekverk Books

I was twenty-one years old, and an editorial assistant at Knopf. It was 1939. I had heard about Mazie Phillips from a few sources, but Fannie Hurst was the first. I had been invited to a dinner party at her house by an older gentleman who I believe was endeavoring to make me one of his fancy lads, though he wasn't quite sure if I would be amenable to that sort of thing. People have always wondered about my sexual proclivities, and I had just approached the moment where I recognized that the mystery surrounding that area of my life could be of benefit to me. That, in fact, I could and should cultivate that mystery even further. And it has certainly helped me in my life. There is power in elusiveness. Even just to be charming is, of course, great assistance to one. But to leave people guessing about you, that adds a whole new layer of memorability.

Fannie Hurst was charming also, professionally so. I felt like I could sit at her elbow for hours, days, weeks, and never tire of her. She was quite famous then, for her books, which were wildly popular, bestsellers always, though obviously quite mainstream, and not particularly literary. She was also famous for having famous friends. The Roosevelts, for example, adored her. I never met them, but we all knew. Anyway, she was extremely well known, even though barely anyone has heard of her these days. Her name pops up and then disappears again. If only the writing had been better.

But she was a delight! Dry as the day, funny, funny, funny. She was an activist, albeit sometimes a misguided one. For example she was supportive of the African-American literary community even if her books weren't viewed as such necessarily, and she liked to slum downtown on occasion. She was fascinated with the lower class. Also the young. People of color, poor people, young people, anyone who didn't have what she had, or had something she didn't. The only people she didn't really care that much for were the Jews—because of course she was a Jew herself.

So at dinner that night, I was a target for her because I was young and pretty and, as I said, indeterminate. Also I was rather handsome. I had inherited my mother's looks—she was a fabulous, glamorous, well-crafted woman—and by then Fannie was on the southward slope of middle age and, to be honest, she had never been known for her great beauty. So there, I had something else she didn't have, too. And I was certainly eager to please her. So she invited me to sit next to her at the table, even going so far as to switch cards at the last moment, sending an editor from Harper's to the other end of the table. What did she care? She was Fannie Hurst.

It was a very long table. And you know, there were chandeliers dripping from the ceiling, a dozen uniformed maids dishing out the food, endless bottles of wine. Another young man might have felt intimidated, but I came from money, early Dutch settlers on my father's side, and then my mother was a Spanish heiress. So I felt right at ease there. I had a trust fund that would secure me for many years. I had been waiting to meet these people for a while. I came from California and had only a few introductions. We were rich but my father marrying the Spaniard had turned him into a bit of an outcast in the family. My mother had wanted to be an actress, that's how we had ended up in Hollywood. Oh, you don't need to know all of this. It's going in my memoirs right now, anyway. You can't have it, it's mine. What you do need to know is that many of the other assistants in publishing were struggling, and I had felt like I had to hide where I came from. And that night I had this sense that at last I was where I belonged.

Over dessert, everyone was arguing about the politics. At the time Fiorello LaGuardia was mayor, and it was his second round at bat. And he was a pretty good mayor, he had installed a lot of good programs, but we were still mocking him for some reason. He was very short. It might have even just been his height. God, who knows. We were very drunk. And Fannie was amused by all of our jokes. but then she very suddenly stopped herself and said, "You cynical bastards. For once I'd like to hear people talk about a New Yorker doing something right instead of wrong." She was right of course. We were a very cynical lot.

So then we started talking about whom we would have liked to see run for mayor instead. When it was time for LaGuardia to go, who would be next? And then it very quickly turned into this kind of parlor game, everyone having to go around the table and nominate who'd they vote for. So there were professional athletes named, and a religious figure or two, and I believe Dorothy Day was in there, and Dorothy Parker too and I think Fannie was hoping someone would nominate her but no one did. And then when it was Fannie's turn she said, "Mazie Gordon." Of course we all said, "Who?" She really treasured it, being able to stump everyone. You know, took a significant sip of wine from her glass, licked her lips, that sort of thing. And then she spilled.

Mazie's Diary, May 12, 1934

I saw Ben again at our regular spot, this all-night no-name diner by the Brooklyn Bridge. He asked about me helping the bums again. I don't know why he's so interested.

He said: I could never do it.

I said: Helping people's the easy part. It's the rest of life that's hard.

George Flicker

About six months after we moved in to Knickerbocker Village I met this nice woman named Alice. She was a nurse at the time, and I had a small accident at a construction site, a brick falling on my hand, and I ended up in the hospital. There, you can still see it, the scar, right there. Alice tended to me with great care. She was from Vermont and had served in the first war and landed in New York City after. She was a very brave and bold woman. We talked about our service and I cracked a joke about people forgetting all the work we did for our country but I wasn't really kidding, of course. And she said, "Forget about what you did already, what have you done lately?" And it was this real kick in the pants that I needed.

I've always been a hard worker, but she was right, I needed to stop worrying about the past. Maybe I needed to let it go. Then she told me that she was applying to medical school, she was going to be a doctor. She had her heart set on University of Michigan because they were the first in the country to accept women to their medical school. She had been watching the doctors for years now and she felt that she could do what they did, though she wasn't so sure they could do what she did. And at the end of this I realized she had cleaned and bandaged my hand and I hadn't even noticed. She had a magic touch, that Alice. So I said, "But if you go away to Michigan how will I ever see you again?" And she said, "You'll just have to wait for me to come back." Well, I married that girl six months later. I wasn't taking no chances on anyone else snapping her up.

Mazie's Diary, June 1, 1934

Maybe I had a little roll in the hay with George Flicker last night. Maybe it was all right. Maybe I didn't mind it one bit.

George Flicker

Are you married? I don't see a ring on that finger. What are you waiting for? Are you in love? I know, I know, I'm a nudge. Only I loved being in love so much, I only wish the same for the good people I meet.

Mazie's Diary, July 12, 1934

It was the strangest thing, seeing George tonight, late, after I got home from the streets. He'd waited up for me. I closed my front door and I heard him knocking a minute later. His face seemed more familiar than it ever had before, even though I've known him all my life. All of a sudden he was glowing like there was a spotlight on him. He looked so handsome. Every part of his face seemed perfect. I don't even know where it came from, I never expect to feel anything for any man anymore, at least not in that way. All I knew was I saw a good man next to me in bed.

Phillip Tekverk

Fannie said, "I know a woman of greater compassion than any I have known before." Someone shouted, "Does that include you?" She said, "I'm not compassionate, I've just got a lot of guilt." Everyone laughed, and she continued. "I know a woman who works long hours in a tiny cage all day long, dealing with the public, which is something none of you could do, you ill-tempered, pampered artists. Then, after fourteen hours in this box, she walks the streets of the Lower East Side helping the homeless and suffering wherever she goes. No matter how filthy or drunk or evil-smelling a bum may be, she treats him as an equal. Just an average woman doing something quite extraordinary. What have you done for humanity lately? Agonize over the placement of a semicolon? This woman gets off her derriere and actually does something important with her life. Mazie Phillips for mayor, I say." There was probably more to this speech, but this is what I can recall, drunk as I was, old as

I am. Everyone hear-hear'ed and cheered, and then moved on to the next subject. I had an idea, though. I told Fannie I wanted to meet her. I said it sounded like she would make a great book, and I wasn't lying to her when I said that. But also I wanted to get in Fannie's good graces because I wanted to go to every single dinner party she threw for eternity.

George Flicker

We had a mind to take over the world, Alice and me. She was going to help provide better medical care to women in New York City. She had seen so many immigrants on the Lower East Side show up at her hospital, in her emergency room, with all kinds of diseases that could have been tended to much sooner, if they had spoken English, if they'd had someone to look out for them. A clinic for women; that was her aim. My plan was to own every building on the Lower East Side and to make them livable. Don't get me wrong, I knew that was impossible. If I could even own one in my lifetime I was going to be one lucky fellow. But if I could just have one to start with I promised myself I'd be the best landlord this city had ever seen. Which I assure you most landlords out there, that is not their mission. So I married my girl and off she went to medical school and we saw each other when we could. We worked very hard for a long time to achieve our dreams. She was my best friend. She was beautiful and brilliant. Her mind and my mind together, we were the tops.

Mazie's Diary, October 15, 1934

It's all over with George but he won't tell me why. He's never home when he used to be home. I'm not going to track him down. I've got better things to do with my time, places to go, people to see.

Fine, he doesn't want me anymore. I won't chase after a man.

Mazie's Diary, November 1, 1934

Closer to forty than thirty. What happens when I get to the other side? Do I tip over?

Mazie's Diary, November 15, 1934

Cold snap. I bought twenty warm wool blankets and handed them out to whoever needed them on the streets. It was pitch dark, only a handful of stars in the sky. Jeanie came with me to help. She brought with her a floppy, coffee-colored hat, a silky red ribbon gathered at the side of it in an enormous bow. It was a real party, this hat. She told me she hadn't brought much home with her from out west, but somehow it had made the trip. She had no occasion to wear it anymore, though. She couldn't bear to look at it any longer, but she couldn't throw it away either. I put it on, and the sides of it collapsed gently around my face and neck. Musk, smoke, California.

Jeanie said: You look very fetching.

She was wearing her hair in braids like she used to when she was a teenager. Her skin looked better, it glowed like the moon again. She rambled on about her life, how everything was fine, great, better than ever, and I was nodding and believing her. She asked me if I was listening and I snapped to it. She's helping Ethan out with the horses, and by the end of the day, she smells like dung.

She said: But so does he, so that makes two of us, smelling like shit.

I asked her if she missed dancing and she told me she doesn't even remember who she was before, and it's easier that way. I got distracted for a second, trying to remember what the moon used to mean to me. Now it's just another light to guide me while I look after these fellas.

Mazie's Diary, November 18, 1934

George told me he's in love with a woman named Alice. A good woman. She'll be a doctor someday.

I said: You find love, you take it.

Phillip Tekverk

In the spring of 1939 I met Fannie Hurst across the street from the Venice Theater, at a place called the King Kong Bar & Grill, the name of it being the most significant thing about the establishment. The bartender seemed to know Fannie. I asked if she were a regular patron. She said she stopped in from time to time when she was downtown. She said, "I like to have a quick one by myself sometimes. They don't seem to mind what you do down here. In my neighborhood they whisper a bit more. I wouldn't call it whispering so much as talking loudly to anyone who might listen. It's not very polite. Not that I can complain, I'm a gossip like the rest of them, like all writers, like all people with too much time on their hands. And I don't mind anyway. You get to a certain age, let them whisper, let them talk, let them scream. Fannie Hurst likes to hang out downtown in bars by herself. Doesn't everyone wish they could do that?"

I said that I could and did all the time, and she said, "But you're a man." And even though she was nearly thirty years older than I was, and an affluent, successful woman, she recognized a gap between our privilege. "Sometimes a girl likes to have a quiet drink away from it all. Read into it however you like." I noticed then she was drinking whiskey, straight. It was one in the afternoon. "Mazie understands," she said. "She's a solo artist. A diva. And she's a warrior queen. Did you know they call her the Queen of the Bowery? I'll never be the queen of anything."

"I've been to one of your dinner parties," I said. "You're a queen, don't worry."

Mazie had just had her appendix out and was no longer drinking hard alcohol, so we purchased her some beer, which at the time you could take away in a cardboard container. Together we crossed the street to this run-down theater Mazie called home. A group of bums shifted around in front of the theater. Before we approached the cage Fannie said to me, "Prepare for greatness."

George Flicker

I'll fill you in on the good stuff, if you care to know it. The good stuff of my life. I married Alice, as I said, and she became a doctor, an obstetrician. She worked at Presbyterian for a long time, decades, but also she volunteered at a clinic downtown one day a week, working with immigrant women. She did that until we had our son, Mel, named after my father, and once he was old enough she went back to volunteer work again, and there's a fund set up there now in her name because she was so instrumental in developing its growth. So I couldn't be any prouder of my wife, Alice. She was a personal hero of mine.

Mel went on to have three children, Max, Miranda, and David, and they each have had two children and they are all gorgeous, just gorgeous. It is never a dull moment at the holidays, I'll tell you that much. I went on to own not one, not two, not three, but five apartment buildings on the Lower East Side. I know, can you believe it? I wouldn't believe it myself only I know what kind of work I put into it.

One of the buildings I bought was actually the tenement I grew up in, all crammed into that tiny apartment with my family. It was the fourth building I bought. I had to wait that long for it to be up for sale. I had my eye on it forever. I probably had my eye on it when I was five years old and didn't even know what that meant yet.

And what I did when I bought it is, I tore everything out. I gutted the place, and I made each floor its own apartment, except for the top two floors, which were joined together in one duplex, which is where Alice and I lived for many years. Each apartment is full of light and space and air. All the things we're entitled to, or should be anyway.

Oh, it's tremendous, you should see it. Call my grandson, sweetheart, and have him invite you over. Tell him I sent you. The skylight in the bedroom is something else. When we finished construction and finally moved in, Alice and I would just sit in bed for hours staring up at the sky. We'd go to bed a few hours early and just lay there looking at the moon and the stars, holding hands and talking. She passed in that bed exactly that way. I was next to her. My beautiful Alice, my gorgeous girl. She was blind by then so I told her what I was seeing. There were clouds that day. Winter clouds. It was January. I said, "Alice, the sun is out barely, and the clouds are gray and blue and they've got a kind of outline around them and there's a bit of white from the sun and it looks like it's going to be a cold, cold day." And then she let go of my hand and was gone.

Phillip Tekverk

People have different definitions of greatness. Was she wry and funny? Yes. Charismatic certainly. Beauty—and I won't apologize for this—is part of my definition of greatness, and she wasn't beautiful anymore, although I suspected she had been. Her hair was straw yellow, bleached for too many years. And she wore this green celluloid shade, which looked ridiculous. I suppose it was to block the sun, but it wasn't flattering in the slightest. Her face seemed sort of hazy around the edges, as if her chin were on the verge of melting into her neck. She was well put together otherwise though. Although she was hunched over, she had a wonderful bosom, which she showed off perfectly, and I come from a family of women obsessed with their personal lighting. And she was direct and sharp and I liked her, and I had been told to admire her and so I did.

It all happened very quickly. Fannie gave her the beer, and they greeted each other like they were sisters; it was all very familiar and loving. Then Fannie said, "You must meet this young upstart in the publishing world." And I said my name and introduced myself and then I lit a cigarette and gave it to Mazie. She eyed me, and I got the sense she trusted absolutely no one on first impression. Yet I could tell it was very clearly a positive appraisal. Perhaps she was flirting with me, I don't know. She was a little long in the tooth for me, but if it hadn't stopped any of the older gentlemen who took me out for drives in the country, why should it stop her? Then it seemed like she caught herself. I wish I could remember more of our conversation. I was quite captivated by her looks even as I rejected them. She was not beautiful but she was a presence. I suppose that could have made her great in someone's book.

Anyway I razzle-dazzled her with the idea that she should write the story of her life and she seemed uninterested at first, but I assured her that she—and I stole this phrase instantly from Fannie, of course—she, as the Queen of the Bowery, should tell her story to her subjects. I don't know if that appealed to her ego but it had a hook to it. She still was uncertain, but I felt that I had gotten under her skin, so I resolved to pursue it.

George Flicker

Rosie and Al lived for a long time in Knickerbocker Village together, though they never married, which would have been scandalous if we'd had anyone left in our lives to care. Their apartment became a haven for all the intellectuals and bohemians that eventually moved into the building. The police came more than a few times to ask him questions about his radical politics, which, as it turns out, he still was very much active in. I guess it's possible he resumed his activities once he settled down with Rosie. Perhaps the building triggered his renewed interest, being around all those thinkers. The Rosenbergs were have said to have dined at their table more than a few times. The police never arrested him or roughed him up though. Those days were done, thank god. He was a frail man now, and Rosie looked after him. Tiger Lady's what we used to call her.

Mazie had long since moved out. I didn't see her very often. Al told me she had an aunt in Boston she'd grown close with and she visited her once a year. I thought that was good for her. Her sisters had never been so reliable. She was a churchgoer too. Al told me she went to workingman's mass every Sunday, late at night, or maybe it was early in the morning. While Al didn't necessarily approve of God, he did approve of the workingman so I remember him telling me that as a point of admiration.

I waved at her sometimes at the theater. But she always seemed busy, and whatever had existed between us once, it was like none of it had happened. I missed her but I guess I didn't have the right to say that or much of anything to her. It was true that there was a crossover in time between her and Alice. I didn't tell you that right away because my wife is the one I think of from that time in my life. Mazie wasn't the girl I was going to marry. Alice was. And some secrets are better left hidden. We don't need to know everything about everyone. I have to admit I'm a little tired now of you digging up the secrets. Just today, just now. I'm tired.

Vera Sung, former resident, Knickerbocker Village

I did not speak English yet, or only a little bit I did, but not very well. I felt very lonely even though the apartment was crowded. We were happy to be there though, because the Knickerbocker was a special place, well kept and beautiful. And we had many family members in the building, too, so there was always someone to feed us or look after us, which was helpful for my mother after the divorce. But in my apartment there was my mother and four brothers. So, the only girl, even harder.

I was silent for a long time, but I was also a daydreamer and an adventurer. I could climb like a little monkey and I could fit through windows that no one else could. There were many passageways to explore there. There is a basement that connects all the buildings, for example, and side entrances and exits where you can escape undetected. All of this was very helpful later when I began to skip school, and then after that when I started hanging out in the East Village with those bad boys in the leather motorcycle jackets and the tight jeans. Those are good stories. I can tell you those too.

But when I was little I had nowhere in particular I wanted to go but the garden. I liked to listen to all the birds chirping. I would pretend I was Snow White. In my daydreams my brothers were my dwarves. I would hold my hands out and wait for the birds to come land on my shoulders and arms and fingers but they never did. In the early mornings, before anyone in the apartment woke up, that's what I would do, I would sneak out to the garden and daydream, sing along with the birds.

This is where I found this couple, the older Jewish couple. I had never met them before, but later I learned their names were Rosie and Al. They were sitting next to each other on one of the benches, hidden behind a row of high hedges. It was September, but they were wearing their winter coats because they were old, and old people get cold sometimes. She was snoring loudly, so loudly that I could hear her over the birds. That's why I had gone over there, to investigate the noise. He was not snoring at all. He had a long gray beard and fisherman's cap, and he was blue in the face. I had never seen a dead person before but I knew right away that's what he was.

Suddenly I realized the birds had stopped chirping. I shook the woman awake. I said, "Miss, wake up, wake up." It was the most I had spoken all year. I was four or five. She finally woke up and I pointed to him and said, "He is sick." Which was a lie but I could not bring myself to say the real truth. She shrieked, and I ran off, back to my apartment. I heard an ambulance soon, and I watched it all through my window. I told my mother nothing.

Two days later I snuck out of my window again, back down to the garden, and I found the woman, Rosie, on the bench. And now it was her time to be dead, and this was when I began to cry. Once stunned me. Twice wounded me. Now there was no way to hide this information from my mother. Someone had to call the police, and it was she who made that call. She hugged me, and she made all my brothers hug me, one by one. After that morning I talked all the time.

Mazie's Diary, December 1, 1934

I'm late, I'm pregnant, all of it, all that could happen, it's true. It's George's and no one else's.

Mazie's Diary, December 3, 1934

Could I keep it and never tell him is what I'm thinking today. I could move away and he might never know. I never wanted one though. Why would I now?

Mazie's Diary, December 4, 1934

What if the mattress turns red again? None of us have ever been able to have a baby. All the Phillips girls, our bellies are made of shit.

Mazie's Diary, December 5, 1934

He loves this Alice. I saw them today together. Across the street from the theater, her in her nurse's uniform, him in his best suit, her carrying flowers, him with his arm around her, her talking, him nodding. The two of them acting like real people in love. Not like we were. We were just horizontal is all.

Mazie's Diary, December 6, 1934

I came in last night late, and he was there, too. In the hallway. And now my heart swells for him a little bit more because I can't have him. His hand was on his door handle and mine was on mine and I thought for a moment I'd tell him the truth, and I know he'd care because he's an all right fella but what good would it do? It wouldn't change a thing. It wouldn't change my mind. It might change his, but not for the right reasons. I don't need to tell him and he doesn't need to know.

So we both stood there with our backs to each other and there was all this silence between us and then we both wished each other good night. No glance over the shoulder. Just the best of wishes for a gentle sleep.

Mazie's Diary, December 7, 1934

Ben was in town on business again. Him with all his meetings, and his high-class suit and now he's gone gray, too. He looks the same though, just more prestigious. Me, I'm looking older. He gets to look important.

He took me out for a honey bun and a coffee after work. I didn't mean to tell him I was pregnant. Especially him. But it came out anyway.

I said: The world is all bitched up. Always was, always will be.

He said: Do you really believe that?

I said: No, I guess I don't.

Ben told me he thought I'd be a great mother, but that I should know children were hard, much harder than he'd imagined. He didn't know why they didn't just listen. Why couldn't they just be quiet when they were told?

He asked what I was going to do and I said I didn't know but I think I do. What do I need a baby for when I got all those men out there needing me?

He gave me a wonderful hug when he left me. He told me no matter what, he'd always respect me and love me.

I think he might be the best friend I have in the world. Who would have thought? The Captain and me, buddies.

Benjamin Hazzard, Jr.

He talked about her ceaselessly, his famous friend Mazie in the city. She was so special to him there was just absolutely no way he wasn't sleeping with her. It's just the way men and women work. I could talk for hours about it but who would want to listen?

You know, I held her no more and no less against him than any of his other girls. She was just the one I thought about because I knew her name. Mazie. You don't forget a name like Mazie.

Mazie's Diary, February 1, 1935

Moving day tomorrow. You'll be packed up again. This table I've sat at so many times with you will be gone, somewhere, in someone else's home. The Salvation Army is coming to take it away in the morning.

Rosie said: I don't want it.

I said: Me neither. What am I going to do with a table like that?

Rosie said: It's just that Al likes the table he has already, and things need to be just so with him. He's so finicky.

I said: You met your match then.

Rosie said: But it's a fine table.

She rapped it with her knuckles.

Rosie said: Are you sure you don't want it?

I said: It's like I'm sitting down to dine with ghosts at that table.

Rosie said: I never minded the ghosts.

I said: I know.

Rosie said: They keep you company.

I said: All I want to do is forget them.

George Flicker

I didn't know about that part. No. That part I didn't know. She never told me. Oh, I'm sorry. Oh, that poor darling. [Puts head in hands for a moment, inhales.] Are we done here? Can we be done now? I'm tired. I'm just an old man now. I've only got so much energy in the day. You're a gorgeous girl. Very convincing. But I'm done now.

Pete Sorensen

And then she was gone for five years. No diary updates, nothing. How dare she, I know. Five years, no Mazie. Five years of using our imagination. Five years of filling in the blanks.

Elio Ferrante

What happened in those five years? You can't stop New York City from changing, don't even try it. And there were global events, obviously. A war was coming. I will spare you the lecture. You're a smart lady. You know your history.

Phillip Tekverk

I'm sorry I've been difficult to reach. I've been out of the country. I had to present a speech in Paris. I gave you all the files I had on her, I thought somehow that would be enough. But apparently it isn't.

Mazie and I met for coffee a few times. We talked about what she would have to do to write a book. I asked her what books she liked and she said she only read magazines, *True Confessions* and *True Romance* and the like. She said, "I can't

believe people would be willing to spill their beans like that."
She did not seem to fully grasp that she would have to spill her
own beans if she were to write an autobiography. This concerned me. I said, "You know you'll be telling your life story,
right? Just like all those people do." She got huffy. She said,
"I'm not like those people. I'm a lady."

I couldn't quite figure out how to handle the situation. I
thought maybe I was in over my head, but at the same time I
was young and headstrong and extremely entitled. I was there
because a smart woman had told me I should be interested,
but at the time I was too foolish to understand why. Mazie
was, to me, a common person, and I believed I should be able
to manage common people. So I told her she would need to
outline what she wanted to say. That if she had an outline I
could go to my boss and show it to him and maybe he would
let me buy this book. And if she needed help we could probably hire someone who would work with her. But the first
thing she needed to do was figure out what she wanted to talk
about. Or rather what story she had to tell.

Lydia Wallach

I just wanted you to know that I unpacked the boxes finally,
and I'm sorry to report there wasn't a picture of her in there.
I did find a picture of a plaque that Mazie had made when my
great-grandfather died. She had put it on the back of the aisle
seat in the last row, where he loved to sneak in and sit at the
end of the last show every night. When they shut down the
movie theater one of my great-uncles managed to remove it
from the theater. It said, "Here sat Rudy Wallach. He was a
good man. Now look up and watch the movie."

Mazie's Diary, March 13, 1939

I don't like reading you. There's good things that happened to me in my life but more sad things it seems. Better just to save some of this thinking for my prayers, that's what I believe, that's how I act. Still, I know some things. I know about these men. I should write about these men. So they won't be forgotten.

Mazie's Diary, March 15, 1939

Last night I walked to the footwalk of the Manhattan Bridge and watched the bums standing by the fires in the old oil drums there. I had myself an illicit cigarette. One of the bums called my name, no one I recognized but that doesn't mean a thing. I'd know him eventually. I know all of them eventually. I slipped him a dime and a bar of soap, pleaded with him to use it.

I stayed there in front of the fires with him for a good while, bathed myself in the smoke. He told me his sob story. Once he was rich, now he's poor. That's a good one. It's very popular. I don't know why I didn't bid him good night. I just kept nodding and listening like he was the most fascinating man. I thought something interesting might happen, like he might become a different man than he already was. But I know that the story always ends the same way. With them on the streets.

Then I realized what I was waiting for. I wanted Tee to show up and walk with me, whisper in my ear, tell me which man was injured and needed my help and which one to let alone, he's sleeping, just needs to rest for the night. I've felt that way before. Not most nights, not anymore anyway. But looking back at you made me remember her, how she walked right next to me on the streets of the Lower East Side. In this city we fight for our space, but Tee was never afraid to be up close.

When he got to the part where he'd managed to lose it all through no fault of his own, I pressed another nickel in his hand and left him. He blessed me, and I blessed him. Our frail blessings. Then I walked up the Bowery, heading toward home. I was with her and without her at the same time. I emptied my pockets of everything they had in them. I didn't want one cent left at the end of the night.

Excerpt from the unpublished autobiography
of Mazie Phillips-Gordon

I'll admit sometimes it's peaceful to watch a man passed out on the street, snoring, curled up, that last lick of whiskey still on their lips. It's hard to tell if they're passed out from pleasure or pain, but my prayers for them always are that it's boozed-up bliss. I never want to wake them up when they're like that. It wouldn't be fair. They spent all night getting there.

Phillip Tekverk

I suppose I was careless with her.

Excerpt from the unpublished autobiography
of Mazie Phillips-Gordon

Flophouses are just that, a place you go to flop face-first. There's only a bit more comfort in sleeping there than on the streets.

They've got bugs and mold, and sheets like paper and mattresses that suck you in like a dirty old hole in the ground. But they've got showers, if you're the kind who cares about showering, and they're warmer than the streets in the winter. And sometimes a warm bed is all it takes to make a man feel like he's champion of the world.

Lydia Wallach

And I wanted to tell you that I was glad that I finally unpacked all of those boxes. A lot of it was garbage, and I just threw it away, but some of it was useful, and even triggered a nice memory or two. So it was good that you asked me these questions, it was good that you wanted me to look. I just wanted to say thanks for that.

Pete Sorensen

Do you remember that day we went down to the Navy Yard? And I pointed to that gap between the fence and the sidewalk? I said that was the exact spot I found the diary but I lied. I couldn't remember where. I just thought you'd feel better thinking you knew it. I didn't feel like there was any harm in lying. But now I want you to know: I lied.

And then we played that game where we tried to figure out how that box got there. Like how does something from the 1930s in Manhattan end up on the Brooklyn waterfront in 1999? My best guess was someone was cleaning out her apartment after she died and it ended up stuck in the trunk of a car for a good long while until the car was impounded by the city. But of course we ended up talking about diary thieves and stolen cars and carrier pigeons for a while. You know, you're just really incredibly good at coming up with elaborate scenarios, Nadine. I never met anyone who knew how to complicate things like you do.

Phillip Tekverk

Ultimately what she delivered to me was unusable. First of all, it was handwritten. I mean, you saw it. I realize it's a copy but I think you get the gist of it. She had been a drinker for many, many years, and I'm presuming she had the shakes. I hadn't noticed it whenever she and I met, but that's really the only explanation for the appearance of it. The papers even smelled as if it had been written in a bar. What little I could translate was entirely useless. She just went on and on about these men, how to care for them, their struggles, their essence. What would I have done with that? I wanted to publish cutting little novels about humanity that people would brag about having read to their friends at dinner, downtown, on a Saturday night. Not a treatise on the care and feeding of the homeless. I kept it though, like I kept every piece of paper that passed across my desk. It felt like something, an artifact.

Pete Sorensen

You let me hold your hand that day and then I put my arm around you and you put your hand around my waist. We kept finding new ways to wrap ourselves around each other. Then we walked down the waterfront to Williamsburg and sat at a dive bar outside on the patio and drank beer and watched the boats. It was a sunny and cool spring day, and it felt like we were a million miles from home, and I thought, "She's my girl. This is my girl."

Phillip Tekverk

And I was cold to her. I was too cold. I regret that now. I didn't even do her the courtesy of coming to meet her in person. I called her at her cage and said I wouldn't be able to work with her. I said, "No one is interested in this story." A different kind of a person would have known what to do with it. I was not that person. I am not that person. It is important to know your strengths and weaknesses and work with them and around them. I was too young to realize it then, but by now I see it, and it's this: I have very little imagination. I think she knew that, because before she hung up on me she said, "Lucky for you, the lord loves all fools."

Excerpt from the unpublished autobiography of Mazie Phillips-Gordon

All I ever needed was my walking stick and my flashlight and I felt safe. No one would touch me or trouble me. They all know my name. They knew I was there to help them. Most of them mean no harm. They just have no home.

Phillip Tekverk

Fannie called me the next day. She was furious about my treatment of Mazie. She said, "I will destroy you." And she did! [Laughs.] For a little while, anyway. She got me fired from my job, and all the new friends I'd made dropped me. But it turned out not to matter in the end because I had my father buy a small, failing publishing company for me that I turned into less of a failure for many years, putting out war sagas by middle-aged men who had never seen a day of combat. Then when I retired my underlings started publishing experimental fiction popular with cerebral midwestern graduate students. For which they win many awards. For which I take all the credit at dinner parties, when I am invited to them. Which is still often. And then six months later Joseph Mitchell wrote about Mazie in the *New Yorker*. So I guess Fannie found the right person to write about her after all.

Elio Ferrante

This was easier information to find than I thought it would be. Jeanie Fallow was buried beside her husband, Ethan Fallow, in a cemetery in Queens. Rosie was buried next to Al Flicker, also in a cemetery in Queens, but not in the same one, as Rosie and Al were buried in a Jewish cemetery and Jeanie and Ethan were buried in a nondenominational one. Mazie was buried in Boston, in a family plot, where her mother, father, and aunt were all buried. If you want to know the names, I can e-mail them to you, but I can't remember them now.

Pete Sorensen

And it doesn't matter anymore that you don't love me and maybe never did. If you hate me, it's fine, but I hope that you don't, because I don't hate you, at least not anymore. If you met someone new, it's fine. If you're obsessed with your work and that's why you don't call me anymore, that's fine. Just disappear, it's fine. No one understands being obsessed with their work more than me. I love my shop. I know what it's like. I'm glad you have something to care about at last besides your goddamn haircut. It's good to have something to care about. But you can't keep the diary. It's mine. I didn't give it to you. I loaned it to you. Whatever you're doing with it, you need to be done. And especially if you're not in my life anymore, you need to be done.

Elio Ferrante

Death, that's the real end of the story; am I right? Now will you turn off the recorder, darling, and come to bed?

Phillip Tekverk

I heard there was a diary though. Fannie said she'd seen her once with one at the theater, that she'd walked up to her at the ticket booth and startled her. But she saw it, this brown leather diary, the words across the cover in gold, and when Fannie rattled on her cage, Mazie looked up, quite shocked, and shut it closed. A diary, could you imagine? What I wouldn't give to read it. That was the real story right there. But I never saw it. Did you?

Mazie's Diary, August 15, 1939

Just for a minute I thought I needed someone to know what I knew, but I can see I was wrong. I've been wrong before. I've talked to enough people about my life already. I've written enough in these pages. It's enough that it happened. It's enough that I survived. It's enough that I have a warm bed to sleep in at night. I got enough. I got more than enough.

Excerpt from the unpublished autobiography
of Mazie Phillips-Gordon
Somebody loved them once, and that's all you need to know.

Acknowledgments

This book was inspired by the life of a woman who was profiled in the essay "Mazie," which appeared in Joseph Mitchell's brilliant and essential essay collection, *Up in the Old Hotel.* Many thanks to John McCormick and Vannesa Shanks for introducing me to the collection, and to John for naming this book.

Lisa Ng took me on an epic tour of the passageways, stairwells, and gardens of Knickerbocker Village. I am grateful for early reads from Kate Christensen, Bex Schwartz, Lauren Groff, and Courtney Sullivan. Thanks for love, support, and housing to: Rosie Schaap, Wendy McClure, Stefan Block, Molly Dilworth, Sunil Thambidurai, Rien Fertel, Alex Chee, Roxane Gay, Brendan Fitzgerald, Ron Currie, Jr., Kerri Mahoney, Gabrielle Bell, Cinde Boutwell, Matt Laska, Jenn Northington, Maris Kreizman, Rachel Fershleiser, and Amanda Bullock. Bright stars all of you.

The stellar Doug Stewart and Sterling Lord Literistic have given me a decade of unwavering support and invaluable wisdom. I write to impress Helen Atsma, my talented, generous editor. She, along with Sonya Cheuse and Grand Central Publishing, have given me their faith, and have changed my life forever, in no small part because they are all extremely good at their jobs. A thousand thanks, a thousand embraces.

With love, as always, to my family.

About the Author

Jami Attenberg is the *New York Times* bestselling author of *The Middlesteins, Instant Love, The Kept Man,* and *The Melting Season.* She has written for the *New York Times* and numerous other publications. She lives in Brooklyn, New York, and is originally from Buffalo Grove, Illinois.

Learn more at:
Twitter: @jamiattenberg
Tumblr: jamiatt.tumblr.com

READING GROUP GUIDE

Questions for Discussion

1. *Saint Mazie* is told through diary entries and snippets of contemporary interviews. How does this narrative style change the story for you? Did you ever find your sympathies or attitudes about the characters shifting as you heard new perspectives?

2. Does anything about Mazie's New York, and the streets she loves, remind you of today's United States? What lessons might a reader learn from exploring this era of history in fiction? Do you often read historical fiction?

3. Is it a compliment or commentary to call Mazie a saint? Is the word *saint* ever used in a negative way?

4. Why might Mazie, a Jew, feel so drawn to nuns like Sister Tee and Catholicism? Did anything about Mazie's relationship with Sister Tee surprise you?

5. Who belongs to Mazie's family? To Rosie's? To Tee's? What does family mean to the characters in this book?

6. In what ways is Mazie's cage a comfort? A constraint? Are there any nonliteral cages that constrain or comfort her as the story progresses?

7. Why do you think Jeanie keeps leaving home? Why does Mazie stay? Does she really stay, or do her and Rosie's many moves make her more like Jeanie than it might at first seem?

8. What do you think motivated Nadine to conduct interviews and track down information about Mazie? In a novel filled with so many first-person perspectives, did you wish you could hear from Nadine in her own words? Why or why not?

9. What comfort does Rosie find in the gypsies? Why does she turn to them in times of need? Who or what does Mazie turn to in similar times?

10. Everyone seems to fall in love with Mazie, even strangers who read her diary after she's gone. Can you identify anything about her character that might explain this phenomenon? Did you fall in love with Mazie?

11. Should Mazie have broken things off with the Captain? When? Does her participation in adultery diminish the good works she did?

12. Did you find the ending of *Saint Mazie* satisfying? Were you left with any questions?

A Conversation with Jami Attenberg

Q. How did you come upon the historical Mazie Phillips?

A. I had a dear friend, John McCormick, tell me about her and suggest I read the essay by Joseph Mitchell in which she originally appeared. (It was first published in *The New Yorker* and then later in the seminal collection *Up in the Old Hotel*.) John had felt deeply inspired by her, so much so that he designed and built a beautiful bar called St. Mazie in Brooklyn. I fell for her instantly too. I was working on another book at the time, but I knew almost immediately that I would write my next book about her.

Q. What kind of research went into the writing of *Saint Mazie*?

A. I read a lot of books. Obviously all of *Up in the Old Hotel* was a huge influence, as was Luc Sante's *Low Life*. *Amusing the Million: Coney Island at the Turn of the Century* by John F. Kasson was very helpful. Lionel Rogosin's *On the Bowery* is a gorgeous film, and the patter and the look and the feel from that was an influence, even though it was made in the 1950s. I also spent some time on The Roaring Twenties, a website that maps the sounds of New York City in the late 1920s and early 1930s. Just in general I spent a good deal of time online watching little films and videos here and there. Although the book doesn't necessarily drip with historical detail, I wanted to know what it looked and sounded like as I was writing it.

Q. Do you keep a journal yourself? Have you always, or ever? What kind of story might it tell, if a stranger were to find it?

A. I do keep a journal, but it's mostly a jumble of things, to-do lists, story ideas, the occasional letter to myself, reminders of how to be in this life, etc. I think if anyone read it they would find it quite repetitive. I actually committed to keeping a daily journal a few years ago when I spent the winter in New Orleans, and I thought I was writing the most brilliant thing ever, but when I look back at it now I realized that our (or at least my) day-to-day existence is usually pretty dull. But it turned out coincidentally to be a good writing exercise for this book. I realized I didn't need to document every little bit of Mazie's life—just the interesting stuff.

Q. Is Mazie your favorite character in the novel? If not, who is?

A. Of course I love Mazie the most! She's the reason why I wrote this book. I fell in love with her, daydreamed about her, heard her in my head chattering at me until I had no choice but write down everything she had to say. I hope people read her as smart and complicated and sexy and strong and as having a beautiful, generous spirit, much as I imagined the real-life Mazie was. This book is really a tribute to her.

Q. Your previous novel, *The Middlesteins,* followed the lives of a Jewish family. In *Saint Mazie,* the heroine is

Jewish but is drawn to Catholicism. Why do you find yourself writing about faith?

A. There are all kinds of faiths, and they can be both specific and fluid. The real-life Mazie did have an interest in Catholicism—she actually did go to Working Man's Mass, for example—but was Jewish. She was also fascinated with true life romance magazines and horoscopes. All of that piqued my interest instantly. It seemed like she was searching for something to believe in, anything that could work for her, could guide her through this life. As a writer I'm compelled by what inspires people, what gives them hope, where people find their strength that enables them to be compassionate and humane. Faith is an excellent place to start.